A Taste For Life

A Taste For Life

©Barbara Knight 2021

Cover illustration: Original artwork by Barbara Knight

Proofing and typesetting: Ryan Curtis and Julia Knight

Published by: Sculptural Images

Printed by: Ingram Spark

Dedication

This book is dedicated to my darling daughter Julia and her much loved husband Ryan, who share my love of good food and wine.

Alice's Story

The Way We Were

I will never forget the first time I met my future in-laws.

Although Robert and I had been walking out together for two years he had never suggested such a meeting, but Mama had insisted on it before we became officially engaged.

We walked to his home one beautiful spring afternoon, with me chattering girlishly away about the blossoms coming on the trees and the sparkle in the air while Robert strode silently beside me. I knew he was nervous about the forthcoming event and tried to calm him with my chatter.

After walking along the main road for about a mile we turned into another road that led to a small, rounded hill. Narrow streets wound round the hill with small, box-like cottages on either side.

Halfway up the hill he stopped abruptly and said, 'This is it,' in a gruff voice.

Holding my hand he headed up the path and knocked on the door before opening it and calling, 'Mum, we're here.'

His mother walked towards us along a narrow passage and I saw a short, solid woman dressed in a stiff black dress and sensible black shoes. I felt frivolous in my new green linen dress and matching shoes. She greeted me very formally before ushering me into a small room on the right of the passage. She cast a brief glance at the sleeping figure in an armchair and said, 'It's better to let him sleep. I'll introduce you when he wakes up. Now take a seat Alice and you come and help me Robert.'

They left and I sat in the dark, immaculate room shifting uncomfortably in the hard wooden chair. The only source of light was a weak ray of sunlight filtering through the white, lace curtaining that decorated the small square window. In the sagging armchair in a corner of the room the old man slept, his breathing loud and ragged, his head slumped in sleep. Drool slithered from his half open mouth. Even in the dim light I could see that the table before me, the sideboard along one wall and the wide, timber skirting boards were all shiny with a polish, the smell of which pervaded the room.

I was beginning to feel very alone and neglected when the door opened and Robert and his mother reappeared. He held the door open for her and she bustled in, tray in hand.

She placed the tray on the table and turned to me, no smile on her face. 'How do you take your tea Alice?' she asked rather gruffly.

When I requested milk and two sugars she made a harrumphing noise to show that she considered this was obviously indicative of my extravagant tastes. She reinforced my perception by saying, 'I likes it plain black. That way you get to taste the tea.'

Robert, ever the peacemaker, came to my aid with, 'Each to their own taste Ma,' and added milk and one sugar to his cup.

He stood to take a similar brew to his father in the corner, and placed the cup on a small table next to his father's chair. Although he shook his shoulder gently the old man still woke with a start and stared unseeingly around the room screaming, 'Where are they? Where are they?'

He became more and more agitated until the mother said in a rather peremptory way, 'Take him to his room Robert.'

After the men left the room we sat in silence sipping our different cups of tea, and I ate one of the rich shortbread biscuits, worrying all the time that I might drop a crumb on the faded but immaculate carpet. I couldn't seem to think of anything to say to this woman and didn't even know how to address her, although she had told me to call her Mildred. I was overwhelmingly pleased when Robert returned to fill in the void that existed between us. I wondered if I would ever get to know and like this woman who would one day be my mother-in-law.

Later that day after Robert has escorted me home and returned to his place I sat around the big dining table with my mother and sister Violet. They wanted to hear all about the visit because it had been a long time coming.

I had known that he was self-conscious about me seeing the small house in which he had grown up, and the fact that his father, a casualty of the Great War, behaved irrationally at times. I had tried to reassure him, insisting that all that mattered was the way we felt about each other. Nevertheless, once he had left and I recounted to my mother and sibling the horrors of the pokey but immaculate room, the lack of friendliness and warmth of his mother and the discomfiture I had felt being alone in the room with his war-damaged father we were soon laughing uproariously about my outing.

That night, when I was lying awake in my bed I felt guilty and disloyal about making light-hearted fun of Robert's home and family, but this visit had reinforced the differences in our upbringing.

My Papa was an educated man, the younger son of wealthy landowners in Somerset, England. He had come to the colonies with his parents' blessings and a small amount of capital. Through dint of hard work and clever investments he was a wealthy bachelor of fifty when he met Mama, the talented and charming daughter of one of the town's leading lawyers. Despite a twenty-year age difference they fell in love and married and made a very happy and comfortable home life for my two sisters and me.

By contrast Robert's parents had battled all their lives. Both grew up in poor circumstances and had little education. His father had been employed as a drayman, but the war had damaged him so badly he could no longer work. For many years the mother cleaned other people's houses to keep a roof over their heads and food on the table. Robert had left school at fourteen to take up an apprenticeship and help with the family finances, but I knew he felt his lack of education and had insisted that his younger brother complete his schooling.

I knew Mama had reservations about our relationship because of our differing backgrounds. From Robert's mother's demeanour towards me today I gathered that she saw me as spoilt and incompetent. Considering how hard I worked and the responsibilities that I shouldered after Papa's death I thought her attitude most unfair.

I lay in my bed tossing and turning and pondering on how we would work things out. I loved Robert with all my heart, but I wondered sometimes if we would ever make a life together.

Robert and I met in the spring of 1926. It was at a party at our house - a sort of combined celebration of my nineteenth birthday and the engagement of Violet to her

Frank, but also to welcome the changing of the season after a long, hard winter and a year of sadness and loss.

Our beloved Papa had died the previous spring just as his carefully tended orchards were bursting into full, creamery blossom. He had turned seventy-two that year but before his illness had had the vigour and energy of a man half his age.

To me Papa had been the centre of my world, the one who tucked me into bed at night and made my breakfast in the morning. He taught me the wonders of the changing seasons and of the growing world. When I was a small child he carried me around our land on his strong, broad shoulders. After I reached my teens I became his helper in the orchards, assisting him with the thinning of the apples, helping put the hessian skirts around the trees to capture codling moths and of course bringing in the harvest of apples, apricots and plums.

My sisters Evie and Violet had never joined in with these activities. They preferred a more genteel life assisting Mother and Mrs. Jones, our household help, with small indoor tasks as well as knitting and sewing for themselves and the poor.

Papa had always said that I was as good as any son could have been and twice as pretty.

His illness had started with a particularly virulent form of influenza, and despite Mother nursing him day and night he couldn't seem to recover his strength and health. I was surprised by how well she coped during that horrible winter because our mother was a rather butterfly sort of person, extremely feminine, seemingly fragile and very spoilt by her doting, older husband. I loved my mother very much, but had grown up always turning to Papa if I were upset or bothered by anything.

When Papa died it was as if the light and energy of our household vanished. Mother and Violet and I just dragged ourselves through each day. Even visits from Evie, who had married the previous year and was now happily and heavily pregnant, couldn't raise us from the doldrums. I would feel especially badly when I wandered through the neglected orchards, but could not summon up the interest or effort to carry out the necessary chores that Papa and I had previously done together. As a consequence by autumn codling moth had infested many of the apples and brown rot ruined much of the apricot crop. Mrs. Jones and her son, Alfie, gathered in some of the fruit, but much of it fell to the ground to rot or was eaten by scavenging parrots and blackbirds.

One day, late in the autumn, as I stood in the orchard surveying the neglected trees and wasted fruit I felt the presence of my father standing next to me. I would swear that I heard his voice saying, 'You're as good as any son and twice as pretty.' The words were so clear I turned, expecting to see him there, but I was alone. I was crying bitterly beneath the trees when I felt a gentle hand on my shoulder and I knew he had come to be with me one last time. From that day I determined to pull myself together, and to get on with living a useful life and doing all I could to help Mama.

With considerable help from Alfie, who was by then a strong and willing fourteen year old, I cleared all the diseased fruit from the ground, pruned the trees that needed attention and cleared much of the long grass from under them. By spring the orchards once more looked a picture. The blossom was dense enough for Violet and me to cut the odd branches from selected trees to decorate the house for the party, the party at which Robert and I met.

Before Papa had died our home had been a joyous and welcoming place. Both Mama and Papa were sociable people and frequently held dinner parties for friends and relatives. They also encouraged us girls to invite friends home, and much of Evie and Violet's time had been spent planning parties for any and every occasion. As you have probably gathered I was not as interested in these rather trivial pursuits and, being younger, had not always participated in their social life. Eventually I joined in, and always had plenty of partners when we danced to tunes played on the piano or our very new wind up gramophone. I had even kissed one or two of the young men out on the verandah, but no one really touched my heart until I met Robert.

That spring party was a big and boisterous affair. Violet and Frank invited all their friends, and all the girls who had attended the same school with me were there, as well as most of the young people from the neighbourhood. I had also told my friends they could bring a partner, and this is how Robert came to be at the party. He came with Jack who was a very dear friend and neighbour, and one of the boys I had kissed on the verandah. I'm afraid he may have had a bit of a crush on me, which was a pity, as I really liked him in a sisterly way but could never have felt romantically inclined towards him.

When I saw him standing at the doorway I crossed the room to welcome him. I knew I was looking really attractive that night. I had on a new silky crepe-de-chine shimmy dress and my hair had been bobbed in the latest fashion. Even though I only thought of Jack as a friend it was flattering to see the look of appreciation in his gaze. As I approached he pulled forward the friend who he had brought and introduced him. When I felt Robert's warm, dry hand in mine and looked up into his solemn, handsome face my heart turned over.

This was how we met and during the next two years our feelings for each other deepened. We knew we loved each other and hoped to marry, but everything seemed to be against this ever happening.

Neither of our mothers wanted us to wed.

Mama was not really a snob but she said things like, 'I have no wish to see a daughter of mine struggling on a tradesman's wage in some little hovel.'

Robert's mother, who was in my opinion an inverted snob, made it clear to me on our first meeting that she didn't see me as a suitable wife for a workingman. Despite Robert telling her how hard I worked, it was many years before she grudgingly changed her mind about me.

As well as the attitudes of our mothers we both felt that they needed us at home with them, Robert because he contributed financially to the household and me because I had taken over much of the work previously done by Papa.

During the next four years Robert saved enough money to put a deposit on a dear little house. His younger brother was now earning a wage, so could help their mother with household expenses. Robert began urging me to name a date when we could marry, but I was worried about how Mama would cope without me.

One night we were sitting in the little parlour when, out of the blue, she said, 'You and Robert should marry. I know you've felt responsible for looking after so much since your father died and I've depended too much on you. I've grown very fond of Robert and I know he's a good man. You two should be together. I've talked to Mrs. Jones and Alfie and I'm sure that with their help I will manage. Alfie will work full-time on the land and Mrs. Jones has offered to collect the rents for a small fee.'

I was glad for Alfie who loved the work we had been doing, but felt sorry for Mrs. Jones with the onerous task of collecting the rents.

The Depression had affected many of our tenants and some were finding it hard to pay the few shillings each week. I'd had some very upsetting experiences with people unable to make their payments. Sometimes they would come to the door with two or three little children clustered behind them, and beg for a few more days to get the money. Others pretended to be out when I called, but I would see the curtains flicked back as I walked away and knew they were hiding from me. I was glad to be relieved of that task.

At last we could begin planning our wedding. We had been going together for six years and been engaged for four of those years. Our little house was slightly derelict when Robert bought it. Because of some legal problems involving inheritance it had been empty for a long time. Together we painted walls, sanded down flaking window frames and laid new linoleums on the floors. I even re-blacked the old fuel stove, and one night baked cheese biscuits in it as a surprise for Robert when he came by after work. I had also brought along a bottle of homemade fruit wine so we could celebrate our house being finished.

Robert held me close and said, 'We will be happy in this home.'

I couldn't help but wonder if this was a statement or a wish.

The day of our wedding dawned bright and sunny and I lay in my single bed for one last time watching the soft white clouds scudding past my window in a bright blue sky. I thought of the old adage, 'Happy the bride the sun shines on,' and felt such joy that this day had finally arrived. I ran my hands over my breasts and down my sides, and imagined how it would feel when Robert did this to me later that night. I was feeling a little nervous about the wedding night, but both Evie and Violet had assured me that it only hurt the first time and I was sure Robert would be gentle.

The wedding ceremony was held in the small church nearby followed by a reception at home. Mama had offered to pay for us to spend our honeymoon night at a fancy hotel because she knew Robert had spent all his savings on our house, but he had politely refused. He said he had planned a surprise and I couldn't wait to see what it was.

The ceremony was to be at two o'clock but I was ready by one, resplendent in my beautiful, white satin dress. Violet, who was my matron of honour, was also ready in a pale pink silk gown but my two bridesmaids were still twittering around fiddling with each other's hairdos. Mama looked delightfully feminine in a floaty, lilac gown of chiffon and a big picture hat. Evie was on hand to help with hairdos and cups of tea. She was seven months pregnant with her second child, and even though her dress was cleverly styled with front panels you could still see the bulge.

Shortly before two she and her husband Don took Mama to the church in their new automobile, and as they were leaving Uncle Spencer arrived in his big black Ford. He was Mama's older brother and was to give me away.

Although I was very fond of him I couldn't help wishing that my beloved Papa were still there for my special day.

Uncle had hired another car for Violet and the bridesmaids and they climbed aboard, a mass of giggles and frothy pink and drove away.

Uncle gave me his arm and said, 'Well come on my pretty one. I'll do my best to stand in for your father, but I know it's not quite the same.'

I squeezed his arm to show my affection for him, but I had to blink back the tears. I felt so emotional that day.

When we arrived at the church all the guests were inside and Violet fussed around me, straightening my train and adjusting the veil. We heard the Wedding March begin and Violet led the way into the church, followed by the bridesmaids and then Uncle and me. I was aware of a sea of smiling faces as I walk down the aisle but I really only saw Robert. He looked almost like a stranger in a dark suit, white shirt and navy tie but his eyes glowed with love as he watched me come towards him. When he stepped forwards and took my hand my heart turned over as it had done the day I met him.

I don't really recall much of the ceremony I was in such a daze. I remember saying my vows and Robert's brother fumbling a little as he handed Robert the ring, but my most vivid memory is of Robert gently lifting my veil and kissing me in front of all those people, and quite passionately too.

The reception at home was progressing noisily and happily when I crept away to change. Robert has told me I would need a comfortable dress and strong shoes so I didn't make the most glamorous exit when we left the reception in a T-model Ford Robert had borrowed from a friend and workmate called Ian. I still didn't know where we were going, but sat back and enjoyed the adventure.

Robert drove through town and up the winding road until we came to the Springs Hotel. This was a large, sprawling weatherboard building and the only dwelling of any size that far up the mountain. I turned to him to ask if we were staying there for the night because I hadn't been aware that they had accommodation, but he pre-empted my query with, 'No we're not staying here. I want you all to myself tonight. You'll see now why I suggested you wear comfortable shoes.'

I retrieved my small holdall from the back seat while Robert pulled a bulging haversack from the boot before guiding me across the road and onto a narrow, shady path. With Robert leading the way we walked for about a mile, and I enjoyed the peace and quiet after what had been a busy and people-filled day.

Just as the sun was disappearing behind the trees we arrived at our destination - a little hut standing in a small clearing and surrounded by tall eucalypts. I had heard about these mountain huts that were built as weekend retreats, but had never seen one. Evidently there were quite a few of them dotted around the mountain. They were built from local timber and various building materials that could be carried up the mountain, so were fairly basic.

I peered into the dim interior and saw that it consisted of one large room with a big stone fireplace on one wall and a rough table and bench in the centre. Against the far wall was a wide wooden bed, which was covered with a multi-coloured woollen spread.

Before I could enter the door Robert scooped me up in his arm and carried me across the threshold saying, 'Welcome to Ian's Hut, his home away from home.'

I snuggled into my new husband's neck and giggled, 'What a lovely surprise,' and I was thrilled with the idea of spending our first night together in such an unusual place.

Ian had left a good stock of water and firewood and there were basic provisions like tea and sugar stored in square metal tins. Robert unpacked his haversack and I saw that he had brought bread, butter, milk, eggs, bacon and cheese as well as my favourite sweet biscuits. Robert lit the fire and boiled the old enamel kettle.

As the sky darkened we sat outside drinking tea, eating biscuits and listening to the evening birdsong and the wind sighing through the surrounding trees. We were both tired from the day's celebrations and I was suddenly feeling strangely shy with this man who I had known and loved for six years. In that time our intimacy never progressed beyond kissing and cuddling. Now that we were married and free to explore each other's bodies without restriction I was fearful that the years of denial would make for difficulties between us.

I finished my tea and went back inside the hut. I took my nightgown from the bag and held it before me. I had made it especially for my wedding night, but now when I looked at it in the faint light the flowers embroidered around the neck and at the cuffs made it look girlish and virginal.

I slipped into it quickly and was standing in the middle of the room feeling a little unsure when Robert came in. He took me in his arm and kissed me then carried me to the rough bed. I felt shy as he stepped out of his clothes then gently removed my gown. He whispered how much he loved me and how beautiful I looked in the firelight. His voice had so much passion in it I felt myself melt. While we kissed he ran his hands all over my body, and I felt such warmth flow through me I thought all would be well. As I lay there Robert rolled over to cover me, and I felt his fingers exploring the part of my body he had never touched before. Suddenly I felt his penis enter me and it hurt, but I tried to relax. Gradually the pain lessened and I even began to find his movement inside me pleasurable.

He finished with a loud gasp and rolled off me but then gathered me in his arms saying, 'I didn't hurt you too much did I Alice?'

I snuggled into his body and sighed, 'No my darling. You were very gentle and I am sure that in time I will come to enjoy our lovemaking as much as you.'

We went to sleep curled up in each other's arms. During the night we woke at the same time. The fire was out and the hut cold and dark. Once more Robert ran his hands all over my body, but this time I responded fully. When he came inside me I experienced the most amazing sensation, like a thrilling shock going right through my body, and I clung to him fiercely.

In the morning Robert restarted the fire and cooked eggs and bacon and fried bread in a big blackened pan, and we ate it ravenously seated outside at a rough wooden table.

As we sat drinking our tea and listening to the magpies warbling in the gum trees I couldn't contain myself and blurted out, 'Robert, do I look different?'

He stared at me solemnly and said, 'To me you always look beautiful.'

This was not the answer I wanted to hear and I said rather impatiently, 'But do I look different now that I am a woman? Does it show in my face that I am no longer a virgin?'

He laughed aloud, his voice ringing around amongst the trees, and I thought he was not taking my question seriously enough so I said rather sharply, 'But I feel so different now that we have really loved each other. I'm sure it must show in my face.'

Robert reached across the rough little table and clasped my hand, 'My darling Alice what we have shared is ours alone, not something the whole world can see, but yes, to me you are different. I have loved Alice the girl for so many years, and now I know that I will love Alice the woman for the rest of my life.'

Oh how happy I felt and how I loved that man of mine.

We finished our tea then tidied up the hut before heading off down the mountain track hand in hand.

We spent Sunday night in our dear little house unwrapping wedding presents and deciding where each item should go. In the morning Robert had to return to work. He only got two weeks annual leave, and at the factory where he was employed time off was tightly rostered and must be taken when the company decreed.

I had always kept myself busy and that had been especially so after Papa died. At first I had thought I might not have enough to do looking after that small house and gardens but soon found that the days passed quickly.

After I cooked Robert's breakfast and saw him off to work I tidied the house and then often went outside. Because the house had been empty for a long time the front was a jungle of neglected shrubs and was full of weeds. I hacked away at the brambles and pulled the weeds, and soon uncovered the remnants of what would once have been a pretty garden. I pruned the many rose bushes that surrounded what was a lawn then cleared this central area of weeds and sowed it with grass seed. Between the rose bushes I planted bulbs that would make a nice show in the spring.

The back yard was quite large and also totally wild. There was a large walnut tree in one corner so I decided that this would be my fruit tree area. I bought an apple, a pear and a quince tree and planted them along the back fence, and then I cleared the rest of the back yard of weeds and dug it over. Part of it I set aside for a vegetable patch and the remainder I sowed as lawn. I wanted plenty of space for our children to play in when they arrived.

Once a week I visited Mama and usually caught up with my sisters at the same time. I also had them and some of my girlfriends around for afternoon teas. I enjoyed baking cakes and biscuits in my refurbished oven and bringing out some of the china we had received as wedding presents. Most of all I enjoyed cooking a good meal for Robert when he returned home tired and hungry from work.

Previously I had never done much cooking because Mrs. Jones always ruled the kitchen at home and she didn't like other people getting in her way. Because of my culinary inexperience our meals were fairly basic, but I always made sure that the meat was of a high quality and the vegetables fresh.

By Christmas I knew I was pregnant. Robert and I painted out one of the spare bedrooms and I spent the next few months making little flannelette nighties and knitting booties and bonnets and jackets. I felt extremely well all through the pregnancy and in early June, almost exactly a year after our wedding, we became the proud parents of a baby girl. She was so beautiful we spent hours just gazing at her in her cradle and feeling very pleased with ourselves. We both liked family names being carried on and had planned to name our daughter after my sister Evelyn, but after some consideration decided that this might lead to confusion. Instead we gave her Evie's second name Ronda.

For the christening Robert's mother wore a stylish black dress with matching gloves and hat. Mama dressed in a floaty gown of pinks and blues and lilacs and wore neither hat nor gloves. Both women thought the other unsuitably dressed. This was their first meeting since the wedding and they exchanged only formal greetings. Obviously these two women would never be anything more to each other than casual acquaintances, even though they shared a grandchild and in time, hopefully, would share more.

Ronda was an extremely good baby. She fed well and by the time she was three months old slept through the night. Even so it was amazing how much time it took to care for one small person. I fed her at six and then she slept while I got Robert off to work and started the copper to wash her nappies and nighties. I'd have time for a cup of tea and some toast and to tidy the kitchen before the water boiled and I could put in the clothes. Usually it was then about ten o'clock and time for baby's bath and second feed for the day. After this feed Ronda slept and I had time to put the clothes through the mangle and hang them on the line in the back yard. For the first few months I worried about going outside for fear Ronda would wake and I wouldn't hear her crying, but I slowly became more relaxed about this as she got older. Often I would even pause a while outside and pull a few weeds, but I am afraid my gardens were not getting the attention they needed.

The afternoons passed quickly as I fitted in another feed with household chores. Sometimes I put Ronda in her pram and went to the shops or to visit Mama, but I didn't get out of the house much. It was fortunate that the grocer, the butcher and the baker all delivered in this area.

When Robert returned home we had tea, I fed our baby and Robert had a chance to hold her and play with her. He was a doting father and loved Ronda very much. I felt it a shame that he got so little time with her for fathers miss out on such a lot because they have to go out to work.

By the time Ronda was nine months old I began to wean her. She had diluted cows' milk and gradually this was increased until she could cope with full strength. I could now supplement this with Milk Arrowroot biscuits and thin porridge and soon she would be eating vegetables. She was a bonny, healthy little girl and brought much joy into our home.

Two years after the birth of Ronda we had another little girl who we named Joan, which was her Aunt Violet's second name, and eighteen months later our third daughter was born. We had used up aunts' names but I had recently seen a newsreel of the little English princesses and was very impressed by Elizabeth, so we gave our baby this name but called her Liz. Robert joked and said that the next one had better be a boy as he was beginning to feel outnumbered in his all-female household. I thought that he was only half joking. He loved his little girls but all men seem to want a son to carry on their name.

Shortly before Christmas in 1938 our much wanted son was born and this time there was no prolonged consideration for a name. He was a miniature of his father with the same dark solemn eyes and brown hair so we named him Robert and called him Bob. He was an angelic baby who fed contentedly, slept soundly and woke happily. His three sisters were fascinated by their little brother, and took it in turns rocking his cradle or wheeling him around the yard in his pram.

At that time Robert's brother William bought a car and he offered Robert a loan of it so that he could take our growing family for Sunday trips. Because we hadn't a vehicle of our own going out anywhere had been difficult so we are thrilled. The only problem, as far as I was concerned, was that we were expected to take my mother-in-law with us, and I still found her a very difficult woman to relate to.

The seat was wide so she sat in the middle of Robert and me. I nursed baby Bob while the three little girls shared the back seat. I would have much preferred it to be just our little family on these outings, but I knew that it was good for Mildred to get out of the house because she rarely relaxed at home. Some days her dour presence put a damper on the day for me, but generally we had enjoyable times.

We always stopped at some pretty place to have our lunch of sandwiches, fruit and billy tea. If we were near a creek the girls and I paddled in the water or searched for watercress to put in our egg sandwiches, or wildflowers to take home for the vases. When we went to the beach I played with the little ones in the water or we wandered along the sand collecting pretty shells.

I loved the freedom of those days. During my childhood and for much of my young adult years I had spent much of my time out of doors. With so many responsibilities I now got little opportunity to walk and play in the sunshine or wind. I was grateful to Robert for the way he always offered to mind the baby and stay with Mildred.

While Robert and I and our little family were managing very happily many people were suffering through those years of the Depression. Sometimes I would answer a knock at my door and there would be a raggedly dressed man asking if he could do chores in exchange for a feed. These men frightened me with their neediness and I would tell them I had no work available and got rid of them with a sandwich.

A road was planned to give access to the top of the mountain, but more importantly to provide paid work for some of the many unemployed. The scar crept up the mountain as men, desperate for any work, laboured in harsh conditions and with basic tools to complete a road to the pinnacle. As I watched the road grow I thought how lucky we were.

Robert had had to take a cut in wages but we still had sufficient to make our house payments and to feed and clothe our family. The only real change I had to make was to be more economical with my food budget.

When we were first married I had always bought the best cuts of meat and a good piece of beef or a leg of lamb for Sunday lunch. With less money coming in and more mouths to feed I knew I would have to learn how to cook more economically. Although relations between my mother-in-law and me were still quite strained I consulted her on this matter, and she was happy to assist with recipes and hints.

We would never be close, but this sharing of recipes improved things between us and Robert quite enjoyed having some of the dishes he'd grown up with being reintroduced into his life.

I had never eaten lamb's fry but cooked with bacon and onion it was quite delicious. Following Mother-in-law's recipes I could feed our family well for two meals with two pounds of sausages by using half in toad-in-the-hole and currying the remainder. I also added Cornish pasties to the menu and the little girls loved helping make them. They made smaller ones for themselves and an extra big one for Daddy.

During the Depression years many men took to hunting at weekends to help feed their families and Robert sometimes went out with friends from work. They often got several rabbits, and cooked carefully this replaced the more expensive cuts of roast meat for Sunday dinner. If the men were lucky they shot a kangaroo or two. Although the flesh was rather dry it made up into very nice patties when minced with some bacon, carrot and onion and the tail made the most delicious soup.

Another inexpensive treat was scallops and during the season a man came around on a cart selling them. When the girls heard his bell they'd rush and tell me and I always bought several scoops of them. This versatile seafood was lovely in a white cheese sauce or curried or fried in batter.

Shortly after Bob's first birthday I realised I was pregnant once more. I had always welcomed the prospect of another baby, but now began to wonder how we would cope. Our little house was already rather cramped. Bob had been moved from our bedroom and was sharing Ronda's room and Joan and Liz took up all the space in the third bedroom. Where would we sleep this little person once he or she was big enough to leave our bedroom?

Besides worrying about this I was not feeling well with that pregnancy. I had always been so healthy when expecting but now I woke every morning and was sick.

I was also concerned about the polio epidemic that had been raging for the past few years, and was glad my girls were not yet old enough to attend school. In the papers there were warnings about avoiding crowded places, being extra careful with hygiene and symptoms to watch for. If any of the children seemed extra tired or complained about an ache in their arms or legs I was inclined to panic. Altogether this was a very worrisome time.

There was also great turbulence occurring in Europe caused by a horrible little man called Adolph Hitler. His troops marched into Poland, and Australia entered the war alongside Britain. From the time Mr. Menzies made the announcement that we were at war Robert listened intently to the evening news on the wireless. I knew he was concerned about the state of the world, but I was too wrapped up in domesticity to give it much thought. Most people were saying that it would soon be over in any case.

At this time Robert and I had our first really big row and for a long time I didn't think I could ever forgive him. He knew I had been worrying and not feeling very well, and then one night he came home and said he thought he should enlist. I just stared at him in amazement. I hadn't thought events happening on the other side of the world could impinge on our lives, and it had certainly never occurred to me that Robert would think of leaving his family to join the fighting.

I shouted at him, 'You must be mad. Where is your sense of responsibility?'

He stood before me and had the gall to say, 'The blokes and I were talking at lunch time, and most of us reckon it's our duty to get over there and help drive back the Hun.'

I was furious and almost spat at him, 'It's your duty to look after me and your children and the baby who's on the way. I don't know how you could even consider such an action.'

I turned on my heels and flounced out of the room, and when he tried to cuddle me later that night I pushed him away and slept right on the very edge of my side of the bed.

In the morning I was still just as angry and my feelings didn't improve as the day progressed. For once I wasn't happy when I heard his footsteps coming up the path, and didn't greet him when the girls gathered round to welcome him home.

We ate our tea in silence except for the children's chatter, and once they were in bed I went straight to our room and pretended to be asleep when he came in. Things continued in this way until Friday. After I had tucked the children up for the night Robert stopped me from going to the bedroom.

He put his arms around me but when I pulled away he held me and said, 'Let's stop this Alice. If you keep on this way the children will notice and get upset.'

I let him lead me over to the couch, but was still feeling so angry with him. Before he could say anything I said, 'I just can't understand how you could even contemplate joining up when you know how much the children and I need you.'

Looking rather shamefaced he said, 'I'm sorry I upset you so much. I guess I just got sort of carried away by the other blokes. Of course you're right and I shouldn't have even considered going. Anyhow none of them could join because our factory has been declared essential to the war effort, as we will now be making munitions.'

I lashed out, 'So you're just saying you're sorry now because you couldn't have gone in any case.'

'No, I didn't try to enlist when I saw how upset you were about the idea.'

I wasn't sure I believed him but I hated feeling so angry. I was worried that it might be affecting the baby. Anyhow we made up, at least on the surface, but it was a long time before I lost the sense of betrayal with which this whole episode left me.

Before that long cold winter was over even worse unhappiness occurred. My mother contracted pneumonia, and despite the concerned administrations of Mrs. Jones she could not seem to rally and died.

I was too overwrought to even attend the funeral but Robert went. Afterwards he told me it was a very moving service and that a lot of people attended. I just lay on my bed, hugging little Bob to my swollen stomach, crying and crying until the poor little fellow squirmed free and ran to his Grandma.

Robert's mother was wonderful during that awful week, caring for the children, preparing meals and keeping the house cleaner than I could ever manage to. This brought us closer, but we would never be real friends for we were just too different.

It seemed ridiculous. I was a grown woman with four children of my own and another on the way, but I missed my mother. At times I just couldn't imagine life without her. I cried as I read a book to my children that she had shared with them, and they looked at me with worried eyes.

One day I saw a small, frail-looking woman ahead of me on the street, and for a moment I thought she was my mother. I almost called out to her, but then I realised how foolish I was being. I really needed to pull myself together.

Spring came and with it our second little boy. After a difficult pregnancy I had an easy birth and I swear he smiled at me straight away. He was a bonny baby with a tuft of blonde hair and the deepest violet-blue eyes I have ever seen. I decided to name him Vincent after Van Gough - not only because that artist was said to have eyes of this colour but also because he was one of Mama's favourites.

Lambs' Fry

1 lamb liver	1 cup milk
3 rashers of bacon *(cut into large pieces)*	1 dsp. tomato sauce
1 onion, finely sliced	1 tsp. Worcestershire sauce
1 tsp. seasoned flour	1 cup water

Fry bacon and onion in a little fat or oil then remove from pan.

Wash and dry liver and remove grisly centre.

Cut into slices and place in the milk for 5 minutes.

Remove from milk and roll in seasoned flour.

Fry liver in pan turning frequently – about 8 minutes.

Add water to pan and extra flour if needed to thicken.

Return bacon and onion to pan and add tomato sauce and Worcestershire sauce.

Simmer gently until heated through and gravy thickened.

Serve sprinkled with parsley.

Delicious served with mashed potatoes and carrots or on toast

Curried Sausages

1 lb. sausages	1 lb. onions
2 tbsp. plain flour	1 tbsp. curry powder
1 dsp. Worcestershire sauce	1 dsp. tomato sauce
2 cups water	

Fry sausages until firm then cut into bite sized pieces.

Slice onions finely then fry in a little dripping until golden.

Add flour and curry powder and cook 1 minute.

Mix in sauces then add water and stir until thickens.

Add sausages and cook for 5 minutes.

Serve with mashed potatoes, carrots and a green vegetable.

Toad-in-the-Hole

1 ½ cups self-raising flour   pinch salt
2 eggs   1 cup milk [approximately]
1 lb. sausages

Sieve flour and salt.

Beat in eggs.

Add enough milk to make a smooth batter.

Allow to rest in a cool place.

Place sausages in an oblong casserole dish with a little melted fat.

Half cook sausages in hot oven [440F].

Remove from oven and pour batter over sausages.

Return to oven for approximately 30 minutes or until well risen and brown around the edges.

Cut into squares and serve.

This is delicious served with mashed potatoes, carrots and peas and brown gravy.

Cornish Pasties

Pastry

4 oz. butter cut into pieces   2 cups plain flour
pinch salt   3 – 4 tblsp. iced water
(Ready-made puff pastry can be used but is not as good)

Sift flour and salt in a bowl.
Rub in butter until mixture resembles fine breadcrumbs.
Add 3 tblsp. water and mix with knife to form dough. *(May need extra water.)*

Filling

1 small swede

8 oz. rump steak
8 oz. potato   salt and pepper to taste
1 small onion   2 tblsp. finely chopped
                                 parsley
1 small carrot   2 tblsp. water

Cut steak into very small cubes and finely cut all vegetables. *(Mince can replace cubed beef.)*
Mix all together with seasonings, parsley and water.
Divide pastry into six pieces.
 Roll out each piece to the size of a saucer.
Place filling on rounds and moisten edges of pastry.
Fold circles over into half-moons and crimp edge together firmly.
Brush with egg and place on greased oven tray.
Bake in hot oven 440F for 20 minutes.
Lower heat to 350F and bake a further 25 minutes.

Kangaroo Patties

3 lbs. kangaroo meat   4 rashers bacon
2 slices bread *(can be stale)*   2 onions
2 carrots

Mince kangaroo meat, bacon, onions and carrots.

Alternate for ease of mincing as meat can clog the mincer.

Soak bread slices in water or milk.

Mix into kangaroo, bacon and vegetable mix to make sausage consistency.

Form into patties and fry in hot fat or oil.

Delicious!

Kangaroo Tail Soup

kangaroo tail	1 stick celery
dripping	1dsp. Vegemite
1 carrot	plain flour
1 onion	finely chopped parsley

Joint tail and brown in dripping.

Add thinly sliced carrot, onion and celery.

Place in large saucepan and cover with water.

Simmer very slowly for 3 hours.

Mix together Vegemite and plain flour with a little water to make a thin paste.

Add to soup and cook a further 5 minutes.

Serve sprinkled with parsley with hot toast.

Scallops in Cheese Sauce

1 lb. scallops	2 oz. grated cheese
1 tbsp. butter	breadcrumbs
1 tbsp. plain flour	milk

Melt butter in a saucepan, add flour and cook for 2 minutes over a gentle heat.

Remove from heat and gradually add milk until thick sauce consistency.

Return to heat and stir, adding extra milk if needed.

Add scallops and cook for 1 minute.

Remove from heat and pour scallop mixture into a casserole dish.

Top with breadcrumbs and grated cheese.

Heat in oven until top is golden brown.

Moving On

It seemed no time at all before Vincent was one year old and would soon need to move out of our bedroom. I had to face the fact that the time had come for us to leave our home. Mama's estate had been settled and my considerable inheritance would enable us to buy a bigger house, but I was loath to leave the home I had come to as a bride. For the most part Robert and I had been very happy there, and it was the only home our children had ever known. Nevertheless I knew I must be practical and so we started the traumatic business of looking at potential properties.

After viewing numerous houses we were shown a lovely weatherboard house in Tower Road, in the suburb of New Town. It had been built for a wealthy, hedonistic bachelor at the turn of the century and reflected his needs. It consisted of a kitchen, bathroom, laundry, formal dining room, long living room and a more intimate lounge room opening onto a sunroom. Upstairs was a large bedroom with a huge walk-in wardrobe and underneath this room a covered indoor/outdoor area with walls of the house on two sides and waist-high walls on the other two.

Because of its lack of bedrooms it was not particularly suitable for a large family, but Robert loved it and I could see that it could be made suitable with some reorganisation of the spaces. The three little girls adored the garden, which had a circle of rose bushes in the middle of a large lawn, and a latticed summerhouse covered with a climbing yellow Banksia rose

During the summer of 41 we moved house and the little girls annexed the upstairs bedroom that was big enough to be both a sleeping and a play area. Robert and I selected the intimate lounge as our bedroom, and the sunroom became the nursery for our two little boys.

As the years progressed we were blessed with another son, who we named Gordon after my beloved Papa. When he was old enough he joined his two older brothers in what had originally been the formal dining room and I turned the sunroom into a sewing room. Finally I had a small space just for myself, and I needed it, as the children seemed to fill nearly every corner of the house.

The war had continued to ravage the world, and soon some of the maimed and damaged men were to be seen in the streets. The first time the girls saw a man with one leg they stared so much I had to reprimand them, but I could understand their shock. Slowly it became commonplace to see these casualties of the war in the streets and on the trams, but it was still heart-breaking to think of so many young lives ruined.

When I saw these men I couldn't help but be glad Robert hadn't gone, even if he felt that he should. I will never understand how he could have even thought of joining up. He was such a loving husband and a great father it seemed out of character that he could even consider leaving us. I guess that's the difference between men and women; we have different priorities. Anyhow I have long forgiven him, but I don't think I will ever forget my anger and sense of desolation of that time.

Except for the sight of the poor maimed boys and the inconvenience of the rationing of food and clothing the war did not impinge greatly on us. Robert's brother tried to enlist but was rejected because of poor eyesight, and I had no brothers. Some of our friends were fighting overseas but luckily none were killed.

The Rawley's man, who called with his suitcase full of soaps and cleaners and essences, was a returned soldier from the First World War. He told me regularly of how lucky he was to get back in one piece, but his hands shook as he opened the cases and he had a constant twitch in one eye. I always invited him in for a cup of tea and cake and bought more from him than I should.

Because I had learnt to cook economically during the Depression years I could prepare nourishing meals for my large family with the amount of meat that rationing allowed and I started a vegetable garden in the back yard that provided us with potatoes, carrots, onions and greens. Many people began growing their own vegetables and even some public spaces were given over for this purpose. We called them Victory Gardens. I'm not sure why but perhaps it was part of our wishful thinking that the war would soon be over and meanwhile we were doing our bit.

My biggest problem during this time was that sugar and butter were rationed and eggs scarce. I liked to have something sweet in the tins for after school snacks, and these had always been essential ingredients in my cakes and biscuits. I experimented in the kitchen, replacing sugar with golden syrup and I also found that custard powder mixed with the flour gave richness to cakes that were low in butter and eggs. I managed to produce a delicious gingerbread, quite a good Madeira cake and a reasonable sultana loaf. These became my standbys during the years of rationing.

Butter was so severely rationed I could no longer make fruit pies and crumbles for dessert as they used such a lot of this commodity. I replaced them with puddings made with suet and jam roly-poly and golden syrup pudding became favourites with the children.

Another problem was the rationing of clothing, as once the children started school most of the coupons went for uniforms. I had always sewn and now made most of the children's out-of-school clothes, sometimes unpicking an adult garment no longer in use to make a dress or a pair of trousers.

I was so glad when rationing ceased as the girls were growing up and were already becoming critical of these homemade garments.

For New Year's Eve we had a big party and my sisters and their families came, as well as some of the girls' friends. We celebrated the start of the new decade, the fifties, with lavish amounts of food, some sparkling wine for the adults and punch for the youngsters. We finished the evening with fireworks on the front lawn.

Once everyone had gone home and all our children were finally in bed, Robert and I sat companionably on the old couch in the inside/outside area and held hands. We toasted each other with the last of the sparkling wine.

He said, 'To my darling Alice, the love of my life.'

In return I said, 'To you Robert, my man,' and leant over to kiss him on the mouth.

Economical Gingerbread

2 oz. butter	1 cup milk
2 oz. sugar	½ tsp. bicarbonate of soda
4 oz. golden syrup	1 tsp. ground ginger
8 oz. self-raising flour	pinch salt

Place butter, golden syrup, milk and bi-carb soda in a pot and heat slowly.

Allow to cool.

Pour mixture onto flour, ginger, salt mixture.

Mix well and beat until smooth.

Bake in a greased loaf tin in a moderate oven for 50 minutes.

Madeira Cake

3 oz. butter	1 egg
2 oz. sugar	1 ½ cups self-raising flour
1 tbsp. golden syrup	¾ cup milk
1 dsp. custard powder	level tsp. bi-carb soda

Cream butter and sugar.

Add egg, then golden syrup and mix well.

Add flour/custard powder mix alternately with the milk in which the bi-carb soda has been dissolved.

Bake in a greased, oblong tin in a moderately slow oven [330F] for 35-40 minutes.

Sultana Loaf

3 oz. butter
¾ cup sugar
1 cup sultanas

1 cup self-raising flour
1 cup water

Cream butter and sugar.

Mix sultanas into flour.

Add to creamed mixture alternately with the water.

Turn into a small loaf tin and bake in a moderate oven for approximately 30 minutes.

This is an immensely quick and easy recipe and makes a great after school snack or a quick afternoon tea cake.

Jam Roly Poly

Suet Pastry

½ lb. flour   4 oz. suet
½ baking powder   ½ tsp. salt
water to mix

Sift flour, baking powder and salt.
Chop suet and mix until it resembles breadcrumbs.
Mix into flour with enough water to form a soft pastry.
Roll pastry into an oblong.
Spread with raspberry jam to within 1 inch of the edges.
Wet edges of pastry and roll up.
Tie and pin in a scalded, floured pudding cloth.
Boil for two hours and serve with sweet, white sauce.

Sweet White Sauce

½ oz. butter   6 drops flavouring
½ tsp. salt   ½ oz. flour
½ oz. sugar   ½ pint milk

Melt butter in small saucepan.
Remove from heat and stir in flour, sugar and salt until
smooth.
Add milk gradually over heat until boiling.
Lower heat and cook for two minutes stirring.
Add flavouring and pour over pudding.

Steamed Golden Syrup Pudding

½ lb. flour
½ tsp. baking powder
½ tsp. salt

4 oz. suet
1 ½ gills milk

Sift flour, baking powder and salt.

Chop suet and mix until resembles breadcrumbs.

Add suet to flour mix.

Mix in milk with spoon.

Tie in scalded, floured cloth – allow room to swell.

Cook in boiling water for 2 hours.

Serve with warm golden syrup.

This dessert would probably not suit the modern palate but it had the advantage of enabling the housewife to provide a dessert for her family without using any of the precious sugar rations.

Liz's Story

While We're Young

Many people say you can't remember anything before the age of seven. They insist that things you think you know about at an earlier age have been told to you and you have stored them as a memory. I know this is not so because I remember quite a lot of my life before we moved to the new house, and I was only five at that time. My memories are not bits and pieces that I could have been told, but are things I know only I felt. Others are like pictures in my head and could not have been put there by other people's words.

By the way, I am Liz, the third daughter of Alice and Robert. I don't profess to remember when Bob was born but I do remember Vincent as a baby, and at that time I would have only been about three and a half. I also remember the months before he was born and that Mummy was very sad a lot of the time. I remember Grandma coming to our house every day for a while, and that we had to be very good when she was there. Grandma used to say, 'Children should be seen but not heard.'

At that time I knew, but only in a part of my brain, our Nanna had gone to Heaven and that we would never be able to see her again. This made me sad because she had always given us hugs and read us stories.

I also have clear recollections of tea parties on the back lawn with Ronda and Joan, and of cooking with Mummy and my sisters and watching as the pasties or cookies came out of the black fuel stove.

Perhaps you remember the things that affect you deeply at the time, and also other things that happen often and so are reinforced by repetition.

My earliest memories of the new house are of climbing the steep staircase and seeing the wondrously big room I was to share with Ronda and Violet. It was so spacious that even with our three beds placed across one wall there was still a large area in which we could play. There was also a small room off it in which we could hang all our clothes. As we grew older we managed to make this dressing room quite crowded, but at that time there was room to spare and some of our toys were stored in there too.

I had a very happy childhood in that house and the teenage years were the best fun ever. Mum and Dad were really great parents and I loved all my brothers and sisters, but especially Joan. She was only one class ahead of me at school because she repeated grade four, and we shared our friends.

To celebrate the start of a new decade, the fifties, we had the most tremendous New Year Party and were allowed to invite anyone we wanted to. Of course Joan and I invited our gang, the girls who we hung out with after school and at weekends, Di, Anne, Margery and Alex. I remember lying in bed after everyone had gone home and hearing Mum and Dad talking quietly below me, and Joan or Ronda snoring softly before I drifted off to sleep.

As I have said my teenage years were fun. Often the decade in which I grew up is called the boring fifties, but for me it was a great time to be young and not at all boring. We didn't drink alcohol, there weren't any drugs around and fear of pregnancy kept most of us on the straight and narrow.

So what did we do for fun, you may ask?

Every Friday night we went to dancing class. This was held in a large hall and was where many of the town's teenagers went to learn to dance, and more importantly, meet members of the opposite sex.

Before the dance we gang members would meet at our house and admire each other's clothes before catching the tram into town. We all wore very full skirts held out by stiff, starched petticoats, pretty blouses and extra wide belts. Sometimes we carried cardigans in case the night turned cold. Our skirts were so full and stiff we had trouble fitting next to each other on the narrow seats on the tram. We would giggle about this and some of the older women would look at us critically, but we didn't care.

When we reached the centre of town we got off the tram and walked to dancing class. The hall had an entry foyer where you paid to go in, and off this was a cloakroom where we left our cardigans before going inside. The room had a highly polished floor and a small raised stage at one end where the three-piece band was set up. If a dance were already in progress when we arrived we would file in sedately and sit on the chairs positioned around the edge of the room. When the dance finished the boys escorted their partners back to their seats before returning to the boys side of the room.

We would look across at the boys and decide whom we wanted to dance with. This was a sort of game we played and it added to the fun, although sometimes it didn't work out in the way you wanted.

Mrs. Hythe-Smith, a prim, middle-aged martinet who ran the dancing classes, insisted on correct dance room etiquette. If a boy asked you to dance you were duty bound to accept, so we spent the interval between dances eyeing off the good-looking lads and avoiding eye contact with the five-foot four midgets looking at us longingly.

When the next dance was announced there would be a scramble of boys across the room and I would be relieved when the boy who I had chosen was standing before me and requesting the pleasure. We danced and tried to make conversation, but one had to concentrate on getting the steps right or one of Mrs. Hythe-Smith's assistants would intercept and correct you.

When the number finished the boy would escort you back to your seat. If you had clicked he would say rather quickly and shyly, 'Perhaps we can have another dance later.'

In between dances my girlfriends and I would discuss our various partners and scan the room for likely conquests.

The evening continued with the quickstep followed by a waltz, a schottische, the pride of Erin and the always-popular progressive barn dance. Before the new or more difficult dances Mrs. Hythe-Smith and her partner gave a demonstration of the steps and then some unlucky boy and girl were chosen to dance a further demonstration. We all breathed a sigh of relief when we were not chosen because the dancing partner was a sleazy little man who had been known to make a pest of himself with some of the girls unlucky enough to dance a demonstration with him.

You were not allowed to dance with the same partner all the time, but if a boy liked you he would ask to have the last dance with you. This was an indication that he wanted to take you home. If you liked him you would agree and look forward to the tram trip home and a cuddle in the street as he walked you to your door. If you really liked him you invited him in for a cup of tea and later a smooch on the couch. Conversely if he didn't appeal on closer inspection you would kiss briefly at the gate and make a half-hearted agreement to see him the following week at dancing class.

Saturday nights were spent at the Jazz House, which was entirely different from dancing class and much more exciting. We spent most of Saturday afternoon deciding what to wear and often borrowed Ronda's more sophisticated clothes. Generally we wore tight skirts, fitted tops or sweaters and lots of makeup.

Once more we caught the tram, but we were quieter and behaved more maturely because we were going to the Jazz House, and this was a place that was not only for kids but attracted people in their twenties. It was also a popular meeting place for the bodgies and widgies who were the fringe group around town, and they fascinated us with their unusual clothes and haircuts and the way they seemed to thumb their noses at normal society.

As we got off the tram we would hear the sounds of a favourite New Orleans blues number throbbing in the air and it became louder as we climbed the narrow staircase that led to the dance hall. It felt as if the music was drawing us into a place of excitement and the unknown.

We paid at the door and left our coats in the cloakroom. As we entered the door to the dark interior and heard the lead clarinettist take a solo bracket we would stand transfixed as he improvised around the melody, going higher and higher until he finished on one long, pure note that sent a shiver down my spine. The rest of the band joined back in to complete the number and everyone clapped. There was a feeling of camaraderie and warmth in the room that you get when a group of people share a momentous moment.

We headed straight to the left hand side of the room just as the bracket finished and were jostled a bit as dancers moved off the floor. The lights were turned up during the intervals and we looked across the room at the widgies in their black, tight dresses and their boyfriend bodgies who all wore big-shouldered zoot suits in various bright colours. They enthralled us because they were the rebels around town, but you didn't dare look at them too closely or a widgie was likely to cross the floor and insult you. Their presence added a sense of danger and willfulness to the evening.

Usually the bodgies and widgies danced together. They were always first on the floor and knew the latest steps that they performed very showily. Occasionally a bodgie sauntered across the floor and ask a "good girl" for a dance but the widgies were definitely out of bounds for the straight guys.

One night I met a particularly nice boy named Gerald and had several dances with him. During the last one he asked if he could take me home and I accepted his offer. Before leaving I checked with the other gang members to see what they were doing and learnt that Joan and Alex were being escorted but the others were going home together. We all caught the tram and Di, Anne and Margery sat at the back of the tram and giggled amongst themselves. I thought that perhaps I would have been better off being with them than sitting here next to an almost stranger, trying to make conversation.

We got off the tram at our stop and I allowed Gerald to put his arm around me as we walked down the street. He told me he worked in a furniture factory and seemed a bit put out when I said I was still at school. We arrived at my house and I invited in for a cup of tea but he said he must be off or he'd miss the last tram home. I allowed him to give me a kiss.

When he asked if I'd be at the Jazz House the following week I just answered nonchalantly, 'Maybe,' even though I knew that I would be. We kissed once more and then he loped off up the street to catch that last tram. I wouldn't be coming home with him again because he had not passed the club rules which included that a boy should be willing to come in and meet your parents and must be prepared to miss the tram and walk home if need be.

Gerald was of no particular importance in my life but this event is typical of how we related to the opposite sex. Many years later, when I watched a program on television about speed dating, it reminded me a bit of the dating methods of my youth. We certainly got to meet a lot of boys but few of them appealed enough to date for very long.

During the summer on Sundays we girls caught the double-decker tram down to Sandy Bay beach. We would sit on the top of a double-decker tram and as it swayed around the bends and rattled along the straight we would sing songs like, "Irene Goodnight" and "On Top of Old Smokey," at the top of our lungs. We were young, brash and exhibitionistic.

Once we arrived at the beach we would head for the lawn that ran down to the sand. Here all the young people congregated. We would settle ourselves on our towels and then proceed to flirt with nearby groups of boys, swim out to the punt that was moored in the bay, eat ice creams and chips and generally have fun.

When autumn arrived and swimming and sunbathing days came to an end for the year we spent Sunday afternoons on the covered verandah. Our gang and various boyfriends who we had acquired at dancing class or the Jazz House got together and we spent the afternoons dancing to an ancient, wind-up gramophone, talking, flirting and eating. I made my special cheese straws and Mum plied all-comers with cups of tea, coconut cake and jam rock cakes.

An outdoor skating rink opened up not far from our street and soon we all became proficient skaters and had our own white skates, instead of the ugly black ones that were for hire. We also had to have proper skating clothes and Mum made Joan and me some lovely short skirts and dresses.

As a group our gang became almost obsessed with skating. From our homes we could hear the music coming from the rink and it acted as a magnet to draw us there. Each night we rushed through our homework, or simply pretended to do it, because then we were free to go skating. Here we glided gracefully alone or in pairs or skated furiously during the speed skating sessions. This was somewhere else where we met boys. Sometimes we allowed them to walk us home and we kissed them goodnight with promises of further meetings at the rink, but if a handsomer boy took our fancy we ignored the boy from the previous night.

We were fascinated by boys, but also treated them with a fair degree of disdain. We flirted with them, allowed them to kiss us but dropped them or swapped them quite heartlessly. We didn't consider what it was like for them walking home late at night through deserted streets, or how they must have felt when we kissed them one week and ignored them the next. For a brief time we were queen bees and made the most of it because we sensed, from watching our mothers, that we were destined to become worker bees in the not too distant future.

Our hedonistic life began to take its toll on school results and at the end of the year I barely scraped through and Joan failed and would have to repeat year ten. Mum and Dad were not happy with our reports and curtailed some of our social activities when school resumed. We were only allowed out on Friday and Saturday nights.

I really did want to train to be a teacher, as Ronda was, so settled down to my school work, but Joan was tired of school and had no interest in further study. When she turned sixteen Mum and Dad let her leave school and she got a job in a dress shop.

I spent the next two years concentrating on improving my grades and at the end of 1953 I matriculated and won a scholarship to university. Mum and Dad were really proud of me and so was Ronda who had just completed her degree and would commence teaching the following year. Joan didn't say much but brought me home a surprise present, a beautiful fine woollen sweater. We had grown apart during the past eighteen months with her at work and I at school so this present was important to me.

During that summer, before Ronda took up her first position as a teacher and I commenced university, we sisters drew together again. Perhaps it was knowing in some way that our paths were diverging made us cling closer to each other, but that summer we spent more time in each other's company. Ronda even came to the Jazz House with us one Saturday night. She found that it was not her scene but she did come to the beach with us and to the pictures a couple of times.

On Sunday mornings we would wander down the narrow staircase, sleepy-eyed and tousle-haired in our candlewick dressing gowns. We'd sit around the kitchen table, drinking tea and talking about how and with whom we had spent the previous night. The room filled with the tantalising smell of the fore-quarter of two-tooth baking slowly in the oven as we listlessly podded peas, peeled innumerable potatoes and sliced apples for the pie, while Mum folded and rolled her puff pastry in a waft of flour.

By one o'clock we were dressed in jeans and sweaters or shirts and we would join the rest of the family for Sunday lunch. Dad carved the roast while Mum dished out the potatoes, peas and carrots. Sometimes we invited our current boyfriends to lunch and extra chairs were fitted around the big pine table. Mum welcomed all comers and made light work of feeding as many as a dozen people. There was always something sweet to finish the meal, be it a slice of boiled chocolate cake, apple pie or a fresh batch of scones.

Cheese Straws

3 oz. flour	1 egg yolk
2 oz. butter	1 tsp. cold water
2oz. grated cheese	½ tsp. lemon juice

Rub butter well into flour, add grated cheese and mix well.

Beat egg yolk with water and lemon juice and mix into dry dough.

Roll out and cut into sticks and rings.

Cook in a moderate oven until golden brown.

Serve by placing a bundle of sticks inside each ring.

Coconut Cake

8 oz. butter	4 ozs. desiccated coconut
grated rind ½ lemon	4 beaten eggs
14 oz. flour [3 ½cups]	6 fluid oz. milk [¾cup]
pinch salt	1 tsp. baking powder
10 oz. caster sugar [1 ¼cups]	

Preheat oven to 350 F

Grease 20 cm. Cake tin and line with greaseproof paper.

Sift the flour, salt and baking powder into a large bowl.

Rub in butter until mixture resembles fine breadcrumbs.

Stir in the sugar and coconut.

Mix together eggs and milk and gradually add to the flour mixture.

Turn into cake tin and smooth the top.

Bake for 1 ½ to 1-¾ hours.

When cool ice with lemon-flavoured icing and sprinkle with coconut.

Jam Rock Cakes

8 oz. self-raising flour
pinch salt
½ tsp. mixed spice
3 oz. butter

3 oz. caster sugar
1 egg beaten
2 – 3 tbsp. milk
raspberry jam

Sift flour, salt and spice into a bowl.

Rub in butter until fine.

Mix in sugar.

Mix together egg and milk then add to dry mixture to produce stiff consistency.

Pile in heaped spoonfuls onto greased biscuit tray.

Make a hole in top of each cake and fill with raspberry jam. [Approx. 1 tsp.]

Bake in moderately hot oven [375F] for 15 minutes.

Turn onto cake rack to cool.

Boiled Chocolate Cake

1 cup water
1 ½ cups sugar
4 oz. butter
2 tbsp. cocoa

2 eggs
1 ½ cups self-raising flour
½ tsp. bi-carb soda

Place sugar, water, cocoa and soda in a saucepan and stir over a low heat until butter melts.

Bring to the boil and simmer very slowly for 5 minutes.

When cool mix in beaten eggs and self-raising flour.

Bake in a moderate oven for 1 hour.

Apple Pie

4 large cooking apples	1/3 cup sugar
Squeeze of lemon juice	Water

Peel apples.
Combine apples with sugar, lemon juice and very little water. Stew until soft.

Pastry

1 oz sugar	1 egg
4 oz butter	4 tbsp. milk
8 oz S.R. Flour	

Cream butter and sugar.
Beat in egg.
Add sifted flour and milk alternately.
Mix to a soft dough and divide into two.
Roll pastry between two sheets of baking paper as it is very soft.
Use half to line a tart case.
Fill with the warm apple and cover with the remainder of the pastry.
Decorate and sprinkle with castor sugar.
Bake in a moderate oven (370 - 400 F) for 30- 40 minutes.

As Time Goes By

Life at university was fun but also a lot of work. I found that I had to organize my time or assignments piled up and I began to panic. Ronda was then teaching in a small country school on the north-east coast and only came home at school holiday times, but we corresponded often and she was helpful and encouraging.

Joan was heavily involved in clothes and fashion and totally disinterested in study of any kind, so we now had little to talk about. My friendships with the gang had also slowly eroded as they were all working, and Alex and Di were engaged and spent all their spare time with their fiancés.

I had made friends with two girls who were in my English tutorials and we hung out together in the refectory between lectures. Betty was tall and dark while Sue was a petite blonde so they looked complete opposites, but they shared a zany sense of humour and were fun to be around.

I also made friends with a couple of boys named Rick and Tom. I met them in the Geography practical sessions and we often worked together on assignments.

I joined the debating society and a bush-walking group, and there were always parties on Friday and Saturday nights at different shared houses so I was having a pretty full social life.

One Saturday I went to a party with Rick. I considered him a friend, but thought he might want to be more intimate so I flirted a bit with the other boys to show him that I wasn't his possession. Rod who was one of the organisers of the bush-walking group was there and I rather fancied him.

Towards the end of the evening he asked me to dance and we went to the darkened room where several couples were moving zombie-like around the floor clinging drunkenly to each other. I thought Rod must also be a bit drunk because he held me very close and ran his hand down my back to my bottom in a rather suggestive way. I was responding to his touch when suddenly I felt a tap on my shoulder and there was Rick looking angry and telling me it was time to go home. Because I had come to the party with my friend I said a hurried goodnight to Rod and left with Rick. When we arrived home he tried to kiss me but I told him I didn't feel that way about him. He refused my offer of a cup of tea or coffee, and seemed in a sulky mood as he said goodnight and left. I hoped I hadn't lost a friend.

The next time Rod and I met was when we all gathered near the Cascade Brewery to walk to the Springs and up to the pinnacle of Mount Wellington, then down a track to Lenah Valley. I was sort of excited about seeing him again after our rather sexy dance together, but he greeted me quite offhandedly with a, 'Hi Liz. Pleased to see you've brought your raincoat because the weather could turn nasty.'

I felt a little put out and assumed that he had probably been too drunk to remember our dance. We set off with Rod and his mate Fred in the lead and the rest of us trailing behind. We considered these two men our leaders as they originally organised the bush-walking club and were both experienced in the bush. They were also big, tall competent men, a little older than most of us students so we followed them happily.

The day had begun bright and clear and we made good time, walking single-file along a narrow track and then over rocky scree slopes until we reached the pinnacle. We were settling ourselves down to enjoy our sandwiches when a sudden squall erupted from the west, and soon we were being pelted with icy rain and the air became thick with a clinging white fog. There was a rough shelter nearby into which we all crowded. We pulled our raincoats from the canvas haversacks that we all carried, but already our jeans and sweaters were damp.

Rod and Fred looked at the darkening sky and Rod said, 'It looks as if this will only get worse so we can't stay here. Our best bet is to make our way down as quickly as possible.'

Fred agreed but then a young fellow who I really didn't know spoke up, ' I think it would be madness to try to make it down in this weather. I'm for staying here until the worst of the weather blows over and then we can walk down.'

Although most of us looked on Rod and Fred as our leaders they had no official standing as such so could not insist on everyone following their advice. Some of the girls and one other boy said they were staying, and the rest of us set out behind Rod and Fred who led us down a narrow path.

We were halfway down the mountain when we came to a stone hut. The weather had continued to deteriorate and we all crowded in gratefully. The hut was open on one side, but it faced away from the worst of the wind and rain and had a large fireplace on one wall. Rod and Fred soon had a good fire going. They instructed us to take off our wet outer-clothing, and while we were getting warm and dry they collected extra firewood and water from a nearby stream. They both had large billies in their haversacks and in no time had hot soup bubbling away over the fire. We were soon warm and relatively dry, so we settled down for the night. There were eight of us and we snuggled together near the fire. During the night I woke briefly to find my head resting on Fred's shoulder and Rod's body close to my other side. I will never forget that feeling of being cared for and protected by those two capable, strong men.

As often happens in Tasmania the next day was clear and sunny and we continued down the mountain without any problems. Unfortunately those who had remained on the pinnacle fared badly as they had been unable to light a fire, and the temperature up so high had dropped well below zero. They were rescued in the morning but were all suffering from hypothermia and needed to be hospitalised.

As a result of this event strict guidelines were put in place regarding the walking club. Weather reports were studied closely, and a designated leader was always made responsible for planning the walk and ensuring that the group stayed together.

For the remainder of the year I continued as a member of the walking club and enjoyed many lovely treks on the mountain and beyond. Rod never showed any special interest in me on these walks, and although I found him attractive there were plenty more fish in the sea. As a group we dispersed at the end of the academic year.

In my second year at university my life settled into a pattern of lectures, tutorials and assignment work through the week and of partying on Friday and Saturday nights. I now had lots of friends at university, and there were always plenty of boys around who wanted to take me to parties or to the pictures. So far I'd not found one who I could love but lots of them were fun to be with.

Often a group of us would pile into the few available cars and drive to one of the Saturday night country dances. These were held at many small towns throughout the state in community halls or large barns. A band from the city sometimes provided the music but often a local group would be playing. Supper was always supplied by the women of the town and was a highlight of the evening.

For me these dances were strangely distorted versions of the Jazz House with "townies" on one side of the room and the country girls and a few under-age boys on the side near the exit.

When the band commenced a bracket we townies were always first on the floor, showing off to our country cousins how to combine the traditional quickstep with the new rock and roll moves that were becoming popular. In this we were a bit like the bodgies and widgies had been at the Jazz House.

The country girls, in their old-fashioned pink or blue taffeta dresses, usually danced together or with the younger boys until the pub closed at ten. Then the local lads arrived. Many of them would be decidedly drunk, but they gradually infiltrated the dancing and the drunkest or bravest tried their luck with the city girls. Frequently these dances ended in fistfights rolling on noisily outside between the city and country boys. Meanwhile a veneer of social nicety continued inside with tea, scones, sponge cakes and delicious egg sandwiches being served.

If any of our boys had been involved in a fight we bathed their faces at an outside tap and laughed uproariously about the whole evening on the way back to town.

I continued as a member of the walking club. Many of the members from the previous year, including Fred, had completed their degrees and left but other new members had joined. As an experienced walker Rod was often the designated leader and sometimes we walked together, but it was only on these fortnightly trips that I saw him. I gathered from one of our conversations during the year that he was determined to excel in his final year of an Economics Degree. He was older than most of the students, having had to work to afford the fees before coming to university. He had set his sights on a highly paid job when he graduated, and knew that good exam results would widen his choices. Although I found him very attractive I felt he considered me a little bit juvenile and frivolous, so I tried not to think about him too much.

Second year finished, results were up on the board and I had a credit and a distinction in my majors. I was feeling really happy and enjoying a couple of celebratory drinks with some friends before we headed off to a party, when I saw Rod across the room with a couple of other men. I gave him a wave and was surprised when he came over to our table. He and his friends sat down and we swapped results. He had done exceedingly well and I gave him a congratulatory kiss on the cheek. My friends insisted that he and his mates join us so we left the pub together and walked to the house where the party was being held. I was very conscious of him walking beside me and was wondering if this were the last time I would see him, as he had now finished his degree.

When we arrived at the house we were handed drinks while informal introductions were being made. Everyone was chattering about their results and commiserating with students who had not done very well.

Rod stood beside me, then whispered, 'Would you care to dance.'

Before I could answer he guided me towards the darkened room from which the powerful tones of Jo Stafford could be heard belting out the popular song, "You Belong to Me." He held me tight, and as we moved around the floor he kissed me. I was quite breathless and when he said, 'I've wanted to do that for a long time,' I could only answer, rather goofily, 'Me too.'

I felt a dizziness that had nothing to do with the alcohol I had consumed or end of year euphoria, but with being kissed by this man who I had secretly cared about for some time even if I hadn't admitted it to myself.

When we left the party we decided to walk home, as it was a beautiful warm star-filled night. We strolled along a narrow footpath, which widened when we reached the main road and as we went we kissed at every second step and talked in lovers' code.

'You are so beautiful.'

'Well why didn't you tell me this before.'

'You were always surrounded by other people and having a fun time. I thought you must think me too serious and boring.'

'But I've always admired you so much, ever since that night on the mountain but you didn't seem to find me attractive. You never made a move.'

In this way we covered the three or four miles to my home. With a final, wondrous kiss we said goodnight and arranged to meet the next day before Rod set out on a long walk home.

I sneaked quietly up the stairs so as not to wake Mum and Dad and my brothers. I was tempted to wake Joan and tell her what had happened to me, but felt it was too new and precious to share.

During the next two weeks while Rod was on vacation and before I started my holiday job in a bookshop we saw each other every day. We went on bush walks and it was a novelty for there to be just the two of us. The weather was glorious so we spent a lot of time at the beach, and at night we went to the pictures or snuggled up on the old couch in the covered verandah. We were really getting to know one another and found that we both loved cats, swimming, and jazz and had enjoyed many of the same books. The chemistry between us was amazing. I couldn't get enough of his kisses and his touch, and I wondered how we had previously managed just to be friends when now my greatest pleasure was to be wrapped up in his arms.

When we kissed at the family party to welcome in the New Year of 1956 I knew that I had found my mate for life. I saw my mother watching us. The little smile on her face told me she recognised our love and that she approved.

The following year was momentous in so many ways. In May Ronda married her fiancé, Frank, and moved to a property in the Midlands. They had a beautiful wedding in our local church followed by a reception at a very posh place. Joan and I were bridesmaids and wore gorgeous aqua dresses. It was strange coming back home after the reception and knowing Ronda would never share that bedroom with us again. Even though she had been away for most of the time during the past two and a half years she had been back home for school vacations. Now she was gone for good and Joan and I both felt a little sad.

In June Rod proposed to me formally in the rose-covered summerhouse and gave me a dear little diamond ring. He had also put a deposit on a cheap block of land on a steep hill. When he showed it to me I was doubtful about whether I would be happy in that particular suburb and the block looked very difficult to build on.

Rod could see the disappointment in my face and said, 'This is the best I can afford at present. It won't be forever but it will give us a start.'

He looked so eager and vulnerable. I put my arms around him and nuzzled his neck whispering, 'Darling I'll be happy wherever we are just as long as we're together.'

After we became engaged Rod took me to meet his parents. His father, Bill, was a big, powerful-looking man and his mother, Penny, a tiny smiling woman, very pretty in a slightly careworn way. Bill treated her like a beloved pet patting her bottom affectionately when she came near, but most of his words to her sounded like commands. She responded with dog-like devotion and was busy all through the visit, plumping cushions, refilling cups, bringing in extra unnecessary food, dithering. It appeared to me that she never really relaxed and I was glad when we could leave.

Rod obviously loved both his parents and they were so proud of him, but I certainly wouldn't want that sort of marriage.

That year I finished my degree and was given a posting to a small seaside town on the East Coast. I was feeling a little nervous about commencing teaching but Ronda gave me lots of encouragement and tips. I decided to just enjoy my vacation so spent much of the time with Rod and read all the books that I hadn't had time to during my three years at university.

At the end of January I started my new job and right from the start found it enjoyable. The school was a small three-room weatherboard building with long windows that let in the afternoon sun. My room overlooked the small asphalt area surrounded by shady trees. Past the trees there was a scrubby patch of natives with a path winding down to the nearby beach.

There were only two of us on the staff, the headmaster and me. Mr. Hinds taught grades three to six and was terrific with the children. He had been teaching there for ten years and he and his wife planned to stay in the town when he retired in a couple of years. He knew every child in the school, and had often taught older brothers and sisters so there was a sort of family feeling about the school.

I had kindergarten plus grades one and two. I loved the little ones, and although organising work for each group required a lot of planning I was enjoying myself and learning as I went.

I stayed in the home of a charming widow called Mrs. Bryson. Evidently she always billeted the new teachers, and she certainly made me very welcome. I had a lovely room overlooking the school oval, and was spoilt with a cooked breakfast each morning and lavish evening meals. If I didn't swim regularly at the nearby beach and run around the oval each morning I knew I would be putting on weight.

Everything should have been good in my world but I missed Rod so much. I hadn't thought that this would be so hard. We wrote to each other every night and I made the long bus trip home each fortnight, but I was desperately lonely for him. When I was home we spent every waking minute together, but then we had to say goodbye at the bus stop and I often cried on the return journey.

I didn't spent much time with Joan during those months because most days when I was at home Rod and I spent lots of the time clearing our block and marking out foundations. We spent the evenings snuggled up on the old couch. Joan was out every Friday and Saturday evening, so we didn't catch up with each other except for a while on Sunday mornings.

Sometime in March she met Derek and had been dating him from then. Evidently he had come into the shop where she worked to buy a sweater for a girlfriend. He left without the sweater, but with a promise from Joan that she would meet him after work. Mum thought him a bit flashy and I didn't think either she or Dad quite approved, but Joan was dotty about him. On the rare occasions when we were together she could talk about nothing but Derek and of how wonderful he was. He wooed her with flowers, chocolates and dinners at the top spots in town. Every weekend he picked her up in his jazzy MG car and they went for long drives in the country. By June, although they have only known one another for such a short time, they planned to marry.

Dad queried her about where they would live and Joan answered airily, 'We'll get a flat.'

When Dad huffed about not giving his permission she said, 'I'm a grown woman Dad and don't need your permission.'

So the marriage was planned, but not with the same enthusiasm from our parents as there had been before Ronda's wedding.

After their wedding Joan and Derek moved into a rather cramped flat underneath a large house. Sometimes Rod and I visited them when I was home for the weekend. Knowing that when we left they could go to bed together and make love increased our frustration at having to wait. This frustration, allied with the time we must spend apart, was causing us such unhappiness that we decided to marry at the end of the year. We had hoped to complete our house before we married, but now planned to finish two rooms and live in them while we built the rest of the house around us.

The House On The Hill

During the remainder of the year Rod, with help from his father, put up the shell of the house and finished two rooms, the bedroom, passage and bathroom. We bought a bed, a chest of drawers and a coffee table and Mum and Dad gave us a little stovette and frypan that we set up in a cupboard in the passage. This would be my kitchen.

Two days before our wedding we were putting the finishing touches to what was to be our home. We made up our bed with new sheets, blankets and bedspread. When we finished I pulled Rod onto it and we lay there then turned to cuddle. He ran his hand over my breasts and kissed me and I felt his erection pushing against my leg. I rubbed him gently through his trousers.

I was becoming very aroused and thought, 'If he persists now I won't stop him. After all we'll soon be married.'

Just then Rod pulled away from me and mumbled, 'We've waited so long. Let's leave before I do something I may regret.'

I tumbled from the bed and straightened the covers, but I couldn't help smiling to myself. So often during the past two years I'd felt mean about not being willing to go all the way, but now I saw it had also been important to Rod that I be a virgin bride.

On the first morning of our honeymoon I remember lying in bed and looking across at my handsome husband sleeping peacefully beside me. In sleep his thick dark lashes shadowed his cheeks making his face look almost childlike. Rod was such a masculine, vital man when awake it was as if I were seeing another side of him. I leant over and gently kissed him awake, and he smiled and pulled me over so that I was on top of him.

He laughed happily, 'Hello wife, you just can't leave me alone,' and I nodded agreement.

For the next few days we spent as much of our time as possible in bed. We were staying at a lovely resort situated a short distance from a beach and so usually swam after breakfast. Then we returned to our unit to shower together which led us back to bed for more lovemaking. Most afternoons we took short drives in Rod's old car and walked to the various beauty spots, then we returned to the resort for dinner and an early night. After waiting so long to consummate our love we couldn't get enough of each other.

Mum had never given us advice on birth control and perhaps she didn't know much about it. After all she and Dad had produced six children. Her only words of wisdom were that it was unnecessary to take precautions during the first three months of marriage if you were a virgin. I'm pretty sure a lot of women found this was not so, but Joan proved Mum's theory correct. By October she was suffering from morning sickness and was due to give birth in June, almost exactly one year after she and Derek married. As I didn't want to take the risk of becoming pregnant until the house was finished I made an appointment to see a doctor two months after we returned from our honeymoon.

I sat in the waiting room feeling very nervous. Mum had brought us up to consider our female parts as very precious, and although I enjoyed lovemaking with Rod I dreaded the thought of having another man touch me there, even if he was a doctor.

As I waited I tried to take my mind off the impending examination by reading an article on growing native plants. Suddenly the door opened and a small boy dashed across the room to a play area in the corner of the surgery. He proceeded to empty a box of blocks onto the floor.

His mother, who followed him in, called out loudly, 'Johnny, you'd better play with them now you've made such a mess.'

I looked up at the sound of that familiar voice and there was my erstwhile girlfriend Alex. I hadn't seen her for years, not since we were scatty teenagers together. I don't know if I would have recognised her except for her voice. She was wearing a full smock over baggy pants and her long hair was pulled back in a severe bun. Besides the boy Johnny, who was about four, there was a small child sleeping in the pusher that she manoeuvred clumsily between the rows of chairs.

After she had given her name at the desk she looked around the room for a seat, and I caught her eye and called her name. She came over and I stood to give her a hug. She felt so big and solid in my arms I found it hard to believe this was my friend with whom I had swapped fitted skirts and cinchy belts.

She said, 'Liz, how great to see you. Gee you look good. What are you doing here? Are you preggers too?'

I mumbled that I was just here for a check up, and told her I'd only been married two months.

'It didn't take John and me that long. We conceived little Johnny on our honeymoon, and now we're expecting our third in four years. John reckons he only has to take his pants off in the same room as me for me to fall.'

She said this with an earthy laugh, and I felt a bit embarrassed when others in the room turned to look at her.

Feeling rather prissy I said, 'Well Rod and I are building our house, and we don't want to start a family until it's finished.'

Alex said rather ruefully, 'We planned to build too, but with the kids coming along so quickly we haven't been able to save enough for a block of land. Now we're still renting, and that's so dear we can't save at all. We've put our name down for a housing department home, but who knows when that'll come up?'

Just then my name was called and I said quickly, 'Lovely to see you again. We must catch up,' before I stood and walked across to the door that was being held open by the nurse.

When I entered the room the doctor came from behind his desk and introduced himself. He was a fatherly-looking man of about sixty and I felt slightly reassured. I explained to him that I had married recently and needed some effective form of birth control.

'How long have you been married?' he asked.

When I told him two months he said, 'Well we'd better check out that you aren't already pregnant.'

I felt inclined to tell him this would be extremely unlikely as I was a virgin when I married, but I resisted. Perhaps members of the medical didn't believe my mother's theory. I stripped to the waist and lay on a high, narrow bed. As the doctor performed an internal examination I closed my eyes and tried to pretend I wasn't there.

While I was still lying on the bed the doctor washed his hands then appeared above me again saying cheerfully, 'No little visitor there yet.'

As I went to get off the bed he said, 'Now just lie there for a moment and I'll show you what I usually recommend.'

He returned with an object in his hand that was round and white and looked as if it were made of some kind of thin rubber. He explained how it worked then demonstrated how easy it was to insert. I was surprised how comfortable it felt when in place. I was also surprised when he called it a diaphragm as I had always thought that this was a part of the body somewhere below the chest.

After he removed the diaphragm I was allowed to get off the bed, but then he suggested that I insert the thing into myself.

I stood as instructed with one leg up on the bed and folded the item as shown. I pushed but did not get it high enough, and it fell back into my hand.

The doctor said, 'Now just relax and try again.'

Feeling flushed and embarrassed I tried again and this time it slipped into place. He told me how to remove it and then got me to insert and remove it once more. Finally I was allowed to dress, and I sat opposite the doctor as he told me about the cleaning and storage of this device.

As I was leaving his office he gave me a reassuring pat on the shoulder and said, 'You'll soon get used to it.'

I checked the waiting room but couldn't see Alex, so she must have been in with one of the other doctors. I was rather relieved not to have to pretend a friendship that no longer existed.

I was also relieved to have obtained a reliable means of birth control, and felt I had taken an important step as a responsible adult. To reward myself I went to a nearby cafe and had a strong cup of coffee and a vanilla slice. I couldn't help feeling a bit smug that, unlike Alex, I would be able to plan my life and decide when Rod and I started a family.

Because I was married I was given a position in a nearby school. It was one of the largest schools in the state with over a thousand pupils and forty-five to fifty children in each class. There had been a rapid increase in the number of births following the end of the war and these babies were now at school. Like many others in the state, this school had had to expand to cope with the sudden increase in the child population. I was allocated one of the demountables that lined a side of the playground. It was actually quite a pleasant room, bright and sunny compared with the older ones in the main brick building.

I had a grade three and there were three other women teaching the same grade so we planned our programmes together. I enjoyed their companionship and gained a lot from the advice of these more experienced teachers, but I rather missed the country children. Generally the city kids were not quite as open and friendly although I did have some lovely pupils in my class.

I also had three very naughty little boys who continually disrupted lessons. At times I felt like shouting at them but I remembered Ronda's adage, "A noisy teacher makes a noisy class," and spoke in a soft and I hoped ominous voice to them. I could have sent them to the headmaster when they misbehaved too badly but resisted this urge, as I knew they would be caned and I didn't want to be responsible for that. Instead I kept them in after school and talked to them, hoping some goodness lurked behind their cheeky grins.

Every weekend Rod and I worked on the house and soon we had the roof on and most of the weatherboards nailed in place.

One wintry day we worked from early morning until dark and were so tired we went straight to bed after a warming meal of soup and toast. During the night we half woke and made slow and gentle love. In the morning I remembered I hadn't put in the diaphragm because I'd thought we would both be too tired for sex. I thought we would be safe as it was past the middle of my menstrual cycle so I didn't bother telling Rod.

By the beginning of September it was six weeks since I'd had a period and I feared I might be pregnant. I didn't know how to break the news to Rod and I finished up just blurting out one night, 'I might be expecting a baby. I didn't put the thing in one night and I haven't had a period since, and now we'll never get the house finished.'

I then promptly burst into tears. Rod hugged me and made soothing noises.

He said, 'We wanted children anyway.'

When I bemoaned the fact that the house was still incomplete he said, 'We'll still be able to finish the house. It will just mean that we'll have to get a loan, but we can certainly manage on my wage.'

I allowed him to comfort me but I still felt I'd let him down.

Our beautiful baby boy was born on a bright April day after twelve hours labour. I had dearly wanted to be awake for his birth but towards the end they put me to sleep, and it was several hours later before I really saw him. It was even longer for Rod because he had to wait until visiting hour at seven o'clock. The nurse brought him in to us and Rod had a little hold of him.

Some people say all babies look the same and that you can't tell how they will turn out until they get older, but I could see already that baby would look like his Daddy. I felt so pleased with myself.

I had taught until the end of the year. Although getting pregnant had been an accident the timing was very good because I could finish the year before I was showing. Unlike many other employers the Education Department allowed women to continue working after marriage, but they were expected to resign before a "bump" started to show.

Rod took out a loan and we worked hard on the house to have it roughly finished and the baby's room completed.

Once I was home alone with my baby I felt tired and vulnerable. My breasts ached because I seemed to have too much milk even though Dale was feeding well. He was a very good baby and slept four hours between feeds and eight hours at night, but I still worried about him. At times I wondered if I were mature enough to be entrusted with the care of this precious, little person and at other times I felt so different from the person I had been only a year ago. I felt as though the youthful, fun-loving me had disappeared forever, and been replaced by this grown-up person I didn't really know.

I tried talking to Mum about these mixed emotions that I was having but she just said, 'You're doing a wonderful job darling. Look how he's thriving.'

She obviously hadn't had those feelings of inadequacy and rebellion when she first became a mother, so I gave up trying to discuss this with her.

My sisters were more understanding. Ronda said she felt somewhat the same with her first baby, but that the feelings didn't last long and she was really looking forward to having more children.

Joan said, 'Well I felt terrible for the first three months and cried nearly every day. Justin had the most dreadful colic and I'd sit in that pokey little flat holding him while he screamed with tears running down both our faces. Things do get better though, especially once the baby sleeps through the night.'

I feel badly that I hadn't known how unhappy she'd been at that time and hadn't given her any support when she obviously needed it.

I determined to pull myself together and stop being so self-centered.

A year later I looked back at the girl I was then and wondered at my immaturity. Perhaps I could blame my moments of depression and self-doubt on hormonal imbalance. Anyhow once more I felt happy. Dale was a gorgeous little boy toddling around the house, playing with his toys and babbling away to himself.

The house was nearly completed and at last I had a kitchen instead of just a space in the passage. I painted the walls different colours, ochre, lime green and pale yellow and the cupboards doors a brighter yellow that exactly matched the laminex bench tops. We could only afford linoleum for the floor but I hoped to replace this with cork tiles later on.

In keeping with my colour scheme I bought canisters in different hues and a harlequin dinner set that I loved. Rod thought it a bit kitsch, but for me it was so nice to have a complete set of crockery after a couple of years of using bits and pieces given to me by Mum.

Because we didn't want to borrow any more money we furnished our home with cast-offs from Mum and Dad and other odds and ends that we picked up at second-hand shops. We did buy a new fridge though. We hadn't had one until I began weaning Dale and then it was necessary for his bottles, so we gave it to each other as a Christmas present.

The following year we were getting an early Christmas present. Rod and I decided that it would be good to have our children close together and our next baby was due in November. I had gained a lot of confidence in myself as a mother and was really looking forward to the arrival of this baby.

When I was six months pregnant Ronda's daughter Jennie turned three and we went to her party. Rod came too because he worried about me driving too far in that condition. I had said I'd be all right, but was rather glad when he insisted because he didn't see much of my extended family.

When we arrived at the property Frank came out to greet us at the car and led us around the side of the house to where there was a barbecue. He and Ronda had set up a long trestle table under a weeping willow. The tree had balloons hanging from the branches and it all looked very festive. Jennie looked very cute in a flowered dress and we all clapped when Dale handed her our present and gave her a kiss. They looked so sweet together.

Shortly after we arrived Mum and Dad drove in with Joan and Justin and behind them came Vincent, Meg and

Gordon. Although Vincent was not yet twenty-one and Meg a year younger they had been going together since high school. They were so in love at such an early age that we in the family called them "The Sweethearts" and the name stuck. They planned to marry at the end of the year after he finished his carpentry apprenticeship and would be on adult wages. They had bought a bush block and a caravan and planned to live in it while they built their house.

Because Ronda was very pregnant Frank had taken over organising the party and he and Mum saw to the food with some help from Joan. Ronda and I sat in the shade, plumply contented, and made the most of being waited on. Joan joined us for a while, but I think she became bored with our talk about our impending babies for she soon wandered off to drink with the men around the barbecue. Mum spent much of the time playing with Justin and Jennie or carrying Dale around. You would think that after bringing up six children she would have tired of the company of little people, but she adored her grandchildren and seemed to have boundless energy when they were around.

It was a lovely day and I was particularly happy to have shared it with Rod. We now seemed to get so little time to do things together as a family.

When my second beautiful boy was born all went well and I was awake for the birth. I held him straight away and he looked at me with such bright, knowing eyes. Mum always said Vincent had smiled at her when he was born but we hadn't really believed her. Now I did because I was convinced Ralph smiled at me. It was such a special moment.

Rod collected Ralph and me from the hospital and we stopped in at Mum's to pick up Dale and for her to have a proper cuddle of her new grandson. My eyes had become accustomed to only seeing babies and Dale looked so big. When I cuddled him he held himself back and was stiff in my arms. I wondered if he'd been traumatised by my absence or was just withholding his affection to punish me for leaving him.

After we arrived home I fed Ralph and put him to bed while Rod made Welsh rarebit for Dale and us. While I was eating Dale slipped down from his chair and came and sat on my lap. I cuddled him to me and knew I was forgiven for absenting myself so unexpectedly.

My days were now so full. I seemed to be rushing from the time I woke at six o'clock to give Ralph his first feed for the day till ten in the evening when he had his last. My days were spent juggling caring for my baby, playing with Dale, tidying the house, making the beds and doing endless loads of washing. I had a twin tub machine so all I had to do was set it going then move the clothes into the spinner once they had been washed. When I thought of how Mum had to heat up a copper to do the washing then manhandle the hot clothes through a mangle I felt very lucky to have that modern machine.

Years later I read an article that said women at home worked sixteen hours a day. My initial reaction to this was disbelief for by that time I had become a lady of leisure. I thought, 'For goodness sake, that's so stupid. You'd have to vacuum and dust every day and iron everything in sight to spend that long on housework.

Then I remembered those early years with a toddler and a baby and I agreed with her. I remembered just how hard I'd worked and how tired I'd been at the end of each day. Sure, it wasn't true that women could spend that long working in the home once their children were at school, but during the early years of your children's lives a sixteen hour day could be par for the course.

During the week our evening meals were simple. I cooked chops, sausages, patties or casseroles. Sometimes I would cook silverside just the way mum always made it. We always had potatoes and a red and a green vegetable. For dessert we had simple things like jellied fruit with custard, flummery with ice cream or ideal cake. Dale would perch on a stool and help put the vegetables in the pots or mix the jelly. On weekends I would try to cook something a bit more special and Rod loved my lemon meringue pie.

Rod generally arrived home at five thirty and I always made sure I had combed my hair and put on fresh lipstick before he arrived. All the women's magazines stressed how important it was to look fresh and attractive for your husband when he arrived home tired from his busy workaday world.

We ate dinner in the dining room and then Rod played with Dale while I gave Ralph his next feed. He'd have a little nurse of Ralph while I did the washing up, bathed Dale and then we'd put our boys to bed. At last we could have a little time together. Often we would sit at the table talking about our day, but other nights we would lounge comfortably on the old couch Mum has given us and read our books until it was time for me to give Ralph his last feed for the day.

At the weekends Rod got some time to spend with Dale while I prepared lunch. We had more elaborate meals on those two days and on Sunday I always cooked a leg of lamb or a good piece of beef. We usually had meat left over so on Mondays shepherd's pie or beef hash was on the menu. For Sunday lunch I also made fancier desserts and chocolate sauce pudding or golden syrup dumplings were great favourites with Rod.

Every Thursday Rod caught the bus to work so that I could have the car. I really looked forward to this day as I got to visit Mum and catch up with Ronda and Joan. Mum fussed over the children and us, and minded the toddlers and babies while we three sisters went to a nearby shopping centre and bought the meat and groceries for the week. Sometimes we'd stop for a cup of coffee on the way back. We all felt a bit guilty to be snatching this time alone, but it was good to be able to talk together without being interrupted by children or babies.

On one of these occasions Joan told us she was expecting again, but when Ronda and I gushed our congratulations she seemed a little tense. On my way home I thought about the expression on her face when she told us her news, and wondered if all was well between her and Derek.

When Ralph was about two Rod received a promotion. He worked so hard and certainly deserved this recognition, but it seemed that he had less and less time to spend with the boys and me. Often he was late home and would miss out on seeing the boys before their bedtime, and we had less time talking of an evening as he now brought work home. If I reproached him he said he was only doing it for us and then I felt guilty, but I did miss the companionable times we had previously enjoyed. I felt as though the boys and I were living a separate life from him.

From that time I remember one particularly glorious autumn day. The little boys were playing happily in the backyard and Rod was keeping an eye on them from the deck where he was entertaining Pete, a young workmate.

Pete had recently married and had sought out his more mature friend for marital advice.

I was amused at this concept for at times I thought Rod could be a better husband. I eavesdropped shamelessly as the men downed copious amounts of beer and the afternoon sun shifted across the suburban skyline. Both men were slightly drunk but I was still shocked when I heard Rod pontificating, 'Keep them bare-foot and pregnant. That's the answer mate.'

I looked over my protruding belly at my bare, brown feet and felt manipulated. This baby had been his idea, lovingly suggested as a way to bring us closer together when I complained about the distance that seemed to be coming between us.

Silverside

4lbs. silverside	1 carrot
½ cup malt vinegar	1 dsp. brown sugar
1 onion	

Place silverside in a saucepan.

Cover with cold water.

Add vinegar, sugar, slice onion and carrot.

Bring to the boil and cook – ½ hour per pound plus ½ hour.

When cooked remove from saucepan and wrap in clean tea towel or foil for 10 minutes to rest.

This has always been a family specialty but no one can cook it quite like Nan did.

Lemon Meringue Pie

1 biscuit or short crust pastry sheet
1 tin condensed milk
2 eggs
¼ pint lemon juice
2 oz, caster sugar
grated rind 1 lemon

Place pastry sheet in pie plate and trim to fit.

Blind bake for 10 minutes.

Mix together condensed milk, lemon juice, lemon rind and egg yolks.

Pour mixture into partially cooked pie shell.

Beat egg whites until stiff, then fold in caster sugar.

Smooth over top of pie and bake in moderate oven until meringue topping is set.

Flummery

1 pkt. jelly crystals [usually raspberry or strawberry]
1 tin Carnation milk
1 cup boiling water

Dissolve jelly crystals in boiling water – leave until cool but not set.

Whip milk until thick.

Add jelly and continue whipping until all jelly mixture is mixed in.

Set in refrigerator.

Delicious served with bananas and whipped cream.

Ideal Cake

1 tin Carnation milk
4 dsp. sugar
6 tsp. gelatine
½ cup boiling water

Beat together milk and sugar until frothy.

Dissolve gelatine in boiling water.

Add to milk/sugar mixture and pour into a round tin.

Refrigerate until set.

Turn out onto a plate and decorate with whipped cream and bananas or other fruit of choice.

Shepherd's Pie

3 cups lamb, minced or chopped finely
1 onion finely chopped
1 dsp. plain flour
1 dsp. oil
left-over gravy if available

mashed potatoes

extra butter
grated cheese
1-cup water

Heat oil in saucepan, add flour and brown well.

Add water and bring to boil.

Add leftover gravy if available or flavour with Vegemite and Worcestershire sauce.

Add lamb and cook slowly for 5 minutes.

Place mixture in a greased casserole.

Cover with mashed potatoes.

Dot with butter and grated cheese.

Place in hot oven [440F] and heat through and brown top.

Beef Hash

3 cups diced leftover roast beef

2 cups diced cooked potatoes

1 cup chopped onion

½ cup sliced green pepper

1 cup stock

salt and pepper to taste

1 tbsp. tomato sauce

1 ½ oz. butter

Mix all ingredients together except butter.

Heat butter in a large pan, add beef mixture and press down.

Cook over medium heat until crust forms [15 to 20 minutes]

Serve with carrots and peas or beans.

Chocolate Sauce Pudding

1 cup self-raising flour
¾ cup sugar
1 tbsp. cocoa

2 oz. butter
½ cup milk
2 cups hot water

Topping

¾ cup brown sugar

1 tbsp. cocoa

Sift together flour, cocoa and sugar.

Heat butter and milk in a saucepan and stir until butter dissolves.

Stir into flour mix.

Smooth into baking dish.

Top with brown sugar/cocoa mix.

Pour on the 2 cups of hot water.

Cook for 40 minutes in a moderate oven.

Serve hot with vanilla ice cream.

Golden Syrup Dumplings

Dumplings

1-¾ cups self-raising flour

1 tbsp. butter

1 egg

½ cup milk

Beat the egg.

Rub butter into flour.

Add beaten egg and enough milk to form walnut size dumplings.

Syrup

2 cups water

¾ cup sugar

2 tbsp. golden syrup

grated rind and juice of 1emon

Mix together syrup ingredients in a saucepan and bring to boil.

Drop dumplings into boiling syrup.

Lower heat and simmer gently covered for 15 to 20 minutes.

Serve with whipped cream or ice cream.

While We're Young

In August I gave birth to a dear little girl. I couldn't believe my luck. When I changed her napkin before each feed I marvelled at her perfect female body. Rod said he was pleased to have a daughter, but he spent even less time with her than he had with the boys. I had hoped having another baby would bring us closer together again as a family, but this was not the case.

The year after Helen was born was a difficult one. The boys had slept through the night from the time they were three months old, but Helen was still waking for a feed when she was five months old. Rod was working long hours and often had to go out in the evening for business meetings. I felt as though the gulf between us was widening, and didn't know how to stop things getting worse.

One cold night I staggered wearily from the bed and felt my way along the passage to Helen's bedroom. I gathered my crying daughter to my aching milky breasts and gazed out the window at the lightening sky. I wondered where the hell Rod was. I knew where he said he'd be, but I no longer believed him. He was living a life apart from the children and me, a life of working breakfasts, business lunches and networking dinners. At least that was what he told me to account for his many absences.

I fed Helen then put her back into her bassinet. As I was making a cup of tea I heard the key turn in the lock and Rod stumbled through the door.

I turned on him in a fury and screamed, 'Where have you been until this hour? No dinner goes on this long.'

He looked at me coldly, not deigning to give an explanation and said, 'For God's sake Liz, keep your voice down. Do you want to wake up the children?'

By the time I had calmed myself with a cup of tea and joined Rod in bed he was snoring peacefully. I lay there beside him, exhausted but wide-awake. Was he having an affair and what would I do if he were? I knew Joan was convinced Derek was playing around, but she turned a blind eye to it. Could I do that and what were the alternatives?

That night I faced the possibility of having to make a life for myself and the children without Rod. I knew I couldn't do it so I took steps to improve things between us.

I weaned Helen over the next few weeks. I felt a bit guilty about this as I had fed the boys much longer, but the clinic sister said she was a good weight and would do well on formula. Helen took to the bottle easily and when I was no longer breast-feeding I could go on the birth control pill, which was an absolute boon after using a diaphragm for so long.

I exercised my baby-bearing body back to its original shape and bought a whole new wardrobe of clothes. Rod appreciated the changes and began taking me out more. Usually we went to one of the few good restaurants in town, sometimes with my sisters and their husbands but more often with Rod's friends or business associates.

During those years our town became more cosmopolitan and Chinese, Italian and even a French restaurant opened, but it didn't last long. Snails and frogs legs were just a bit too adventurous for our parochial palates.

Inspired by these new tastes I began adding new dishes to the meals I prepared. I began ringing the changes with sweet and sour pork, chow-mien and pasta dishes such as spaghetti Bolognese. I tried my hand at Greek meatballs and they became a standard entertaining entree. Inspired by a meal at the French restaurant I also made a beef

Burgundy with lots of red wine. and a cheese soufflé. As the only cookbook I owned was the Central Cookery Book I had to improvise with these foreign dishes, but I had fun doing it. Rod usually enjoyed the results although the children seemed to prefer the plainer meals.

Besides going out more together Rod and I began entertaining at home quite a lot after we had been able to afford new furniture for the house.

It was quite difficult to organise the evening meal for the family as well as prepare supper, but Helen was soon a help and loved to work with me in the kitchen. She sat up at the breakfast bar and carefully patted tomato slices dry before I put them on Sao biscuits. She also became quite adept at wrapping pickled onions in Belgium meat and pineapple pieces in bacon before I fixed them with a toothpick. I adored my boys, but it was somehow extra special to have this little female person who was so helpful and efficient for one so young.

In some ways I enjoyed those evenings at home more than the dinners out. We just sat around and ate and drank and listened to the peaceful melodies of Peter, Paul and Mary, Simon and Garfunkel and of course our own Australian group, The Seekers.

Sometimes we discussed the war in Vietnam, the student protests and the changes that were occurring in society. We talked of the flower people in San Francisco and of their drug taking, of tales we had heard of wife swapping in the suburbs of Melbourne and Sydney and of the eruption of feminist groups around the country, but we participated in none if these things. The swinging sixties passed us by.

We were most concerned about the war in Vietnam when conscription was introduced and eighteen-year-old boys were subjected to a form of Russian roulette. Their birth dates were placed in a barrel and if their number came up they were sent off to war. Our own sons were much too young to be affected by this appalling procedure and my brother Gordon just too old. One of our friends had a brother who was the right age, and she was so relieved when he didn't have to go away and fight.

Some nights I would look at my two beautiful boys sleeping peacefully and think that surely the war couldn't drag on long enough for them to be affected.

When Helen started school I felt quite bereft. I had thought I would enjoy having time to myself and planned a day in town after I left her at the classroom door. I was going to buy myself a new dress, and then lunch with my old university friend Betty at a fairly posh restaurant. After parking the car I wandered aimlessly from shop to shop unable to find anything that I even liked enough to try on, so I was early for lunch.

When Betty arrived she said, 'What's the matter? You look so sad.'

I felt it would sound too silly to say I was missing Helen so I just answered, 'Doing a bit of wool gathering I guess.'

We had a pleasant lunch and planned to meet up again, but I was glad when it was time for me to collect my children from school. That day made me realise how much I depended emotionally on being needed by them. I really would have to find something constructive to do with my time.

After Helen had been at school for nearly a term I was still missing her company around the house, and found that the days dragged slowly by until it was time for me to collect her and the boys from school.

One day when I was crossing the playground I ran into Beth, one of the women with whom I had taught the year before I had Dale.

We stopped for a chat and when I told her that my youngest was now at school she said, 'Well, when are you coming back?'

I answered rather diffidently, 'I don't know if I could teach any more. It's been so many years and I guess things have changed a lot.'

'Not that much,' she laughed, 'We're still overworked and underpaid and the classes are too big, but it has its rewards. Actually there is a vacancy coming up next term in one of the grade threes. You should apply for it. There's still a shortage of teachers and I'm sure you could get it. I'm teaching one of the other threes and could help you out with curriculum and weekly planning.'

As she was saying this, the siren went and I said hurriedly, ' I'll think about it but I must rush. I like to be at the classroom door when Helen comes out. I'll be in touch.'

I gathered up my little family and drove home, my mind awhirl with thoughts of returning to work. Could I do it? How would it affect the children having a mother teaching at their school? Would Rod agree?

After dinner I put the children to bed and joined Rod on the couch where he was reading. I felt a bit apprehensive about how he would react but I'd never been any good at approaching a subject tactfully so simply asked. 'What would you think about me going back to work?'

Rod turned to me, a slightly quizzical look on his face and said, 'What's brought this on? I'm earning enough money to keep us and you really have plenty to do looking after the kids and me.'

'But that's it. I don't have enough to do, and I ran into one of the women I used to teach with. She said there is a vacancy coming up next term, and that she was sure I could fill it if I applied.'

I knew I was babbling but I had suddenly realised how important this was to me.

Rod breathed a heavy sigh, 'I'd really hate you working. I see enough harried women at work trying to juggle looking after their homes and families while employed. They finish up not doing either job properly and are completely stressed out. I don't want that happening to you. It's not as if we need the money.'

I tried to convince him this would not be the case with me, but I guess I lacked enough certainty in my ability to marshal my arguments. We concluded the discussion with me agreeing to forget about returning to work. That night Rod was especially passionate in bed.

Do we colour reality to rationalise our decisions? During the next four years I felt I was very busy. I worked long hours outside making our steep, rocky piece of land into a beautiful garden, I attended an art class once a week and joined a tennis club. I made acquaintances but not friends. My main friends were still my sisters, but I saw them less and less once our children were at school as both sisters had returned to work.

We would catch up during school holidays when we all went to Mum's on Thursdays as we used to do when our children were babies and toddlers.

While the kids played in the garden or helped their Grandfather in his vegetable patch we three sat in the kitchen as before drinking copious cups of tea, smoking until the room was quite hazy and talking, talking, talking as before, but now the conversations had an edge. There was a gap between us because they were working wives and I was a stay-at-home mother. At times they seemed to be implying that I was not leading a fulfilling life because I wasn't at work. I in return implied that my children were doing better academically, which they were, because I could devote more time to helping them.

Mum smoothed over any possible rancour by saying, 'You're all doing such wonderful jobs,' while she whipped up a batch of scones and an enormous pile of corned-beef sandwiches.

After the scones came out of the oven we called our children inside for hand- washing before we all gathered around the big pine table for a feast of sandwiches, kiss biscuits, coconut cake and hot scones dripping with butter and raspberry jam.

The other times that we got together were for the children's birthdays. We had always celebrated birthdays in a big way in our family, so the children had fairly gala parties. They were always held on a Saturday because most of the cousins were now at school and aunts were working. Rod and Frank always attend but Derek never came. Vincent and Meg had two little girls, Alicia and Sally, close to Helen's age and a little boy called William and they always came for my children's birthdays and put on lovely parties for their little ones. Bob had been working on the mainland for several years as a journalist and we only saw him at Christmas. Gordon was teaching in the north of the state, but he usually made it down south for birthday parties.

I always began preparations several days before the event making long-keeping goodies like chocolate crackles, coconut roughs and coconut ice and storing them in tins. The day before I made patty cakes, little apple tarts, sausage rolls and egg and bacon pies and of course the birthday cake. On the day jelly and cream was added to the butterfly cakes, fairy bread made and cocktail saveloys separated. The boys and Helen helped with these last minute chores and Rod blew up the balloons.

Besides cousins the children also invited school friends now so the parties were always boisterous and noisy but lots of fun.

Helen had a lovely party for her seventh birthday. All the guests had left and we were clearing up the last of the debris when the phone rang.

Rod answered it and I heard him say, 'Yes, she'll come right away,' before hanging up.

I turned to him, 'Who was that?'

'Police,' he answered a strained expression on his face, 'Derek's been killed in a car accident. Joan has asked for you.'

Shocked I asked, ' When did it happen? Where? The kids weren't with him?'

'No, he was alone in the car. I think it must've happened while Joan and Justin and Sara were still here. I didn't ask much. The police woman mainly wanted to be sure you'd go to be with your sister.'

I grabbed a coat and my car keys, and with hasty instructions about the cleaning up and checking on the children was out the door in less than a minute.

I drove the six or so kilometres as fast as I dared and soon arrived at Joan and Derek's house. There were lights blazing in every room and a police car was parked out the front. As I walked up the front path I saw a curtain twitch next door, and over the road there were people standing on their verandah blatantly staring across at my sister's house.

When I pushed open the door and walked into the lounge room I saw Joan sitting on the couch with her arms around Justin and Sara who were both crying softly. She lifted her face to me and I was shocked at the expression I saw there.

In a harsh voice she said to me, 'Will you take the kids home with you? I need to be alone.'

I could see the surprised look on the policewoman's face as I crossed the floor. When I reached the couch Joan stood up and clutched my arm so hard it hurt.

'I don't want them to see me like this. You will take them won't you?'

I wanted to comfort my sister, give her a hug, let her talk out her grief but she was not asking for this. All I could do was agree to her request. I hugged the kids and then helped them pack some overnight gear.

When I tried to hug and talk to Joan she just waved me away and said, 'Just do what I ask,' so I left with the children, after being reassured by the police woman that she would stay with my sister for the night.

After I'd settled Justin on the couch in the lounge room and Sara on a blow up mattress in Helen's room Rod and I went to bed, and I told him about Joan's strange behaviour. I knew if anything happened to Rod I would want our children as close to me as they could be.

He agreed with me that her reaction was unusual but then said, 'You knew he was having an affair didn't you?'

'I think he has had lots of affairs during their marriage but Joan seemed to accept them. I don't see how his infidelity would explain her bizarre behaviour now.'

'I don't either but perhaps you'll be able to talk to her better when she calms down and gets over the shock.'

We spent a restless night. At one time I heard sobbing coming from the lounge room and went out to give Justin a cuddle, but he seemed to be crying in his sleep.

The next morning I rang Joan. She thanked me abruptly for minding the kids and said she would pick them up in the afternoon. I said I'd bring them home but she said she was all right to drive.

She arrived at about two o'clock and once more rebuffed my attempts to comfort her. She appeared dry-eyed and brittle, but was loving and compassionate with the children. I hoped that when they were home she would grieve with them.

I rang Joan every day before the funeral offering to help her in any way I could, but she said she was coping.

On the day of the funeral we gathered at Mum and Dad's so that we could car pool to the crematorium where the service was to be held. We had all offered to accompany Joan and her children, but she refused everyone saying, 'I prefer just to be with my children.'

We felt saddened by her rejection, and worried about the way she was pushing us away at a time like that.

Ronda and Frank came in our car and Mum and Dad went with Vincent and Meg. When we arrived Gordon, who has driven down from the country town where he was teaching, was already there. We stood around talking awkwardly about the weather, the flowers and other trivialities, and were relieved when the hearse and the accompanying black car arrived. An attendant helped Joan from the car and we approached as a group as Justin and Sara scrambled out.

When Mum tried to hug Joan she stood stiffly then shrugged her off saying, 'Let's get this over with.'

I was shocked by the hardness in her voice.

The service was brief and as the coffin slid slowly behind the curtain I felt tears coursing down my face. I knew he hadn't always been a good husband to Joan, but he was a loving father and always fun to be with. I heard loud crying coming from the back of the chapel. I turned to see who it was but couldn't make out where the sound was coming from. As we are leaving I noticed a young blonde girl huddled in a corner her face wet with tears.

Behind me I heard Mum say, 'Poor little thing. She must be someone who worked with Derek.'

Dad just harrumphs in reply.

We had a sort of brief wake at Mum and Dad's, but neighbours were minding our children so we couldn't stay long. Throughout the whole ghastly day I hadn't seen Joan shed a tear. She seemed to have put a barrier around herself that none of us could break through. I worried for my sister for this calm was not natural.

A week after the funeral I rang her and invited myself around for the evening. When I arrived the children were in bed and Joan opened the door, a glass of red wine in her hand. She allowed me to give her a sisterly kiss on the cheek before ushering me into the lounge and pouring me a glass of the wine.

I gulped it down before garbling, 'Oh darling, I know what a terrible time you're going through and what you must be feeling, but you're just making it harder for yourself by shutting us all out. We all love you and want to help, but you won't let us.'

She turned to me a look almost of dislike on her face, ' No Liz you don't know what I am feeling. You can't even imagine it.'

'Well tell me then,' I entreated, 'I want to help you.'

'For God's sake Liz, I don't need any help. What you don't realise is how glad I am that Derek is dead.'

I gasped in shock as she continued, 'For years I put up with his little affairs. At first it hurt so much, but gradually I became immured to them. Although I no longer loved him, the children and the mortgage on this house tied us together. I could live with that compromise but then he fell in love.' She said this sneeringly as she reached for the bottle and topped up our glasses before continuing, 'You probably saw her at the back of the chapel bawling her silly head off. He was coming back from a rendezvous with her when he crashed his car.'

I must have looked sympathetic or at least had a look on my face that Joan didn't like because she continued quite angrily. 'Look, what you haven't known is that a few months ago Derek asked me for a divorce and I refused. I didn't want the children upset, or everyone knowing that he'd left me for a younger woman. Most of all I didn't want to risk losing this house that I've worked so hard to get after years of living in crummy flats.'

Surprised by what she was saying I stammered, 'But why would you have lost the house? He wouldn't have kicked you out.'

'Oh God Liz you really don't live in the real world, do you?' she almost shouted at me. 'Although I saved the deposit and made all the house payments the bank would only lend to a man, and so the loan and the house was in Derek's name. And no, he wouldn't have kicked me out, but I wouldn't have been able to keep the kids and myself and make the payments. Now, because the bank insisted on Derek being insured, the insurance will pay off the loan. So you see, dear sister, his death is a blessing as far as I'm concerned, and I'm not going to pretend otherwise. When I heard about the accident I felt like celebrating, not grieving. That's why I wanted to be alone.'

Now I partially understood my sister's behaviour, but didn't know what to say. I was so sorry for the bitterness she was feeling and the sadness she had experienced through the years and kept hidden from Ronda and me.

We finished the bottle of wine and I drove home deep in thought about who we really are, and how we want the world to see us. I also felt very lucky to be married to Rod. I'd never been sure whether or not he'd had a brief affair after Helen was born, but I had always known he loved me. It must have been awful for Joan, keeping up the pretence for so long while Derek had one affair after another, but then for him to fall in love with someone else would have been devastating. No wonder my poor sister was so bitter.

The years passed happily for my little family and me, although at times I felt as though I should be doing something more constructive with my time. Rod was very successful and the children were all progressing well at school, but often I felt frustrated at being so dependent. So many other women were now working and a part of me envied the fact that they had financial independence and broader experiences.

When Helen turned ten she had a big party. She invited several of her school friends and of course all the cousins were there. For the first time I found it difficult to organise all those children, for now so many of them were teenagers and naturally didn't want to join in pass the parcel and treasure hunts.

Jennie, the oldest of the cousins and a really sweet girl, helped me with the games, but the big boys just absented themselves. Justin was fifteen, Dale fourteen, Ronda's Tom thirteen and Ralph would soon be. They took themselves off to the boys' room and didn't reappear until it was time to eat.

That evening, after everyone had gone home and the children were in bed, I said to Rod that I had felt sorry for the big boys, and worried that they were bored, cramped together in that rather small room.

He put his arm around me and said, 'Well, actually darling, I've felt we're all becoming rather cramped in this house, and that it's time we started looking around for something bigger.'

Startled by his suggestion I said, 'You mean sell this house? I don't want to do that. Couldn't we just build a rumpus room on at the back? That'd give the kids their own space and could be great for when we have parties.'

Obviously Rod had been thinking about this for some time for he said definitely, 'That wouldn't make the boys' bedroom any less cramped and would just be a makeshift solution. No, I think we should move, and to a better suburb. I'd also like a house more suited to entertaining clients. If you remember Liz we always said this would only be our first home, and that we'd get something better when we could afford it.'

I had to agree that this was so, but I didn't want to leave our dear little house. I pleaded and finally cried, but Rod was adamant that we needed to move. Once again Helen's birthday was marred by something awful.

I was so unhappy at the thought of leaving my home. The next day, after finishing the housework I wandered around the garden pulling a weed here and deadheading a plant there until it was time to start dinner. The kids now caught a bus home so I didn't even have the distraction of chauffeur duty.

When Helen came into the kitchen she asked, 'What's the matter Mummy? You're looking sad.'

I gave her a hug and answered, 'Nothing darling,' then turned to put the casserole I had been preparing into the oven so she wouldn't see tears filling my eyes.

Rod arrived home with an enormous bunch of early spring flowers, and when we sat down to dinner he told the children we were soon going to buy a new house, something bigger and better than our present one. They were all excited and talked eagerly about a new place, with Dale and Ralph opting for one at the beach and Helen wanting to move to the country.

Rod just said, 'We'll see what's around. We'll start looking next weekend.'

I felt totally outnumbered and in some sense betrayed.

Because Rod was busy at work and the children were at school all day it became my responsibility to check out possible houses during the week. I looked at some lovely homes both in town and further out, on bush blocks or near beaches. At the weekends we checked out my shortlist, the attentive real estate agent in tow. The boys and Helen were quite keen on a couple of houses near the beach but Rod vetoed them as too far out of town.

After several weekends we viewed a house in West Hobart and Rod loved it on sight. It had five bedrooms, a separate living area for the kids and magnificent views of the city from the extensive deck that ran the width of the house. I had to admit that I loved the kitchen with its Blackwood cupboards, tiled counter tops and a huge walk-in pantry. It also had an enormous stove with dual oven and copper range-hood and a preparation island topped with marble. I thought if I had to move this kitchen could be a compensation

Rod signed for the property on the spot and in a few short weeks our house was sold.

On moving day Rod and the boys went ahead with the removalists' van and Helen and I did the final vacuuming and cleaning. While Helen was outside emptying the vacuum bag I sat on the floor and was suddenly overwhelmed with sorrow. I didn't want to leave the house Rod and I had built together, the place to which we'd brought our three precious babies and the home and gardens I have tended so lovingly for so long.

There was also something else bothering me. For years I had fooled myself that Rod and I were equal partners, but this forced move had made me realise what little say I had in decision-making. I had let myself be financially dependent, and the one who earns the money wields the power.

When Helen returned with the empty vacuum cleaner bag she found me crouched on the floor crying and put her strong little arms around me to cheer me up.

She seemed to understand a little of what I was feeling when she said, 'Don't cry Mummy. I know this house is special but you'll get to like the new one.'

We gathered the last of our things together and I drove us to our new home.

Helen was right, for in time I did get to like my new home, but the relationship between Rod and me would never be the same. It seemed to me that we lost an essential sense of camaraderie when we left the house we had built together and it was never regained.

Sweet and Sour pork

1 lb. pork fillet
1 dsp. oil
1 dsp. corn flour
1 tbsp. vinegar
1 dsp. brown sugar
1 small green pepper, sliced

1 dsp. finely chopped onion
1/3 cup water
1 dsp. soy sauce
½ cup pineapple juice
½ tsp. salt
¾ cup pineapple pieces

Chop pork into small cubes.

Heat oil in deep pan or wok.

Add pork and onion and fry until brown.

Add water and lower the heat.

Mix together corn flour, brown sugar, salt, pineapple juice, vinegar and soy sauce and add to the pork and onion mixture.

Simmer gently for 10 minutes.

Add pineapple pieces and sliced pepper.

Simmer for further 10 minutes.

Serve with rice or noodles.

Chow Mien

1 lb. mince	1 pkt. chicken noodle soup
½ cup rice	1 dsp. curry powder
2 onions diced	½ tin pineapple pieces
1 carrot cut in rings	4 cups boiling water
½ small cabbage shredded	

Fry mince and onion in fry pan, in a little butter, until brown.

Add carrots and cook for 2 minutes.

Add rice, soup, curry powder, pineapple and water.

Cook for 20 minutes.

Add the shredded cabbage and cook for a further 5 – 10 minutes.

When this was popular Chinese cabbage was not available but it is preferable and needs only 5 minutes cooking time.

Greek Meatballs

1 lb. lamb mince, pounded to almost a paste
2-3 slices bread with crusts removed
1 tbsp. olive oil
4 tbsp. onion, grated finely
4 tbsp each parsley and mint, finely chopped
1 dsp. each oregano and coriander, finely chopped
¼ tsp. each ground nutmeg, cinnamon, cumin and cayenne
salt and black pepper
½ cup dry red wine
flour for dusting

Moisten bread then squeeze out liquid.

Mix bread, meat paste and all other ingredients together, except for flour.

Shape into small balls and dust with flour.

Fry in oil until brown on the outside and still moist on inside.

Can be served as hors d'oeuvres or mixed into homemade tomato sauce and served with rice as a main course.

Can also be cooked on skewers as kebabs at a barbecue.

Spaghetti Bolognese

2 tbsp. olive oil
2 large onions chopped
1 kg minced beef
3 cloves garlic finely chopped
2 tins tomatoes

2 tbsp. tomato paste
3 cups beef stock
salt and pepper to taste

shaved Parmesan cheese

½ cup chopped, fresh mixed herbs – oregano, thyme and sage
Cooked spaghetti

Heat oil in large fry pan.

Brown onions and mince then add garlic and cook for approximately 5 minutes.

Add tomatoes, tomato paste, beef stock and chopped herbs.

Simmer slowly until cooked, approximately 30 minutes. [*may need to add extra stock*]

Season to taste and serve over cooked spaghetti and sprinkled with Parmesan cheese.

This recipe produces a large quantity but can be divided into small batches and frozen for later use.

Beef Burgundy

2 lbs. topside steak
2 oz. butter
6 small onions
2 rashers bacon
4 oz. mushrooms
1 dsp. plain flour

1 cup red wine
stock
salt and pepper to taste
slices of bread
grated cheese

Cut meat into cubes, brown in heated butter.

Remove meat, add whole onions, diced bacon and quartered mushrooms to remaining butter and brown slowly.

Remove onions, bacon and mushrooms, sprinkle in flour and cook slowly until browned.

Pour wine into flour mixture and stir constantly while bringing to boil.

Return meat, onions, bacon and mushrooms and pour in stock. Add salt and pepper to taste. Cover tightly.

Cook in slow oven until meat is tender [approx. 1 ½ hours].

Remove casserole lid. Top beef mixture with slices of bread and grated cheese.

Return to oven until topping has browned.

Cheese Soufflé

60 grams butter

Breadcrumbs to coat dish
2 tbsp. plain flour
salt and pepper

pinch each cayenne
pepper and nutmeg
1 cup milk
3 eggs, separated
1 ½ cups grated cheese

Grease a four-cup soufflé dish with butter and sprinkle with breadcrumbs.

Tie a collar of well greased paper around dish to extend 2 inches above rim.

Melt butter over medium heat, stir in flour and seasonings and cook for 1 minute. Gradually stir in the milk and continue stirring until mixture is smooth and thickened.

Beat egg yolks and add slowly then stir in the cheese.

Whisk egg whites until stiff, fold a couple of spoonfuls through the mixture then fold in the rest.

Pour into prepared dish and place dish on a metal dish that has been heated in a moderately hot oven [190C].

Bake for 35 minutes or until soufflé is puffed and golden and feels firm to the touch.

Chocolate Crackles

4 cups Rice bubbles

1-½ cups icing sugar

1 ½ cups coconut

3 tbsp. cocoa

4 oz copha

Mix together all ingredients except for copha

Melt copha on slow heat then pour onto other ingredients mixing well.

Spoon into paper patty cake cases and allow to set.

Makes approximately 2 dozen.

Coconut Roughs

1/3 cup mashed potato
1 oz. melted butter
1 2cups icing sugar
1 ¼ tbsp. cocoa

1 ¾ cups coconut
1 tsp. vanilla essence
pinch salt

Beat butter into hot potato.

Gradually beat in sifted icing sugar, salt and cocoa.

Add coconut and vanilla essence.

Spoon teaspoonfuls on to greaseproof paper and refrigerate.

Coconut Ice

3 cups sugar
1 cup icing sugar
1 cup milk

1 oz, butter
2 cups coconut
pink food colouring

Combine sugar, icing sugar, milk and butter in saucepan.

Stir over a low heat until sugar dissolves.

Bring to the boil and cook for 4 minutes.

Add coconut and boil 2 minutes more.

Divide mixture and colour half pink.

Beat white half in mixer for 2 minutes or until thick.

Press into bar tin.

Beat pink half and, when thick, place on top of white layer.

Cut into squares when set.

Butterfly Cakes

4 oz. butter

4 oz. caster sugar

2 eggs

4 oz. Self-raising flour

Cream butter and sugar.

Gradually add eggs. Make sure curdling doesn't occur by adding some of the flour.

Fold in remainder of flour – mixture should be dropping consistency.

Half fill greased patty tins.

Bake for 10 minutes in hot oven [400F] until well risen and firm to touch.

Allow to cool.

Cut top off each cake.

Cut the cake tops in two and put aside.

Place 1 tsp. red jelly [set] on cake and top with 1 tsp. whipped cream.

Place the two cake slices on top as wings and sprinkle with icing sugar.

This recipe makes approximately 14 – 15 cakes. Can be doubled to produce more for a party.

Egg and Bacon Pies

puff pastry sheets
bacon – cut into strips and fried until just cooked.
cheese – tasty cheddar cut into thin strips
eggs – beaten

Cut circles from pastry sheet to fit patty tins. [Each sheet makes 12 pies]

Place 3 slices bacon and 3 slices cheese into each circle.

Pour dsp. beaten egg into each pie.

Bake in moderate oven – approximately 10 minutes until egg set and cheese golden.

May be eaten hot or cold.

Barbara Knight

Helen's Story

The Times They Are A' Changing

I don't think I had ever seen my mother crying until the day we moved to our new house. She and I had just finished the last minute cleaning up and I had gone outside to empty the vacuum cleaner bag. When I returned she was sitting on the floor, her head on her knees and she was sobbing. I tried to comfort her and she seemed to cheer up, but I knew she didn't want to move.

On the night of my tenth birthday I'd heard Mum and Dad arguing and I think I heard Mummy crying, but the next morning she seemed okay. The following night Dad had come home with a big bouquet of flowers for her and they had kissed as usual. After dinner Dad announced to us kids that he was putting our house on the market, and soon we would be moving to a bigger and better place. Mummy had sat silently sniffing the flowers.

I loved the new house for I had a beautiful big bedroom and my own ensuite, such luxury. The boys were very happy with their rooms too because they'd always had to share a bedroom and had been fairly cramped. Best of all about this house was that we had our own living room with a pool table at one end and a television set at the other. We even had our own refrigerator that Dad stocked up with soft drinks and ice cream.

Mum slowly got used to the change. She certainly loved her new kitchen and soon began planning alterations she would make to the garden The first weekend after the move we went to a nursery and bought some fruit trees to go along the back fence. While we were unloading the car a woman swanked up the drive, a big smile on her face and a bottle of champagne in her hand.

'Hi, I'm Carolyn,' she said in a very deep, rich voice. 'Welcome to the neighbourhood.'

'Oh! How lovely.' said my mother and I felt an instant warmth between the two women.

Mum led the way into the lounge room and found suitable glasses while I stood shyly by and looked at this stranger.

She was tall, at least 175 centimetres, very slim and with smooth golden brown skin. Her hair was a dark russet brown and cut close to her face, unlike the bouffant style most women were favouring. She had enormous, golden coloured eyes, a thin nose and high, prominent cheekbones, and even I could see she had a presence. Her clothes were plain, compared with the colourful shirts and pretty dresses my mother usually wore, but she made a pair of khaki slacks and a cream shirt look the height of fashion.

Mummy told me to get my father so I went off to find him. By the time I returned they were chatting happily on the lounge, the glasses filled and laughter in the air.

That was the beginning of one of the most important relationships in my mother's life. From that day Carolyn took my mother under her wing, so to speak, and introduced her around the neighbourhood. Those two women soon became close companions and their friendship was of enormous importance in helping Mum adjust to the move from our old home.

It was good for Mum to have a close female friend because she and her sisters had drifted apart. When we first moved into the new house they came to visit that first weekend and sat in the spacious lounge room, drinking sherry, smoking cigarettes and talking as they had in the past, but they rarely came again. They were both working and so were too busy catching up on household chores to spend Saturdays socialising.

I knew Mum had wanted to go back to teaching when I started school, but Dad had been very strongly against it so she'd stayed at home. She had started art classes and joined a tennis club but I think sometimes she was lonely. The other women in our neighbourhood seemed to spend all their time doing housework or having more babies, and I don't think they ever read books like Mum did.

With the move to the new house she had more congenial neighbours. They all seemed to belong to the local library and often met in each other's houses for morning or afternoon tea and shared around books they had enjoyed.

Most of the women in this suburb had a "little woman" who came in a couple of times a week to vacuum and dust, wash and iron the clothes and generally take care of the house. When Dad heard about this he suggested that Mum should also get help as the house was so large, and he didn't want her wearing herself out with housework.

Soon Mondays and Wednesdays began with a flurry for all of us as we rough tidied our bedrooms and collected dirty clothes before the housekeeper arrived.

Because Mum now had more time to spare she threw herself enthusiastically into the neighbourhood activities.

As I mentioned Mum and some of the other women in the neighbourhood shared around books they had enjoyed. Carolyn decided that they should form a Book Discussion Group and she and Mum organised it through the local library. Several of the other women were roped in and each month they met at Carolyn's or our house to discuss the most recent book.

These sessions commenced seriously enough with each woman allocated a question to be answered about the book, and tea and sandwiches were served after the discussion. Gradually these afternoons became more like parties. Wine replaced the tea and more elaborate delights were served instead of sandwiches. Mum and Carolyn would spend the morning, laughing like schoolgirls, while they concocted delicious little savouries that they called canapés.

Although the book of the month was still discussed often the text led the conversation off on tangents to everything from husbands, sex and problems with children to films, politics and environmental concerns. I knew this because sometimes they were still going when I got home and I listened in.

One day when I returned from school I peered into the lounge room. It was awash with cigarette fumes and loud music. The women were limbo dancing which involved trying to get under a limbo stick, or in this case a broom, while leaning backwards. Their faces were flushed and they were giggling raucously like teenagers.

I went to my bedroom and started my homework, feeling very mature and virtuous and slightly disgusted with the way these mothers were behaving. I heard the sounds of farewells and looked through my window, fully expecting to see the mothers doing a conga line down the street with the new book of the month balanced on their heads. Instead they walked off, relatively sedately, heading home to prepare dinners for their families. It occurred to me that, perhaps, they could only be light-hearted and scatty when they were away from their husbands and children.

When I was about twelve or thirteen I noticed that Mum was reading a book with a really gross cover, a woman's headless body hanging from a hook. I asked her what it was about.

She said, 'It's called "The Female Eunuch", and is written by a very clever woman about women and their lives in our society. I think her views are rather jaundiced but it's very interesting. You're probably old enough to read it if you want to when I've finished.'

Because I was rather pleased that Mum considered me mature enough now to read an adult book I ploughed my way through it. I must admit it was over my head, for at that age I hadn't really analysed the lives of adults. I heard Carolyn and Mum discussing it and it seemed to make them angry. From what I had understood the author, Germaine Greer, was fairly critical of relationships between men and women and of women being dependent or subservient to men. I didn't understand why they were taking the book so personally. Neither of them seemed to me to be particularly subservient, and in fact appeared to have pretty good lives.

Not long after this book had been discussed at the monthly Book discussion meeting my friend Janet told me that her mother had decided to go back to university to finish a degree. Another one of the neighbours went back to work because of that book.

As I said it was over my head, but it seemed to have a strong influence, so Germaine proved to be influential as well as clever and jaundiced.

Around this time Carolyn, Mum and some of the other women, the ones still at home that is, organised card afternoons, theoretically to raise money for Red Cross. They played tennis twice a week to keep fit and began having girl's afternoons at the casino, where they regularly gambled away some of their housekeeping money. I don't think that this was the reaction that Germaine had hoped to achieve with her book but I saw it happen. My mother became a social butterfly, filling in the hours to prove how busy she was.

She now spent less time in the kitchen and meals could be scrappy if it was a tennis day. She still, however, enjoyed making elaborate meals if friends were coming to dinner or Dad's business associates needed to be impressed.

Of course the habits of many years did not disappear and Mum still ensured her family was well fed, but she now bought ready-cooked chickens for her fricassees and salads, used bought stock for soups and ready-made bases for pizzas. She also bought an appliance called a slow cooker in which a casserole or a piece of silverside could simmer away all day while she went off to play.

When Book Discussion had been at our place we had entrée for dinner, a selection of the leftover canapés, but Mum still always prepared a substantial meal as well – even if she was "three sheets to the wind" as my father would say.

An important element in my mother's social life was the dinner party. These were held either to entertain Dad's business associates or, more frequently, our neighbours. Dinner parties were fairly formal events. The food was lavish and the guests dressed up. The women wore smart cocktail dresses, slim and sleek and often black or dark blue, or long floaty dresses or kaftans. The men usually wore colourful fitted shirts and flares.

I always liked to see what Carolyn was wearing because it was bound to be unusual. She was the first woman I saw wearing hot pants and she started the fashion for jump suits in the neighbourhood.

The food Mum served became more elaborate and sophisticated and her favourites were Beef Wellington and crown of lamb. Often she would use us for practice runs so we got to try some of the dishes before the night of the dinner party. Beef Wellington took a few trial runs; once it was too rare and the next time overcooked and dried out, but she mastered it in the end. The crown of lamb was tasty and certainly looked festive. I personally thought grilled loin chops tasted just as good and were nothing like the trouble, but I guess they didn't look as attractive.

Desserts for those occasions had to be something that could be made in advance so the hostess appeared calm and unflustered while feeding her guests. As well she had to ensure that her children had eaten earlier and were not committing mayhem in another part of the house. It was also considered necessary that the desserts looked spectacular when served. All this required careful planning on the part of the hostess.

Mum's favourite desserts were an amazing black forest cake that was delicious and looked good and a glorious apple and apricot cheesecake that took a long time to make but everyone raved about it. For one memorable dinner party Mum tried to make Bombe Alaska. She hadn't tried it out on us first and the results were a limp melting mess and an even limper hostess. Fortunately that dinner was for friends, not for business associates, but she didn't ever try to make it again.

On the nights Mum and Dad were hosting a dinner party we kids were fed early. We usually had something that could be prepared in advance like egg and bacon pie or quiche and, once fed, we were banished to our part of the house while the grown-ups played. The boys didn't mind this arrangement at all because we had that great living room of our own, but I liked to see at least the start of these parties. I don't know if it is a gender thing but I always felt I was missing out on something by being sent off. Once I was older I was allowed to greet the guests, especially if Mum was behind with the food preparations. I'd take their coats, if they were wearing outdoor gear, and show them into the lounge room where Dad would be waiting near the cocktail cabinet. It was his job to organise the pre-dinner drinks. He had a large array of bottles and glasses and a little refrigerator for storing ice, white wine and the fruit trimmings for cocktails.

For me it was fun to see the parents of my neighbourhood friends dressed up as if pretending to be grown-ups. Usually I saw the mothers dashing around in jeans or shorts with their hair in ponytails. During the week the men wore dark suits, white shirts and ties. In their more glamorous and colourful clothing both the men and the women looked different.

If Mum was particularly tardy with the food preparation, or had tried something too elaborate and was having problems, I was allowed to hand around the canapés. These were often the same as those served at the Book Discussion meetings but Mum was always adding to her repertoire of these tasty starters. Two of my favourites were toast fingers topped with oyster dip and little prawn tartlets. I often sneaked some of these to my brothers who were in our living room.

After handing around the canapés I would say goodnight to the guests and join my brothers to watch television or play pool so I didn't see any more of the dinner party. Later as I lay in bed, listening to the music and laughter wafting through the house I would think what fun it must be to be grown-up.

By the mid-seventies Mum and Dad's favourite way of entertaining had become Sunday barbecues. We had always enjoyed family barbecues and regularly cooked them on the concrete block structure that was in the back yard when we bought the house. It was always Dad's job to start the fire and the boys would help him while Mum and I marinated the steaks and prepared the salads. We would wait until informed that the barbecue was right for cooking. We'd then carry out the food and Dad would cook the meat while Mum relaxed with a glass of wine and be gallantly served by the chef.

A change in our barbecues came about with the arrival of a large gas contraption that was given pride of place on the wide front deck. More outdoor furniture was bought, and soon as many as thirty people were entertained and fed by my parents on most Sundays through the summer and autumn months.

I know that barbecues didn't start in Australia, but we stamped our very distinctive mark on this form of eating.

The Aussie barbecue was where the men gave the impression that they were responsible for the whole meal while their wives went along with this illusion because it was nearly impossible to get their men involved in any other form of culinary pursuit.

Behind the scenes the women marinated steaks, prepared kebabs and made patties. They also tossed together several different salads and made sure the bread was sliced. Some even baked their own bread for these occasions. The male person then took over, stubby or glass of wine in hand, and proceeded to cook the meat in kingly glory, and take full credit for the whole meal.

I know this sounds cynical and is no longer the case. In recent times many men have become much more involved in the preparation of meals, but when I was fourteen this was before that change. I spend most Sunday mornings in the kitchen with Mum preparing salads, kebabs and patties and buttering bread. Despite my cynicism I really enjoyed these times and Mum and I worked well together. We always made coleslaw, because everyone seemed to like it, and potato salad if pinkeye potatoes were in season. I liked making the Greek salad because it always looked so pretty when it was finished especially if we had been able to get different coloured capsicums.

Unlike the dinner parties the barbecues were more family affairs in that we kids were expected to attend. The guests were varied. Sometimes there would be mainly people from Dad's work and other times mainly neighbours and their families. Auntie Ronda and Uncle Frank came occasionally and brought their kids. I liked to see them, especially Richard who was a few months older than I. Less frequently Auntie Joan came with Sara, but Justin was studying at A.N.U. and I hadn't seen him for a couple of years.

According to Dale he couldn't wait to get away from home as he felt his mother's dislike of men extended to him. I don't know whether or not this was true but Auntie Joan did seem to spend a lot of time saying critical things about men. She didn't even seem to like Dad, and he was always very friendly towards her.

Carolyn and her husband, Matt, were regulars and she always looked stunning in smart lightweight slacks with colourful tops or slinky sundresses.

Another regular was Fred, Dad's friend from university days. Evidently Dad had run into him in the street one day and, over a beer, had learnt about Fred's divorce, his move back to Tasmania and the semi-reclusive life that he was now living. Being Dad he invited him to our next barbecue and Fred turned up regularly from then on. He often came early and brought fresh seasonal vegetables from his garden for Mum and me to incorporate into our salads.

My brothers usually ate and ran. Dale was then nineteen and had his own car and the beginnings of a separate life. Ralph, at seventeen, was still around most of the time, but he would often go back to his room and read rather than socialise with grownups.

In contrast I loved the opportunity to be amongst people and to listen to them talking. I suppose I had always been more curious about the world of grownups than my brothers, or perhaps I was just a sticky beak. Anyhow I loved wandering round the groups, sometimes being included in the conversations.

I noticed that barbecue parties often seemed to split. At one end of the deck would be the people who talked. At the other end of the deck the noisy ones gathered and played music, which they sang along to. Often they would finish up dancing on the deck or lawn.

Dad was always in the thick of the noisy ones and seemed to flirt with all the women. In contrast Mum would be with the other group, which always included Carolyn and Matt and often Fred. In my wisdom I thought Fred probably fancied Carolyn because she was so stunning, and even though she was married he just liked to be near her.

During the next year Dale had almost completed an Economics Degree, following in Dad's footsteps, and Ralph was doing a Bachelor of Arts Degree and planned to do a Diploma of Education and teach. I had almost completed high school and was due to start Matriculation College the following year when my world disintegrated around me.

For months there had been tension between Mum and Dad, but they tried to hide it from us. Often Dad worked late so we didn't see much of him through the week, but this had not been that unusual. What had been strange was that they stopped entertaining at weekends and I wondered about this. Because the house was so big we were sometimes only seeing our parents together at mealtimes, and there seemed to be a frostiness and formality between them that hadn't there before. I asked Mum if anything was wrong. Although she assured me that there wasn't I didn't find her answer totally convincing.

Towards the end of the year quite fierce arguments began and Dale, Ralph and I could no longer pretend all was right between our parents. We did not, however, know what was going on but Dale just said, 'They'll tell us when they're ready,' which I didn't find at all comforting.

One night Mum and Dad came down to our living room. Ralph and I were playing pool and Dale was watching television. Dad walked across the room and turned off the TV. Dad was the sort of man who dominated a room just by entering it but now he had an expression on his face that I found quite scary.

Dale began to complain about the television being turned off but Dad said, 'We've got something important to tell you,' and his tone of voice stopped Dale's objections.

Ralph and I stood back from the pool table, still holding our cues, and Mum said, 'Come over here and sit on the couch.'

She seemed edgy and nervous and I felt my heart miss a beat. Something was very wrong.

Dad sat in the only armchair and Ralph and I moved to the couch to be next to Mum. Dale slouched against a wall.

After clearing his throat rather noisily Dad said, 'Your mother and I have been having problems lately and have decided to spend a little time apart. She wants to move out and into a flat for a few months and will take Helen with her. I reckon that we guys can look after ourselves for a while until your mother and I get our problems sorted. What do you say guys?'

As I'm not a guy I didn't answer but I was also completely stunned. All I could think was that at least I'd be going to be with Mum.

Ralph just sat beside me looking totally bewildered and Dale looked impassive. Neither said anything.

Having dropped their bombshell our parents departed, leaving behind a silent room and the three of us staring after them.

Dale broke the silence, 'Well I don't care what they do. I'll be out of here by the beginning of next year.'

I looked at his closed face and asked, 'Do you know what's caused this or what's going on?'

He looked down at me, a funny quizzical look on his face, and answered, 'Oh, Dad's probably been playing around again and Mum's taking a stand.'

'What do you mean again,' I asked in surprise.

'Well little Sis, you probably didn't know, but I'm pretty sure the old man had an affair a few years ago. I think

Mum found out about it and forgave him, but perhaps he's done it again and this time she's not going to be so forgiving.'

The next day, after Dad had gone to work, I sat down with Mum in the kitchen and tried to get her to tell me exactly what was happening by saying; 'I know you've been unhappy during the past few months, but I thought that you could talk to me about anything. What's going on Mum?'

She looked uncomfortable as she sat next to me at the preparation island and put her hands around her teacup as if she needed to draw warmth into her body.

With a sigh she said, 'Oh Baby, I don't want to give you our grownup problems to deal with. Just believe me that I need to get away from your father for a few months and that I want you with me.'

I touched her hand, 'Mum, please tell me what's happened. I'm fifteen for God's sake. You can tell me what the problem is. Dale says Dad was unfaithful to you a few years ago. Has that happened again?'

She sighed and answered, 'Please darling, go along with this for the time being and I'll tell you all about it eventually.'

All I could do was agree with her request. I finished my tea then wandered off to my bedroom where I sat for the rest of the day, watching the clouds pass across the sky and wondering what would happen next. I felt powerless and vulnerable.

Beef Wellington

2 - 2 ½lbs. fillet beef
4 oz. butter
2 oz. pate
1 small onion
1-cup beef stock

4 oz. mushrooms
1 lb. puff pastry
salt and pepper
1 egg yolk
¼cup red wine

Spread beef with 1 oz. softened butter, bake in hot oven 10 – 15 minutes or until browned all over.

Remove from oven, allow to cool completely, reserve pan juices.

Chop onion finely, slice mushrooms and sauté in 1 oz. butter until tender – cool.

Combine 2 oz. butter with pate, season with salt and pepper and spread over beef fillet with onion/mushroom mixture.

Roll out pastry, place beef fillet with topping in centre of pastry and wrap firmly.

Brush with beaten egg yolk and bake in a very hot oven for 10 minutes.

Reduce heat to hot and cook further 10-15 minutes.

Add 1-cup beef stock, ¼cup red wine to any pan juices and cook until slightly reduced.

Cut beef into thick slices and pour over sauce just before serving.

Crown of Lamb

1 crown roast of lamb [12 –16] chops
¼ cup oil
2 cloves garlic, crushed
salt and pepper
pitted olives
selection of vegetables

Mix seasonings into oil, stand 15 minutes.

Brush roast inside and out with seasoned oil and place in a greased baking dish on a rack.

Cover bone ends with foil to prevent charring.

Roast in moderate oven [180C] for 20 minutes for each pound.

To serve place on heated plate and fill centre with attractive, cooked vegetables e.g. button mushrooms, small onions and julienne carrots.

Remove foil and replace with pitted olives.

This is a spectacular dish to bring to the table but can be dished up in the kitchen and arranged attractively on individual plates.

Black Forest Cake

Cake

6 eggs

1½ cups caster sugar

½cup cocoa

½ tsp. vanilla essence

½ cup plain flour

5 oz. melted butter.

Beat eggs and vanilla until light and creamy.

Add sugar slowly and beat for 5 minutes.

Fold in sifted flour and cocoa and then slowly add the melted butter.

Grease3 round 8-inch cake tins and divide mixture into them.

Bake in moderate oven for 30 minutes and turn out when cool.

Syrup

1 cup sugar

½cup Kirsch

1 cup water

Place sugar and water in a saucepan and dissolve sugar over slow heat.

Bring to the boil then simmer for 5 minutes.

Remove from the heat and add Kirsch.

Place cooled cakes on tray and pierce with a skewer.

Pour syrup over and allow to soak into cakes.

Filling and Topping

2 cups whipped cream   ⅓cup icing sugar
3 tbsp. Kirsch   Grated chocolate
1 can drained Maraschino cherries.

Combine whipped cream, icing sugar and Kirsch

Fold cherries into half this mixture and use to sandwich cakes together.

Cover top and sides with remaining cream mixture.

Decorate with grated chocolate and cherries.

Refrigerate.

Apple and Apricot Cheese Cake

1 ¼cups plain flour
¼cup sugar
1 tsp. cinnamon
pinch salt
grated rind ½ lemon

1 tsp baking powder 1
4 oz. butter
1 egg yolk
1 tsp. Sherry
2 cooking apples
[stewed]

Sift dry ingredients together.
Rub in butter
Combine egg yolk and sherry and add to flour mixture and
work to a dough.
Roll out and place in a spring-form tin
Top with stewed apples.

Filling
2 eggs
1 tbs. plain flour
¼cup sultanas
½cup sugar

½ cup cream
1 ½cups cream cheese
grated rind I lemon

Combine all ingredients, spoon over stewed fruit and bake
in moderate oven for 1½hours.

Topping
Can apricots
1 tbsp. Sugar

1 ½ dsp. Cornflour
whipped cream

Mash apricot and heat with sugar.

Dissolve cornflour in a little water, add to apricot/sugar
mixture and cook until thickened.

Cool slightly and spread over cake then top with whipped
cream. Serve cold.

Quiche

1 sheet short crust pastry
6 oz. cheese [gruyere or cheddar]
1 small onion, finely chopped
4 rashers bacon
3 eggs
¾ cup cream
½ tsp. nutmeg
salt and pepper to taste

Place pastry sheet in round tin or pie dish and trim edges.

Cut bacon into fine strips and fry until crisp – drain on paper towel.

Slice cheese into small strips and place cheese and bacon into pie.

Sprinkle with chopped onion.

Beat eggs lightly, combine with cream and seasonings and pour over cheese and bacon.

Bake in hot oven for 10 minutes.

Reduce heat to moderately slow and cook further 20 minutes or until set.

Oyster Dip

1 small can smoked oysters
½ lb. cream cheese
1 tbsp. cream
1 tsp. grated onion
chopped parsley

Blend cream cheese and cream until softened.

Stir in chopped oysters, grated onion, chopped parsley
and a little oil from the oyster can.

Leave for an hour or so to allow the flavours to meld.

Serve with plain biscuits or toast fingers.

Prawn Tartlets

2 sheets puff pastry
fresh coriander leaves
18 green prawns
1 small red capsicum, finely diced
1 tbsp, butter
1 clove crushed garlic
2 tbsp. Thai sweet chilli sauce
½ tsp. powdered ginger

Preheat oven to 220C.

Cut pastry circles and place in patty tins

Line base of each tart with coriander leaves.

Add 1 tsp. capsicum, then cut up prawns.

Mix remaining ingredients and heat together until butter is melted.

Spoon mixture over prawns.

Cook for 10 – 15 minutes.

Good served either hot or cold.

Kebabs

Beef Kebabs

Marinade

2 tbsp. olive oil

2 tbsp. peanut oil

2 tbsp balsamic vinegar

1 dsp. horseradish cream

salt and pepper

tsp. chopped oregano

Thread beef cubes onto skewers and marinate for 2 hours.

Cook on barbecue.

Chicken Kebabs

Marinade

100 ml. coconut milk

1 tsp. curry powder

salt and pepper

1 tsp. finely chopped coriander

2 tbsp. peanut oil

Chicken cubes can be from the breast or thighs.

Thread chicken cubes onto skewers and marinate for two hours.

Cook on barbecue

Kebabs can be just meat or poultry but delicious ones can be made by alternating meat or chicken with onions, capsicums or mushrooms or a combination.

Greek Salad

Mixed salad greens
1 red pepper
1 green pepper
1 red onion
3 oz. feta cheese

2 oz black olives
3 tbsp. olive oil
2 tbsp. balsamic vinegar
1 clove garlic minced

Wash greens and place in bowl.

Deseed and slice peppers into rings.

Slice red onion finely into rings.

Add to salad greens.

Mix together garlic, vinegar and oil and toss through salad.

Sprinkle top with crumbled feta and dot salad with olives.

Secret Love

In the beginning I sort of enjoyed moving into a flat with Mum. It was an end to the tensions; an end to worrying about what was going on and what would happen next.

During the previous weeks I had felt absolutely helpless to comfort Mum. I hadn't even been able to talk to Dad as I felt everything that was happening was his fault. I felt totally bewildered about what would become of our family. All I really knew was that I was glad that I was going to be with Mum.

Shortly after our conversation in the kitchen, Mum and I started looking at flats. I felt kind of special being consulted in all this decision-making.

We looked at several places before choosing one. There were flats behind houses, flats that were part of old houses and others in modern blocks. The one we finally chose was in a relatively new block and on the third floor. It had a tiny deck that looked out into the branches of a tall gum tree. I loved it on sight and said I'd like us to live there. For the first time in my life I was allowed to make an important decision. Mum agreed with me that it was very nice and we moved in.

We hadn't taken much from the big house. Mum said she didn't need to, but I think that what she really wanted was to make this space different. We had a wonderful time shopping after we worked out together what basics we really needed. In one afternoon we bought orange and purple sheets and colourful duvet covers, new crockery, all blue and white and very cheap, and a few pots and a pan. We also bought a small round dining table with four chairs and a cheap foam lounge.

For the first few weeks it was a bit like a continuing girls' night out. We had left the male dominated house and the terrible tensions with which we had been living. Although I still didn't really know what was going on I felt secure because I was with Mum and she seemed to be coping and even happy.

After the first few weeks Mum started work at a bookshop that belonged to an old school friend and she loved it. I started at Matriculation College.

Mum had to work from nine o'clock until six so I always came home to an empty flat. We had talked about this and I'd told Mum this would be okay with me even though it would actually be the first time I'd ever come home without her being there.

As I walked along the narrow road towards the apartment block and then climbed the stairs I thought, 'Shit, I'm sixteen. It's no big deal. Some of my cousins have been doing this for years.'

Nevertheless I felt a little bereft that first time. I went to my bedroom and started an English assignment, but was listening all the time for the sound of Mum's key turning in the lock.

We settled into a routine, and it was somehow so special because this was the only time I had lived just with my mother. I don't know whether it was special for her too, but she seemed to be happy enough.

Of course we weren't totally alone. The boys came to dinner one night a week and often dropped in at the weekend, but basically it was just we two living together and alone.

Mum and I had a tiny kitchen in the flat. The breakfast bar, where we sat to eat breakfast and sometimes lunch at the weekends, was only as wide as two stools and looked out on a yard with a lovely deciduous tree growing in it. Mum put pots of herbs on the window ledge so we breakfasted close to this sweet-smelling greenery and saw natural beauty through the window. This was important to me because, although I loved the flat, living so high above the ground I felt a bit isolated from the natural world.

With the move to the flat Mum seemed to lose interest in preparing food and of course this was understandable as she came home late and was often tired. We had some very scrappy meals, hastily prepared stir-fries, precooked chicken with salads and sometimes shop-bought pizzas. The only times she seemed interested in cooking was when Dale and Ralph were coming to dinner.

They came every Thursday night so on Wednesday evenings she often prepared casseroles that she could cook in the pre-set oven. Sometimes she did chicken or silverside in the slow cooker that she had brought from home. She also organised to leave work at five on Thursdays so that she has time to make a dessert for her boys. It was good to see my brothers, but I felt a little put out that she made these culinary efforts for them when we were mainly living on quick-fix meals.

At times she seemed a little scatty and overburdened but I understood why she was this way. This was the first time she had worked to earn a living in over two decades. I also knew how much she was missing my brothers now that she only saw them once or twice a week.

In addition she was coping with the absence of someone very special to her, but at the time I knew nothing of this.

Anyhow for three months we lived like that and for me it was a good time. I felt we were supporting each other through a critical period and that we were a unit. Obviously my brothers' visits impinge on this "girlie" time but I felt confident enough about my place in this familial connection to enjoy seeing them.

Dale was always fairly upbeat and full of talk about his job, where he was obviously doing very well. He also told us about the house he was buying and the work that he was doing on it. Ralph didn't say anything about his life at "home" but he talked about his university course and an interesting psychology study in which he was involved.

To make up for our sometimes-scrappy meals Mum introduced the Gourmets' Delight for Monday nights. This was always quite a feast and consisted of all the foods that we both loved – tasty cheeses, black olives, pates, artichoke hearts, hams and salamis, smoked salmon and crusty bread. We'd have this with a good bottle of red wine that Mum now shared with me.

One night, after we have been in the flat for three months, we were just finishing off one of those special dinners when there was a knock at our door. I went to the door and looked through the spy-hole and saw my father, looking small and misshapen through the distorting lens. When I opened the door he gave me a cursory hello and a brief hug, then walked into the room. He stood there looking rather awkward until Mum offered him a cup of tea or a glass of wine.

After he had accepted a glass of wine he sat down on a dining chair. I thought I should make myself scarce, as this was the first time they had seen each other for three months and they obviously needed to talk. I kissed them both goodnight and went to my bedroom, saying that I was feeling terribly tired.

As I lay in bed I heard the arguments and accusations begin and wondered if I should get up again. Should I go out there and plead with them to stop and try to make them see exactly what they were doing to all of us as a family. But then I thought they wouldn't listen to me. I felt so impotent, unable to change a course that had been set in motion. I was as helpless as a leaf floating on a swiftly moving stream.

I didn't get back up but lay in bed and through the not very thick walls heard my parents finally destroy their marriage. I heard my father plead in a way I had never thought such a strong man could and my mother answer coldly in a way that was totally alien to the warm, loving woman she had always seemed to be.

That night I finally learnt the real reason why my mother could leave the father of her children, her beautiful home and daily contact with her sons. The tensions and traumas of the last months at home hadn't been because of my father's infidelity but because of my mother's love of another man. I heard the name Fred mentioned, and thought of the scraps of phone conversations I had heard during the past months. I put my head under my pillow in an attempt to shut out the sounds of my parents shattering each other and the life they had once had together.

I woke with a sick feeling of loss in my stomach and gradually let the words I had heard the previous night register on my conscious mind. Things had been said that I didn't understand and didn't want to know. I felt as though I had been living a sort of blinkered life for years. I was bone weary, so tired that I ached all over, but knew that this feeling was totally mind-influenced. Crawling out of bed I headed for the shower, hoping the hot water would rejuvenate my body, which seemed to have aged overnight.

After my shower I peered into Mum's bedroom. She was lying on her side, facing the wall. When I touched her on the shoulder she turned a tear-sodden face to me and said, 'Darling, I can't cope today. Will you ring work for me and tell them I'm sick?'

I looked at her, without an ounce of pity, and answered, 'You're responsible for all that's happened and for how you feel now, so you'd better cope with it.'

I grabbed my backpack and left the flat, so angry with my mother I felt like vomiting.

During the day I went to classes, took notes and talked to friends, but I felt as though I was floating somewhere above my body.

When I arrived home Mum was in the kitchen.

I approached her and asked angrily, 'Why'd you let me and the boys and everyone else think you left Dad because he was playing around when all the time it was you?'

She looked at me sadly then turned away saying, 'It was how he wanted it. To save his pride.'

After what I'd heard the night before and how she had humbled my father I could only look at her in disgust, 'As if you cared about his pride. You just didn't want us to know your dirty little secret.'

There was a look of sadness in her eyes as she said, 'Darling, I should've told you everything before. I know how loyal you've been, and that now you're hurt and angry because I kept something so important from you. If you'll calm down we'll sort this out. I'll tell you anything you want to know.'

I left the kitchen and slumped down on the couch. Mum followed and sat next to me.

'Okay,' I began, 'How long have you and Fred been lovers?'

She pondered a while then answered, 'Well, I suppose I've loved him for a long time. At first it was just great to catch up with him again; he's so interesting to talk to and he values my opinions. Also he was very comfortable to be around, so relaxed compared with your father who always lives at such a frenetic pace.'

'Oh, so now it Dad's fault,' I jumped in with. 'What I asked you was when did you and he become lovers? When did you have sex with Fred and be unfaithful to my father?'

Mum began, 'I guess I was unfaithful to him the first time I met Fred secretly for coffee. It was after a barbecue last year. As he was leaving, he held my hand and asked if we could meet somewhere. We arranged to have a coffee together that week and from then on we met regularly. Within a few weeks those meetings became so important to us that we wanted to see each other more. One day we went for a drive to Richmond and we kissed down by the river. That was it. I knew I loved him as he obviously loved me.'

'All very romantic,' I sneered, 'but you still haven't answered my question.'

Mum sighed, 'To answer your very blunt question we had sex a few months ago. I knew then that I had to leave your father and I told him the reason. You know the results of that; the arguments and tensions that followed.'

'I sure do, but I'm still don't quite get it. Why did you go through this charade of needing a little time apart from Dad if you thought it was going to be permanent?'

Mum answered slowly, 'It was your father's decision that I move into a flat and not see either him or Fred for three months. I think his idea was that I'd see reason and come back to him. He couldn't accept that what he and I once had was gone forever. I don't know how much you heard last night, and I wish I could have saved you from that. I'm also terribly sorry I didn't let you into my confidence when we first moved into here. You had a right to know. I guess I was still thinking of you as my little girl, and not as the young woman you've become.'

After that long speech Mum stood up from the couch and walked to the cupboard where we kept our few bottles of wine. She opened one and filled two glasses, then handed one to me saying, 'No more secrets.'

Once the restriction imposed by Dad was lifted Mum and Fred began to see each other again. He became a regular visitor to the flat on Tuesday nights and most weekends. They kissed hello at the door, and after dinner sat on the couch holding hands. Even though they were not overtly demonstrative in front of me I still found it embarrassing to watch my mother being affectionate with a man who wasn't my father.

Often Fred would bring a pre-cooked meal in his fry pan, 'To save your mother cooking,' and he always stayed the night. I don't know whether they made love or if out of consideration for me they abstained, but they certainly were quiet.

Pork Stir Fry

Pork

150 g. pork fillet cubed
1 apple sliced
½ green capsicum sliced into strips
1 stick celery sliced
2 spring onions sliced diagonally
¼ Chinese cabbage shredded

small piece ginger grated
½ cup water or stock
1 dsp. soy sauce

1 tsp. chilli sauce
1 dsp finely chopped sage

Preparation

Heat oil in wok

Add vegetables in order as they appear tossing after each addition.

Cook for a few minutes then remove to a bowl.

Place meat in wok, add extra oil if necessary and cook until tender.

Return vegetables to wok stirring through then add stock and flavourings.

Heat through, sprinkle with fresh herbs and serve with noodle or rice.

With a change in ingredients the same simple technique provides a tasty range of alternatives.

Stir Fries - alternatives

Preparation

Heat oil in wok

Add vegetables in order as they appear tossing after each addition.

Cook for a few minutes then remove to a bowl.

Place meat in wok, add extra oil if necessary and cook until tender.

Return vegetables to wok stirring through then add stock and flavourings.

Heat through, sprinkle with fresh herbs and serve with noodle or rice.

Beef

150 g. lean beef cut in strips	½ cup beef stock
2 small onions quartered	1 dsp. oyster sauce
½ red capsicum sliced into strips	1 dsp. Soy sauce
4 mushrooms sliced	1 dsp. tomato paste
3 oz green beans sliced diagonally	1 dsp. chopped oregano

Chicken

150 g chicken breast sliced	½cup chicken stock
½ red capsicum sliced	1 tbsp. lemon juice
2 spring onions sliced diagonally	1 dsp soy sauce
1 zucchini, thinly sliced	1 dsp. chopped thyme
3 oz snow peas	few florets broccoli

Stir Fry Prawns

1 lb. deveined, shelled prawns
2 cloves garlic, crushed
small piece ginger, finely sliced
2 spring onions
1 dsp. chilli sauce
1 dsp. black bean sauce
1 dsp. tomato paste
2 tomatoes, skinned and sliced
1 dsp. soy sauce
1 dsp. dry sherry

Heat wok with a little olive oil.

Place garlic, ginger, and white part of onions in wok and cook quickly.

Add prawns then remaining ingredients and cook for a few minutes, tossing to mix.

Finally add the green part of the onions, finely sliced.

Serve with noodles or boiled rice.

This is an extremely quick meal and can be prepared and cooked in 10 minutes.

Girl You'll Be a Woman Soon

There have been countless books written about the affect of divorce on young children, but very little concerning how older children may react to or be influenced by what is usually a life-changing event.

As that first year in the flat progressed I felt an increasing sense of isolation from both of my parents, and an aloneness that couldn't always be banished by friends.

After that ghastly night in the flat and my subsequent conversation with Mum I began to worry about my father, and so made a point of visiting him at the big house at weekends. It was generally a mess. Dad was always hung-over, as he had been drinking quite heavily, and Ralph appeared to spend most of his time studying. My visits were not much fun and gradually my discomfort overcame my sense of duty and I went there only rarely.

At Matriculation College I was enjoying the freedom of self-motivated study and the easier relationships with the teachers, who treated us more like young adults than wayward children. I also had an expanded circle of friends because there was an easier camaraderie there between the boys and the girls than there had been at high school.

I developed close friendships with a group of boys and hung out with them at lunch times. I'd known Ian and David at high school and the other two were Paul, a hunk of eighteen, and Kent his sidekick. The group adopted me as a sort of mascot. I don't know if, subconsciously, I had been missing the daily contact with my father and my two brothers, but I gravitated towards this male group and was soon an integral part of it.

At the weekends they were always going off doing interesting things and I was now included in their trips. We went bush walking all over the mountain, hired canoes and explored the Huon River, went on camping trips to deserted beaches and even on a caverneering expedition, which was scary but exciting.

Mum met the boys and seemed quite happy to let me go wherever I wanted after she had verified the trustworthiness of our designated driver Paul, who was the oldest in our group and the only one with a car. I think she was glad to be left alone in the flat at weekends because it gave her and Fred a chance to be together without me around.

Although I was fond of all the boys, and had actually gone to the Leavers' Dinner at the end of year ten with David, I liked Paul the best. He was the organiser and this competence allied with a wacky sense of humour and good looks made him very appealing. I felt safe and protected with him around. Compared with the other three Paul seemed so much more mature and together.

I began to single him out to be next to on our bush walks and made opportunities to be alone with him when we were camping. When he came into my tent one night, while the others are sleeping, I unzipped my sleeping bag and we had sex. This was my first time and it hurt quite a lot, although I was ready and willing. Afterwards Paul held me for a while before returning to his own tent.

Somehow I knew it was better that the others not know about what had happened between Paul and me so I avoided him that day as we packed up to go home.

I hoped he would drop the others off first so that we could be alone together again but he headed straight to my flat. I was left, a little bewildered, standing on the footpath while the boys drove off into the night. As I watched the taillight disappear I couldn't help wondering if our lovemaking meant as much to Paul as it had to me.

Our secret relationship continued for several months. During that time we made love in some funny places, on a secluded beach, under a giant tree and beneath a dinghy as well as in the flat when Mum wasn't around. We were more like two playful puppies than lovers and enjoyed each other's bodies totally.

Paul said sweet and funny things like, 'I love tangling myself in your hair,' and, 'Your body is like a beautiful vase.'

He never, however, said he loved me, and because of this I kept hidden from him how deeply I was beginning to care for him.

I was subsequently shocked and surprised when Paul turned up for one of our bush walks with a girl called Moira. I'd seen her around college but didn't know her, and was stunned to see how Paul behaved towards her – helping her over fallen trees and across boggy or rocky spots as if she were precious. The other guys seemed to accept this mollycoddling, but I seethed with jealousy and took pleasure in showing off my superior walking ability.

That evening I rang Paul and asked him what was going on between him and Moira and he told me, unhesitatingly, that he was going with her.

I stammered, 'But what about us?'

I took no comfort from his answer, ' Oh Helen you've been a great mate and the sex has been fun, but I feel really different about Moira.'

I did my best not to show my hurt and just said, 'Well you could have let me know before you brought her along today,' and hung up on his excuses.

I was heartbroken, but felt that at least no one need know of my loss and embarrassment. I'd thought Mum couldn't care less about me as she was so wrapped up with Fred and so I hadn't told her about my feelings for Paul. I'd also thought the other guys hadn't known about our affair. Wrong!

Paul had obviously bragged because during the next week David dropped into the flat and suggested we have sex, Ian rang with an invitation for a night on the town and even Kent, small, innocuous and intense, made a suggestive remark to me during a break at school.

Suddenly I was being seen, not as the mascot and friend, but as the potential group lay. I was absolutely shattered. I had lost my companions, my social life and my very delicately balanced sense of worth.

Fortunately this all happened towards the end of the school year so I threw myself into study. Preparation for the impending exams gave me the excuse to become reclusive.

As soon as the school year ended I applied for and got a job as a waitress at a resort in Swansea, on the East Coast. Because the owners of the resort needed their casual staff from mid-December Mum and the boys and I had an early Christmas dinner before I left. We wore silly paper hats and pulled cheap crackers and Mum served the traditional ham and turkey and trifle, but there was a false of gaiety about the evening. I was glad when it was over.

Mum was going to spend the real Christmas with Fred, and Dale was going to Dad's to share it with him and Ralph. I would be spending it working amongst strangers, and as I boarded the bus and waved goodbye to Mum I felt an unreasonable flare of anger with her for changing my life so much.

When I arrived at the resort the co-owner Maggie Jones showed me to my room. I had spoken to her on the phone, but this was the first time we'd met and she was older than I had imagined. Her voice was soft and light like a young girl's, but she had lined and leathery skin under a thick layer of makeup and her blonde hair was dry and frizzy from years of bleaching. She showed me to my room, which was in the staff block and was small and very basic. Before leaving me to unpack she told me there would be a meeting of all staff in an hour so that we could get to know each other.

After I had unpacked I made my way as directed to the staff room that was a long narrow room off the kitchen. It looked as though it might have been an extension of the verandah that ran around two sides of the motel, but was now glassed in and furnished with a couple of tables and numerous odd chairs. I was one of the last to arrive and people were already talking and laughing while they helped themselves to the quite lavish spread of finger foods that were on the tables. I stood at the door feeling shy and unsure of myself, but then Maggie saw me and pulled me into the room. She took my arm and we did the rounds while she introduced me to everyone, before leaving me with a tall attractive girl called Wanda. This was the third year that Wanda had waitressed at the motel during university vacations, and she was to show me the ropes.

Those first two weeks leading up to Christmas were a big learning curve for me and Wanda was great. We waitresses were rostered on for all meals so the days were long, but there was plenty of free time. Breakfasts were easy because they were buffet style and we only had to make sure the teapots and coffee percolators were refilled and that cereals and juices were replenished. Many of the guests took packed lunches and spent their days away from the motel so the lunch shifts were fairly quiet, but the dining room was always full for dinner and things could be very hectic. Wanda and I shared half of the dining room during the evening shift, and I was very grateful for her help and guidance during those first weeks

There were six of us casuals. Phoebe was the other waitress and Joel, Matt and Ron were the bar staff. The boys were all at university and this was the third year they had worked at the motel during vacation. Phoebe was from Queensland and had been backpacking around Australia for the past year. She seemed so worldly and sophisticated and I was in awe of her. To be wandering around the country by herself seemed to me to be very brave.

The six of us hung out together during our breaks. The beach was only a few metres from the motel and we swam and sun baked together most mornings and afternoons and shared a quiet drink at the bar after closing time. Sometimes Maggie joined us at the end of the evening, but we never saw her husband who was the other owner of the motel. Rumour had it he'd been crippled in a car accident and didn't leave their chalet, that he was a hopeless alcoholic who spent his days drinking or that he had run off with another woman and was no longer on the premises. No one seemed to know which version was true, but we all liked Maggie so didn't pry.

For Christmas Eve we had a full house and an extensive menu so we were all flat out. I fell into bed at one o'clock and slept like a log. Christmas day lunch was much easier as there was a set menu of seafood cocktail, turkey and ham and pudding with brandy sauce and custard. By four o'clock all the guests had left the dining room and we cleared the tables and set up for the next day. The bar was closed for the remainder of the day and everyone headed to the staff room for our own belated Christmas celebration.

The chef and kitchen staff were locals and most of them had gone home to spend the remainder of the day with their families, but they'd left us a feast of prawns, cold ham and turkey, salads and cold plum pudding with pouring custard. Maggie joined us carrying several bottles of champagne, but left after drinking one toast and thanking us all for the way we had worked during this busy time. I wondered if she was going back to an empty chalet or to give comfort and kindness to a grumpy or drunken husband. Not much of a Christmas either way.

By late afternoon all the local staff members had gone and only we six casuals were left. We were all more than slightly tipsy, but managed to clear up and load the dishwashers without breaking anything. Joel suggested we go for a swim so we all changed into bathers and then staggered drunkenly down to the beach. The sun was beginning to set and we swam along the path made by its rays on the water. I felt as though I could keep going like that forever, and was surprised when I turned and saw the others far away and how distant the shore was. I turned and swam back.

As I staggered up onto the beach Joel put a towel around my shoulders and said, 'What did you think you were doing? You went out way too far.'

I giggled drunkenly, 'I didn't know you cared,' knowing full well that he rather fancied me.

Wanda gave me a drunken hug, 'Well she's back now so everything's okay.'

Matt handed me a glass of champagne and said, 'Welcome back.'

Phoebe and Ron had disappeared and we four sat on the cooling sand to watch as the sun disappeared below the horizon and the sky changed from a riot of pinks and reds and gold to an inky black. I felt the warmth of Joel's arm around my shoulder and heard the sounds of Wanda and Matt making out nearby. I was reminded of the last night Paul and I had spent on a beach and suddenly felt so sad. When Joel tried to kiss me I pushed him away, said an abrupt goodnight and went to my room.

The next morning I had the most frightful headache and felt slightly queasy. I staggered from my bed to the bathroom and vomited into the toilet. By the time I had showered I was feeling better physically, but I now had the most horrendous thought.

I suppose it was to do with thinking about Paul the previous night, but suddenly I realised my periods were long overdue. The last two months had been so busy and I had been in such emotional turmoil I hadn't really given much thought to what my body should be doing. I scrabbled in my bag to find my diary with the calendar in the front. I ran my finger down the tiny columns and thought back to when Paul and I last made love, or had sex, as he would put it. It would have been some time in October and my periods were usually in the middle of the month. This meant that I had now missed two periods. How could I not have noticed? If I were pregnant what was I going to do? I felt desolate and alone and would have loved to crawl back into bed and sleep forever, but I was on breakfast duty in ten minutes.

That day was very busy but I found it hard to concentrate on my work. The fear that I might be pregnant dominated my thinking and I mixed up an order. Wanda saw I was being berated by the customers and came to my aid, apologising and settling things down in her diplomatic way.

Every time I went to the toilet I checked for a sign of blood in my panties, and by the end of the day I was a nervous wreck. Instead of joining the others in the bar for our usual late night drinks I went straight to my room and lay in bed with random thoughts swirling in my head. I thought of the ramifications if I were pregnant. I certainly didn't want to have a baby. It would ruin my life. How could I get an abortion? I definitely couldn't ask Mum to help. She would rabbit on about every life being precious and would probably offer to bring it up for me. Dad would just be shocked. I think a lot of fathers continue to think of their daughters as pure and virginal until the day they marry, but with Dad and me it was even more complex. Because we hadn't lived together since I was fifteen he still seemed to think of me as that age and treated me accordingly. He just wouldn't cope with the idea of his girl child being pregnant. Telling Paul was out of the question so what was I to do?

I felt utterly alone and miserable and was sobbing wetly into my pillow when there came a soft knock on my door and Wanda whispered, 'Are you okay Helen?'

I mumbled a reply and she came into the darkened room. I felt her weight next to me on the bed and her arms around my shaking shoulders.

Slowly I told her everything about Paul and me and how I now thought I might be pregnant, and that I didn't know what to do.

She shushed me as though I were a child and said, 'Look I'll help you organise an abortion if it's necessary, but you might be worrying about nothing. Have you had any other symptoms? Do you feel sick in the mornings, are your breasts more sensitive than usual?'

Except for that morning I hadn't felt sick and my breast felt normal.

When I told her this she gave a little laugh, 'I think we all felt a bit under the weather this morning, and with good reason when you consider the amount of champagne we drank. You know you could be worrying about nothing. You've been through a lot during the past couple of months and stress and overwork can cause periods to stop. Anyhow if the worst comes to the worst and you're pregnant I'm here for you. Now go to sleep and try to stop worrying.'

She kissed me on the forehead and left the room, and I lay there feeling much calmer and soon drifted off to sleep.

I spent the next week working and hanging out with the others during our breaks. I tried not to obsess about the possibility that I was pregnant, but this was hard. I checked hopefully every time I went to the toilet. While lying in bed each night I'd run my hands over my stomach and think of how horrible it would be if I did in fact have a tiny creature growing in there. I didn't know if I would ever want to bear a child, and I certainly didn't want one now.

On New Year's Eve we worked flat out because the restaurant was fully booked. After Auld Lange Syne had been sung and the last of the guests staggered out the door we all breathed sighs of relief. We six planned a little celebration on the beach, and went to our rooms for warm coats as the night had turned cold and there was a strong wind blowing in across the bay. As I turned to leave my room I felt a crampy pain in my stomach and warm wetness between my legs. I rushed to the toilet and hurrah, I had my period.

I smiled broadly as I joined the others and whispered my news to Wanda. We celebrated wildly and well, and all had shocking hangovers in the morning.

During the next two months I worked hard and partied even harder. I had a fling with Joel, but made sure he always used a condom.

When I returned to town I made an appointment to see a doctor at the Family Planning Clinic and was prescribed the pill. I didn't bother telling Mum about this.

I felt I had done a lot of growing during those two months and that I was now genuinely independent.

I matriculated in one year and also won a Commonwealth Government Scholarship that would be a marvellous help financially. I enrolled to do a science degree majoring in mathematics and computer science. Soon I developed new friendships, mainly with girls. Because of my experience with the gang of four, as I now thought of Paul and the others, I was wary of friendly advances from male students. I took the pill religiously, but as a precaution rather than a necessity.

During this time my particular friend was Jenny, who came from a town in the north of the state and lived in one of the university dorms. Mum and Fred now spent every weekend at his place so I had the flat to myself. Most Saturdays and Sundays Jenny joined me there, and we studied together before going out to a disco or on a pub-crawl. It was fun getting dressed and trying out different make up and hairdos with another girl, almost like having a sister. We became very close.

At some time in the second year in the flat my parents' divorce became final. Mum had filed for a divorce in the middle of the year 1980 and by the following June it went through with three months until the decree nisi was granted. Neither of my parents attended the court proceedings. To me it seemed totally bizarre that a marriage of twenty-four years could be ended without either of the participants being present.

At times during the previous two years I'd secretly hoped Mum and Dad would somehow get back together again. I knew how much Mum loved Fred and that Dad was seeing other women, but I still couldn't quite believe my old life had gone forever. Sometimes I lay in bed and fantasised about them meeting unexpectedly, on a street or in a café, and suddenly realising that the events of the past two years had been a terrible mistake. Occasionally I even tried to think of ways in which I could bring about a reunion, but short of contracting a rare disease or injuring myself in some terrible accident I was at a loss as to the ways and means – and I didn't wish to be either ill or injured.

The divorce brought to an end these vague longings for a return to the life I'd lived before.

It also marked a change in my attitude towards Mum. I felt as though she and I were now set on separate paths. I felt by ceasing to be the wife of our father she had also cut the family ties with my brothers and me.

As the year progressed it seemed to me that, as I became more mature and independent, Mum became less responsible. She certainly was no less conscientious with regard to her job and continued to enjoy the stimulation of meeting lots of people and helping select, display and sell books. I suppose this sounds bitchy, but her love for Fred seemed to take away some of the maternal love and sense of connectedness that she'd previously felt for my brothers and me. When the boys came to dinner she didn't behave quite as lovingly with them as she had before, and she seemed unaware of the changes in them that were obvious to me.

Dale was becoming somehow tougher, more cynical and macho. He seemed harder than he'd been before.

Ralph, who had dropped out of university and was living in a shared house, appeared lost. As the year progressed he changed dramatically and I became very worried about him.

Blowin' In The Wind

Ralph continued to live in the big house with Dad during his third year at university. Early in the year Dale had bought a house and moved out.

During the first three months of my parents' separation Dad had evidently been quite upbeat, confident Mum would come to her senses and move back home. Most of the time Dad and the boys lived on fast foods, but occasionally they had barbecues and Dad tried his hand at cooking a roast meal a couple of times.

According to Ralph, after Mum and Dad had their big showdown Dad changed dramatically. He spiralled downwards into the blackest of depression, where he drank too much, hardly ate anything and even missed a couple of days from work – something unheard of for our father.

Ralph told me that at this time he felt very critical of our mother and found it difficult to continue the weekly visits to dinner. However he knew he would miss seeing her and me and Dale if he didn't come.

Fortunately one of Dad's friends, who had been through a divorce, became concerned about him and his emotional state. He took it upon himself to get Dad back on track and organized all-male weekends away where they would fish, cook, play cards, and of course drink but among companions. This guy also introduced Dad to some of his lady friends, and soon Ralph would encounter strange women in what had been Mum's kitchen on Saturday and Sunday mornings.

With the change in Dad's attitude Ralph felt he could relax a bit and stop worrying about him, but the strains of the past year had affected his studies and he struggled to complete his degree. He told me that by the end of the year he felt emotionally drained and also isolated from both of our parents and from Dale and me.

When he told Dad that he didn't intend returning to do a Diploma of Education the following year they had an enormous row. This finished up with him moving out of home and into a shared house with some art students who he'd met in the university bar.

Shortly after he moved into this house he invited me to visit. It was in an inner-city area that had once been one of the more desirable suburbs, but was now gently declining into a place of decaying old dwellings and neglected gardens.

When I knocked on the door it was opened by Ralph and he led me along a passage and into the lounge room. It was rather a large room with high dusty windows along one wall, a fireplace topped by a very elaborately scrolled mantelpiece and worn carpeting which partially covered the timber floors. Not an impressive room but sort of cosy.

Three of his new housemates were seated on an old flowered couch while the fourth, a slim blonde man, lounged back in a rather sagging chair.

They all greeted me cheerfully as Ralph made the introductions. There was Mara, a dark-haired beauty with a tiny, curvaceous body and big green eyes. Ralph had told me she was specialising in photography at art school and that he'd actually met the group when she had approached him in the bar and asked if he'd sit for her. Sometime later she told me she'd never seen such a sadly beautiful face as Ralph's and I'd thought it a sort of backhand compliment.

The other female in the flat was Cheryl, a rather busty, pretty blonde who was a talented weaver and also sang in a jazz band.

Jake was also an art student. He was dark and intense. Later, when I saw his room that was painted black and full of gloomy surrealistic paintings, I was concerned about the state of his mind

Rickie, who was the man in the sagging chair, rose to greet me as Ralph made the introductions. He was very tall and his white-blonde hair combined with deep-set black eyes gave him an almost alien look. I felt a small shiver pass through me as he shook my hand. There was something about this man I didn't like. He was the only one of the group not attending art school, but he had been the original renter and had paid the bond.

After Ralph had made the introductions I was given a tour of the house. It was quite large and consisted of two big front bedrooms, two smaller bedrooms, a quite substantial kitchen and the lounge room. These rooms all opened off a central passage that was wide enough to contain the narrow staircase leading up to the attic room where Rickie lived, while still leaving plenty of space to walk through.

The girls proudly showed me their rooms, which were the big ones at the front of the house. Both rooms bore the marks of their personalities and pursuits. Cheryl's was painted a stark white, but the walls were covered with her jewel-coloured woven wall hangings and the effect was quite beautiful. Mara's room was also painted white and decorated with a few large black and white photographs. It wasn't stark, however, because she had added touches of brilliant colour including a crimson bedspread, orange and purple cushions on the window seat and a large bronze vase on the mantelpiece.

As I have mentioned Jake's room was black. Rickie didn't suggest a viewing of his room at the top of the stairs, but Ralph proudly showed me into his. It was about the same size as Jake's but painted blue so looked bigger. It contained a wardrobe and chest of drawers but no bed. Rather than ask Dad if he could take his bed from home Ralph had gone to the Salvation Army shop and bought a double bed mattress. Evidently he felt much the same way as Mum had about bringing possessions from their past life into the present one.

After they had shown me around the house the others returned to the lounge room and Ralph and I sat on the mattress and he filled me in on what had been happening in his life. He had enrolled to do three units, History of Art, Drawing and Photography. He told me he'd chosen this final subject so that he would be sharing some classes with Mara. Although he didn't have a camera she had helped him buy a good second-hand one, and said that the college supplied much of the other equipment. He had applied for TEAS and it was backdated to the beginning of the year so he had a little money to buy an old wooden desk and drawing supplies.

During the first few months Ralph was in the share house I visited him about once a month. He seemed to be happier than I had seen him since our parents' separation. He was enjoying the classes, living in the house was fun and most importantly Mara and he had become lovers. She was bright, creative, fun to be with and very affectionate – a tonic for him after the last sad and rather lonely year.

The house had few rules. They pooled their money for food and cooked when they were hungry. Once they decided that they should have a Sunday roast and Ralph invited me to join them. I think he and some of the others might have been feeling a bit nostalgic or homesick. Mara and he had bought a leg of lamb, potatoes, pumpkin and frozen peas. I took along a ready-made apple pie, as I was pretty sure none of them would know how to make a dessert.

Together we prepared the vegetables and put them around the lamb. After an hour the vegetables were cooked but the lamb wasn't, so we put it back in the oven by itself for a further hour and retired to the lounge room to smoke and drink. Two hour later we remembered the meat. It was now dark brown and overcooked, the vegetables had gone soggy and the peas were still frozen.

At this stage Ralph thought about what our mother would have done and took over. He reheated the vegetables in a hot oven, cooked the frozen peas and rested the lamb wrapped in foil to make it moist again. He even found some mint in the cramped backyard and made mint sauce.

Eventually, at about four o'clock, we sat down to what I remember as a magnificent meal. I think we had fun, but were we all just lost young people trying to emulate the family dinners that, for various reasons, were no longer a part of our lives? I don't know.

The only other time I shared a meal in that house was one night when I dropped in unexpectedly. Evidently the food money had run out and supplies were scarce. They were all in the kitchen; a large room with green walls, very old and somewhat dirty linoleum on the floor, open shelves for food storage and a big table in the centre of the room. They only had loaves of two-day old bread, bought cheaply at a nearby bakery, and lots of eggs so were making French toast.

I joined them around the table and shared the main course of French toast with tomato sauce, salt and pepper and then the dessert of French toast with sugar and cinnamon. I enjoyed myself immensely and everyone made me feel at home.

After we'd eaten and piled the plates into the sink we moved into the lounge room and Rickie rolled a joint while Cheryl opened a wine cask. I accepted a glass of wine and even took a turn with the joint, but didn't want to outstay my welcome so I said I had a date.

When I'd said goodbye to everyone and Ralph was seeing me out I put my hand on his skinny waist and said, 'Mum's a bit worried about you. Are you okay?'

He kissed my cheek and said, 'Tell her I'm a big boy now and she's not to worry. I've started a whole new life and it's great.'

That was one of the last times I visited him there and Mum never did. I thought it odd that Mum never went to see Ralph while he lived in the share house. I knew she worried about him dropping out of university and about the life he was living. It was as though she didn't want to actually see and face up to the changes she'd caused in the life of this beloved son.

The next time I went to the house was during vacation and the atmosphere of the place had changed. I knew that as the year had progressed Ralph had begun to lose interest in the art classes. He said it was because he knew he didn't have enough talent in this field, but I think the main problem was that he was drinking and smoking pot every night.

From what I'd seen Rickie appeared to be able to consume quantities of alcohol combined it with various other drugs with little affect. Cheryl drank quite copiously but rarely smoked and Mara was a very moderate user of both. Jake would share a smoke early in the evening, but then would leave the lounge room to work on one of his dark surreal paintings.

On this occasion when I knocked on the door Mara opened it and greeted me with a hug then pulled me into her room and shut the door. She had obviously been crying, and when I looked around her room I saw she was in the middle of packing.

I was taken aback but before I could say anything Mara answered my unspoken question, 'Yes, I'm leaving. Ralph and I have had the most awful row. I'm going back home to live with Mum and Dad. Your brother's become a total druggy. He'll try anything Rickie gives him and he's dropped out of art school. I'm not staying around to watch him destroy himself. Perhaps you can talk some sense into him.'

I gave her a hug and then left her room to find Ralph. He was in the lounge with Rickie and, even though it was early afternoon, Ralph looked wasted.

He greeted me with a slurred, 'Hello little sister. To what do we owe the pleasure?'

I sat down next to him on the couch and put my arm around his bony shoulder, 'Oh Ralph, what are you doing to yourself? I've been talking to Mara...'

I didn't get any further before he threw my arm off his shoulder and staggered to his feet shouting, 'Don't you start on at me. I've had enough of women telling me what to do.'

Rickie looked on a small, sinister smile on his face. There was a feeling of evil in the room. I turned and left the house.

Shortly after that episode I met Dale for coffee and asked him to go and see Ralph, but I didn't know whether he would and I wasn't sure if he would have any influence on Ralph if he did go. I guess I was clutching at straws.

I went one last time to that house and once more things have changed. Ralph had moved into Mara's old room and a friend of Jake's was in what had been Ralph's room. This time my brother was sober and didn't appear to be drug affected. He apologised for his behaviour on my previous visit, but said he had been upset because of splitting up with Mara. I gave him a hug and we chatted over a cup of coffee in the kitchen. I didn't stay long because Rickie joined us and he really did give me the creeps.

The next time I saw Ralph was a few months later and a dramatic change had occurred in his life.

French Toast

slices white bread [can be stale]
eggs
milk
butter

Melt butter in pan

Beat eggs and mix in milk.

Dip slices of bread into egg/milk mixture.

Fry in pan until golden brown then turn and cook other side.

Serve with tomato sauce, salt and pepper or sugar and cinnamon combined.

This is so simple but some people have never experienced the pleasure of eating this cheap and simple treat.

Lucky, Lucky Me

At the end of second semester Jenny went home for the holidays, and Mum was always at Fred's for the weekends so I was alone in the flat. I decided to invite my two brothers around for dinner so that we could catch up without Mum around. I was hoping that with just the three of us together I would be able to find out exactly what was going on in their lives.

When I rang Dale he said he would love to come, but Ralph was evasive and said he'd make it if he could.

I wasn't sure whether I was cooking for two or three, but I bought a big piece of beef and baked it with potatoes, parsnips and onions and even made Yorkshire pudding to go with it. For dessert I made an apple crumble.

Everything was nearly ready when I heard doorbell ring. I checked the spy hole and saw it was Dale. As I let him in he handed me a bottle of wine and kissed me on the cheek.

His first words to me were, 'Is Ralph coming?'

'I hope so,' I answered, 'He didn't say definitely, but you know what he's like now.'

'No I don't really.' He moved to join me near the breakfast bar where I was opening the bottle of wine and continued, 'You know how you wanted me to go and see him.'

I nodded remembering how I'd asked Dale to visit him after Ralph dropped out of art school. I had thought he hadn't bothered to go.

'Well I went to that house where he's living and knocked on the door. It was opened by a skinny bird in a raggedy black tee shirt and a skirt up round her thighs. When I asked to see Ralph and said that I was his brother she screeched, "You brother's here to see you Ralph" and led me to the lounge room. You should have seen it Helen. The place was like a tip.'

I interjected with, 'Well I've been there a few times, and I didn't think it was that bad.'

'I can assure you it was a mess. The room was full of smoke, there were empty wine casks all along the mantelpiece, and the floor was virtually covered with greasy pizza boxes. Worst of all was the state Ralph was in. He was lying on an old, sagging couch, a joint in one hand and a glass of wine in the other. He looked decidedly scruffy and was unsteady on his feet when he came towards me. I grabbed his arm and asked if we could go somewhere to talk but he got all belligerent and accused me of not wanting to meet his friends. Honestly I didn't know what to do so I just said he knew where I lived, and if he needed help to come around. Of course he never has. I was hoping he'd pulled himself together and that we'd catch up tonight.'

I look at the little clock on the wall. 'I have a feeling that he won't show. He wouldn't give me a definite yes and he should be here by now if he's coming. Anyhow it's lovely to see you and I've cooked us a pretty good meal, but I'd better dish up or it'll be ruined.'

As I was making the gravy and Dale poured two glasses of wine I reminisced, 'Do you remember how Mum would be when Dad was late for dinner? She'd say, "The meal is for the man not the man for the meal," some old French saying. She'd worry about reheating it so that it wouldn't dry out.'

Dale grimaced, 'She always did fuss over him too much. Funny isn't it when you think of how things have turned out.'

He carried the glasses of wine and the bottle to the table as I carved up the beef.

I served up our dinner and put a plate aside in case Ralph should show up later, but I wasn't optimistic. I was worried about Ralph but was also concerned for Dale, and wanted to hear about his life and how he was coping with living alone.

I asked him if he ever got lonely and he laughed, 'You don't have to worry about me Helen. I was lucky the folks decided to split when I was nearly ready to strike out on my own. I was also lucky the government was offering that first homeowners grant. With the bit I'd saved it was enough to put a deposit on my house. I'm earning good money so the payments aren't a problem, and I have money over to make renovations.'

I had seen Dale's house a couple of times and he was doing a terrific job fixing it up, but I still thought that he must miss family life so I repeated, 'But are you lonely? Don't you miss being part of a family?'

'I did to start with. I missed not seeing Mum every day and believe it or not I missed you and Ralph. I used to meet the old man in the pub after work a couple of times a week. That was as much as I'd been seeing him during those last few months before you and Mum moved out so that wasn't very different. But to answer your question, no I'm rarely lonely and I love having my own house. After the split I would've hated living with either of our parents and I couldn't have stood sharing a house with strangers.'

'There's something else I've wanted to ask you. When they told us about the planned separation you said Dad had probably been playing around again. Because you said that I'd blamed Dad for what happened, and then I was so shocked when I found out about Mum and Fred. Had Dad been unfaithful to Mum?'

He looks at me, a serious expression in his dark eyes, 'I think so. When I was about eighteen I went into a pub and saw Dad chatting to a blonde woman, and from the body language they looked pretty darned familiar. I walked over and put him in the position where he had to introduce us. The next day he took me aside and said not to tell Mum about the meeting. He said it didn't mean anything, but I felt that there was something going on between them. Anyhow I kept quiet, but from then on I watched Mum and Dad together and became more aware of the flaws in their relationship. In a way I was relieved when the split came. For years I'd watched Dad dominate Mum and wondered when she would rebel.'

'You know I just always thought they were happy. The only time I saw Mum really sad was when we left the old house, but then she seemed to get over that pretty quickly. To me Mum looked to have a pretty good life. I didn't realise how she really felt.'

'Would you want to have that sort of marriage? I can't see you kowtowing to a man the way Mum did to Dad.' Dale suddenly looked very serious, 'One thing I'm sure about is that if I ever get married, and it's a big if, I want to have a relationship of equals.'

I laughed, 'I don't think you'll have any problems with that. We women of the 80s expect it. I certainly wouldn't ever marry a man who didn't treat me as an equal in every way, but I guess I've just accepted that things were different with our parents' generation.'

While we had been talking we finished our roast and I cleared the table and served the apple crumble. I made a joke of it bowing low as I place the bowl in front of Dale and said 'Your dessert oh Master?' and he laughed and pulled my hair.

This bit of levity brought to a halt to our serious family talk, and for the remainder of the evening Dale talked about his job, which he loved, and I told him about my university courses and of some of the people I had met.

When he was leaving he said, 'Thanks for a great meal little sister. I do love a roast, but I'd never cook it just for myself. And it's so much more enjoyable sharing a meal than eating alone.'

For a fleeting moment there was a look of sadness in his eyes then he grinned, 'It's been great really catching up, just the two of us, although it's a shame Ralph didn't make it. I hope he's all right.'

As he walked to his car I watched and he gave one last wave before driving away. It had been a lovely evening and I was glad we'd had a chance to talk, just the two of us. I felt I'd touched base with one of my brothers. I was also pleased that he had at least tried to talk to Ralph even if it hadn't worked out. I felt happy with the way Dale's life was going for him, and confident he had a bright and successful future ahead of him.

I wished I could feel the same confidence about Ralph.

Starting Over

Except for worrying about Ralph I quite enjoyed the second year in the flat. I was doing well at university and had a good social life.

I had done a lot of growing up and began to understand how difficult the past couple of years had been for Mum. We seemed to be developing a relationship that was more like two friends and flat mates than mother and daughter. This led me to feel that I should take over some of the domestic chores.

Because I was always home before Mum I offered to prepare dinner one night a week. I decided my specialty would be soups and I experiment with different combinations of vegetables and flavourings. I set myself the challenge of making soup without using ready-made stock. Perhaps I was just being my mother's daughter with these experimentations. We had some revolting combinations but several were delicious including a rich French onion.

On other nights I experimented with meat loaf and another staple was Tuna a la King.. We didn't have much money so the challenge was to make the most interesting meals from the cheapest ingredients. We still had our Gourmet Nights on Mondays and these continued to be the times when we related best and talked about our personal concerns.

Shortly after my evening with Dale I asked Mum how she and Fred would manage financially when they were married and she moved into his house. She enjoyed her job so much at the bookshop, and had told me how the years of financial dependence had slowly destroyed her sense of worth and feeling of control over her life. I didn't want to see that happening to her again. Talking to Dale about her and Dad had made me think about this.

She raised her glass to mine and said, 'Don't worry about that darling. I'll just have to find a job locally. Fred says we can live on his salary and investments, but I'm not going down that path again. I'll get something.'

She spoke with such confidence I felt sure she would convince someone to employ her. Obviously she was not going to let her love for Fred swamp her regained sense of self and independence. I felt happy and relieved she wasn't going to make the same mistake with Fred that she had with Dad.

That was one of our last girls' nights where we really talk about our personal concerns. Our previously close bond was unravelling and we were both preparing to go off in different directions.

Mum and Fred were to marry at the beginning of the following year. They had planned a small outdoor ceremony at The Cove, with only their children with a partner or friend and Carolyn and Matt as their witnesses.

Fred had spent the year extending his house to make it suitable for their life together. He and Mum designed the extension, and although they had tried to interest me in their plans I really didn't care what they did. I would never live there and was making plans of my own for the following year.

I did, however, go down with Mum one weekend towards the end of the year. I had been there a couple of times before and was now amazed by the transformation.

The original house had consisted of four rooms; two bedrooms at the front, a third bedroom that had been changed into a bathroom and a large kitchen cum living room with an open fireplace. A narrow passage ran between the front bedrooms and opened into this room. I had thought it was all fairly basic and old, although the land and the setting were lovely.

I was quite impressed with the changes. All the existing rooms had been painted and recarpeted, a magnificent claw-foot bath had been installed in the middle of the bathroom and the combined kitchen–living room had become a comfortable lounge room.

The small side porch off this room now led to the extension, which was large, light and absolutely beautiful. It had a pale grey slate floor, soft grey-green walls and high French doors that opened onto a wide deck that overlooked the bay. Along one wall was the stove, sink and preparation bench. The high, slim windows on that side faced the dam and the land where a vineyard would be planted.

The back wall was dominated be a huge Huon pine dresser and in the centre of the room was a pine table with matching chairs, all of which have been lovingly restored by Fred.

The room had incorporated the old porch and the building had been extended behind this to make a large walk-in pantry that also housed the refrigerator.

Although in real-estate speak it might have been appraised as an unsympathetic addition from the outside, as a liveable space inside it was absolutely right for Mum and Fred and a superb blend of old and new.

I spent the latter part of the year studying hard and was feeling confident about achieving good university results.

Mum and I had more girlie Monday nights, but they were mainly spent discussing my future plans and the wedding.

Dale continued to come to dinner on Thursday nights but Ralph didn't always make it and when he did he wasn't looking well. I had tried to ring him after he hadn't turned up for dinner with Dale and me, but their phone had been cut off and I no longer liked to visit that house.

I was alone in the flat one Saturday swotting for the impending exams when there was a knock on the door, and through the spy hole I saw Ralph standing on the landing, his shoulders hunched and his arms wrapped around his skinny frame.

I let him in with a nonchalant, 'Long time no see stranger.'

He hugged me fiercely and then asked, 'Is Mum here?'

'No, she's down at the Cove with Fred. What's up? You look dreadful.'

Suddenly he just crumpled up onto the couch and began to sob. I thought he said, 'Rickie's dead,' but I wasn't sure as his voice was so muffled. I put my arms around him and held him close while he cried, and then disentangled myself to find him tissues and put on the jug for coffee.

Slowly he regained his composure and when I handed him his cup he said rather sheepishly, 'Sorry about that, but the most terrible thing has happened and I just had to share it with someone I could trust. I was hoping Mum would be here.'

Feeling a bit miffed I asked, 'Will I do? Nothing you've done can be so bad that you can't tell me.'

'It's not something bad I've done. It's something that has happened and it has to be kept a secret, but I need to talk about it.'

I was now totally mystified, so I urged him to tell me what it was that had upset him so much. I listened intently as he told me what had happened.

'At the house last night we all spent the evening apart. Jake and Stephen were busy finishing paintings for end of year assessment and Cheryl was working on an enormous wall hanging that is her major work for the year. Rickie was entertaining some unseen woman up in his room and I had taken myself to bed after a couple of bongs and some glasses of wine.'

He paused and took a sip of coffee before continuing. 'I had been asleep some hours when I was woken by a loud thudding noise followed by piercing screams. I was feeling slightly woozy from the drink and drugs so took a while to react. By the time I reached my door and opened it Cheryl, Jake and Stephen were already in the passage. Rickie was lying at the foot of the stairs with his head at an unnatural angle and his legs splayed on the lower steps. Above stood a slim, frail-looking girl with only a slip on and she was screaming over and over, "I didn't mean to, I didn't mean to."

'God, what ever had happened?' I interjected.

Ralph continued, 'I couldn't take it in at first and stood there like a dummy but Cheryl walked carefully around Rickie and headed up the stairs to comfort the girl. Jake leant over him and felt for a pulse and then looked up and said, "He's dead."

Stephen was all for us getting the police but Jake said we'd better find out how it happened first and suggested we make the girl a cup of tea. It was amazing how calm he stayed. I was shaking like a leaf and so was Stephen, but Jake put on the kettle and by the time Cheryl and brought the girl downstairs he'd made tea for all of us.

Cheryl led the girl into the kitchen and introduced her as Sue. She was now dressed and had one of Cheryl's throws around her shoulders, but she was still shivering and whimpering.'

Here he paused and I put an arm around his shoulders and said, 'Go on.'

Taking a deep breath he continued, 'Jake sat across the table from Sue and asked her to tell us exactly what'd happened. She said she'd only met Rickie that night but that he'd seemed nice so she'd thought that it would be all right to go home with him. They'd smoked some joints and then had sex and gone to sleep, but when they woke up he suggested she try some heroin. Evidently she was terrified at the thought of using hard drugs and when she refused Rickie became angry and abusive. He told her to leave and pushed her out the door. She was angry at being treated like that and pushed back. He must've been off balance because he fell heavily and then rolled all the way down the stairs. After she finished telling us what'd happened she became quite hysterical again saying she'd go to jail and that she hadn't meant it to happen.'

Nervously I asked, 'So what's happened now? Did you call the police?'

Ralph shook his head, 'No, Jake reckoned it wouldn't be right for the girl to have to face a manslaughter charge, in view of the way it happened. He said if we all kept quiet about Sue being there and said that Rickie must have stumbled while affected by drugs it would be seen as an accident.'

'And is that what you did?' I asked breathlessly.

'Yes. Cheryl took Sue home and then we called the police. There'll be a coroner's inquest but the police accepted our story.'

'What a ghastly thing to happen. I didn't ever like Rickie and he was a bad influence on you, but even I wouldn't have wished him dead.'

'Promise me you won't ever tell anyone about this will you Helen, not even Mum. I know I shouldn't have told you but I just had to talk it out.'

I assured Ralph that I wouldn't ever repeat what he had told me and even offered to come to the funeral with him if he would like me to.

Rickie was buried on a wet, windy day and his housemates and I were the only ones to attend his funeral. Ralph said he had never mentioned parents or siblings and when asked about family would say, "I just fell to earth from the sky." When I think of the way in which he died I can't help but think how ironical life is.

After that appalling event none of them felt comfortable living in that house and when the lease was up at the end of the year they didn't renew it.

Cheryl moved in with a boyfriend and Jake and Stephen decided to share a flat.

Ralph moved back in with Dad, but said it was only for a couple of months until the university year commenced.

The wedding day, in early January, was actually lovely. The sun was shining, the garden looked colourful and lush and Fred, in a cream shirt and grey moleskins, looked quite handsome and totally besotted.

Jenny and I drove Mum down and she looked very pretty in a long, pale cream dress that set off to perfection her blonde, shoulder-length hair and blue eyes. When Fred greeted her with a bouquet of apricot roses and kissed her we girls had to turn away to cover our embarrassment at the open emotion between those two, and also to hide our sentimental tears.

Dale and his girlfriend arrived early and Mum showed them the house while Fred opened a magnum of champagne.

Carolyn and Matt drove in, noisily bipping the horn of their BMW, and then proceeded to laughingly carry from the car an enormous present that they stowed on the new deck before accepting glasses of champagne.

Shortly after them the marriage celebrant arrived, a gentle, fussy little man who lived nearby. Straight away he began organising where the ceremony would take place and put up a little table.

I could see Mum looking up the road and knew from her expression that she was worrying about whether or not Ralph would come. He had been through such a disturbed year and was finally getting his life in order, but was still not quite recovered from past events. He was also staying temporarily with Dad and I suppose she may have been worrying about whether he would try to influence Ralph against attending the wedding. Dad still felt very embittered about her love affair with Fred.

Seeing Mum's concern I went over to her and put my arm around her shoulders. Just then down the road came a noisy Datsun, billowing black smoke as it turned into the driveway. I felt Mum's body relax as Ralph stepped out of the car, looking lean and pale but smartly dressed and with a big smile on his face. Mum rushed towards him and hugged him close.

Perhaps she hadn't divorced us after all.

The wedding ceremony was brief but moving and followed by a scrumptious lunch prepared by Fred, cold salmon served in a vinaigrette and roast chicken with delicious salads made from his homegrown vegetables. Jenny and I had bought a big mud-cake decorated with brown and white chocolate roses for wedding-cake and dessert.

After lunch the celebrant left and presents were opened. Dale and I had bought identical beautifully decorated pottery casserole dishes. I had been assured that the potter had only made two such dishes. Just shows how quirky family tastes or influences can be. Ralph's gift was an olive tree and Carolyn and Matt's present a big terracotta love goddess that was immediately placed in the garden, under a tree, and looked as if she'd been there forever.

Fred's son, who had sent a rather stilted note saying he could not attend, had sent them towels.

Jenny and I helped clean up after everyone else had gone so we were late getting away. I let Jenny drive my car home as I had drunk more champagne than she. As we turned out of the drive I looked back and saw Mum and Fred locked in each other's arms like a pair of teenagers.

During my final year at university I mainly only saw Mum once a week, when she drove up to town and took Ralph and me out to lunch. Ralph was doing a Master of Psychology Degree and planned to become a student counsellor at the end of the year

With my scholarship and extra financial assistance from Dad I had been able to afford a dear little flat near the university. I was sharing it with Jenny who was my dearest friend.

I liked those lunches for Mum was always happy. She and Fred were enjoying their life together, enlarging the vegetable garden, fishing in the bay and preparing the empty paddock near the dam for a vineyard. She was also enjoying a part-time job in a nursery that doubled as a second-hand bookshop. This combination of plants and books was so bizarre and so suited to Mum's interests and skills I would have thought it a figment of her imagination had I not seen the place myself.

Ralph was also so much happier, living in a shared house with other university students and really enjoying his studies.

I didn't see Dale much during that year, but evidently he occasionally went down to The Cove with his girlfriend to spend the weekend with Mum and Fred.

I also saw Dad rarely. We still met sometimes for a coffee but I hardly ever went to see him at "home." I felt uncomfortable there, as if I were an interloper in that space. When I'd look into my old bedroom I'd feel as though I was fragmenting into bits of the old and the new me and it was not a good way to feel. I'd shut the door and walk away.

During my years at university I often dropped in to see Nanna Alice and Granddad. Quite often Auntie Meg and Uncle Vincent and their kids would be there. Sometimes Uncle Gordon would turn up with his two little boys. I really enjoyed those visits because they reminded me of when I was young, and my brothers and I would play with our cousins, while our mothers talked and smoked in the kitchen.

Nanna seemed almost unchanged. Although her hair was now white it was still shoulder length and abundant and her skin was almost unlined. I'd watch her as she'd pull a batch of scones from the oven and slather them with butter and jam while they were still hot, and remember how she had done this for us when we were kids.

While Nanna hadn't changed much the years had taken their toll on Granddad. He no longer worked his garden because arthritis in his hands and knees made such physical work too painful. He had also become very deaf so a conversation with him was difficult. Generally when I visited he was sitting in his armchair with the daily paper in his hands, but he'd be sleeping and snoring loudly. He died peacefully in that chair the following year and all his children and grandchildren attended the funeral. We worried about how Nanna would cope without her man, but after the first sad months of sorrow she pulled herself together and seemed to get back her joy of life.

At the end of the year Dale moved to Sydney to work in the head office of his company. Mum, Fred, Ralph and I took him out to dinner to celebrate before he left.

Ralph had been given a position providing a counselling service to students in a number of schools on the northeast coast. We promised to ring each other occasionally to keep in touch.

That summer Jenny and I spent a fortnight at The Cove with Mum and Fred, where we filled our lazy days walking around the rocky foreshore, swimming and fishing in the bay and reading under the fruit trees in the orchard.

Every evening we had long, slow boozy barbecues with flathead, flavoured with lemon, fresh dill and butter and cooked in foil or salmon steaks that have been marinated first in garlic, lime and chilli. The accompanying salads were made from their homegrown vegetables. In the cool of the evening I'd join Mum for the picking and pulling of lettuce, sorrel, baby beets, carrots, red onions and early tomatoes.

During the day Mum and Fred always seemed to be busy, working away together digging and weeding in the vegetable garden and new vineyard, clearing branches from the back paddocks and collecting firewood, or setting nets in the late afternoon and cleaning the early morning catch. They had a few chooks and seemed to be especially proud of how nothing was ever wasted. They appeared to be idyllically happy and a very complete unit.

On our last day they spent the afternoon in the kitchen-dining room from which Jenny and I had been banished and that evening we had a gala feast. We ate homemade pate, dolmades, made using lush leaves from an old sultana grape, Fred's special roast chicken served with potatoes, carrots and snow peas and loganberry sponge for dessert. They were like kids in their pleasure at the degree of self-sufficiency that they were already achieving, and talked optimistically of being able to live off the land.

I couldn't see how they would ever do this, as they would still need to buy the basics like tea, sugar and flour not to mention petrol. However, their long-term hope was to grow a commercial crop, of something yet to be determined, and also to eventually have a cash flow from the vineyard.

Jenny and I left the next morning laden with lettuces, potatoes, spring onions and carrots. We didn't have the heart to tell them that the potatoes and carrots would probably sprout in the cardboard box and the lettuces and onions go limp in our refrigerator, as we weren't into cooking much. Our fridge was mainly a repository for breakfast yoghurt, our salute to a healthy diet, casks of white wine and cartons of milk for tea and coffee.

I enjoyed my three years at university and Jenny and I grew very close. We both studied hard but also played hard, and helped each other through examination nerves, minor heartbreaks and the odd bout of flu. Mum continued to come to town once a week and we lunched together but I rarely went to The Cove during that time.

At the end of the year I obtained a position with the Taxation Department and the following year transferred to Canberra, where the central computer system was located.

That year Ralph also left Tasmania. He had met and fallen in love with a girl called Maureen who came from Melbourne. She had been teaching at one of the schools at which Ralph worked as a counsellor. When they met she had only been in Tasmania for a year, but she was missing her family and friends and the slightly warmer climate of her home state. They moved to Melbourne and both obtained work with the Education Department.

I'm not sure how Mum felt about all her children moving interstate. She told me later that it had made her very conscious of living on an island. It concerned her that if something happened to any of us she couldn't just get in her car and drive to where we were.

Basically, though, she had made a new life for herself and so had we.

Helen's Soup [made without stock]

2 large or 4 medium onions
1 tbsp. butter
pinch sugar
3 – 4 cloves garlic
1 tsp. plain flour
4 cups water

1 dsp. Vegemite
1 tsp. Dijon mustard
½ tsp paprika
salt and pepper to taste
2 oz. grated, tasty cheese
tbsp. finely chopped, fresh herbs

Peel onions and cut into rings.

Heat butter in saucepan, add onions and pinch sugar and cook, stirring, until golden and transparent.

Add finely chopped garlic and cook further 1 minute.

Stir in flour then add water.

Stir in Vegemite, mustard and paprika

Season to taste with salt and pepper.

Cover and simmer for 30 minutes.

Spoon into warm bowls and sprinkle with grated cheese and fresh herbs.

Sausage Meat Loaf

1 rasher bacon	1 tbsp. butter
1 onion	2 eggs
1 kg. sausage meat	salt and pepper to taste
1 cup soft breadcrumbs	½ cup plain flour
1 cup mashed potatoes	

Chop bacon and onion finely.

Place in mixing bowl with sausage meat, breadcrumbs, mashed potato, melted butter and seasoning.

Beat eggs, add to mixture reserving a little for glazing.

Mix well, form into rectangular, loaf shape making sure it is free from cracks

Place on greased baking dish, brush with remaining egg and sprinkle with flour.

Bake uncovered in moderate oven for approximately 1 ½ hours, basting with pan juices after 30 minutes and repeat 30 minutes later.

Do not turn during cooking.

Serve hot or cold.

Tuna a la King

2 oz. mushrooms	1 ½ cups water
1 small green pepper	2 chicken cubes
2 oz. butter	¼ pint cream
¼ cup flour	15 oz. can tuna

Slice mushrooms thinly.

Remove seeds and dice green pepper.

Melt butter in pan, add mushrooms and green pepper and sauté 2-3 minutes

Remove vegetables and set aside.

Add flour to pan and cook for 1 minute in pan juices.

Remove pan from heat and gradually add water and crumbled stock cubes.

Liquid drained from the tuna can replace some of the water for extra flavour.

Return to heat and stir until mixture boils and thickens.

Season to taste with salt and pepper.

Add cream, drained tuna and vegetables and heat gently

Serve with hot, boiled rice.

Pate

8 oz. cream cheese
4 oz. liverwurst
1 tbsp. finely chopped onion
1 dsp. lemon juice
1 dsp. chopped parsley
1 dsp. brandy

Blend together cream cheese and liverwurst.

Stir in remaining ingredients and season to taste.

Serve with toast triangles.

Dolmades

1 large onion
3 tbsp. olive oil
6 tbsp. rice [uncooked]
4 tbsp. pine nuts
340 g raw minced beef

1 tsp. finely chopped mint
pinch cinnamon
30 vine leaves
140 ml dry white wine
water if needed

Chop onion and fry in hot oil for a few minutes.

Add rice and fry gently until golden.

Add pine nuts and cook 1 minute.

Remove from heat and add the meat, mint, cinnamon, salt and pepper and mix well.

Dip vine leaves in hot water for 1 minute to soften them.

Remove carefully and spread out flat.

Put a tsp. of mixture in centre of each leaf, fold in ends and roll up into tight rolls. This needs to be done quickly so that leaves do not dry out.

Put rolls in deep pan; pour in wine and extra water if needed to cover rolls.

Cook for approximately 25 minutes over low heat with lid on then remove lid and cook until liquid evaporates. (*May need to put plate on rolls to hold them down*).

Serve hot or cold as an appetiser.

Lemon Roast Chicken

Rinse chicken and pat dry

Halve several cloves of garlic and push beneath the skin on the breast and thighs.

Rub garlic on skin and squeeze lemon juice all over.

Fill cavity of chicken with sliced lemon, stems of lemon thyme and extra garlic.

Oil skin and rub on sea salt.

Bake in moderate oven, approximately one hour.

Serve with jacket potatoes and cucumber, tomato and red onion salad.

We've Only Just Begun

Weddings are a problem when there are divorced parents unless the divorce has been amicable, which is rare, or has occurred a long time in the past.

Ralph and Maureen announced their wedding plans one year after moving to Melbourne. I was happy for them because they seemed so suited and very much in love.

About once a month my work mates and I felt the need to escape from the land-locked, claustrophobic atmosphere of Canberra so we drove down to Melbourne or up to Sydney for the weekend. In this way I managed to keep in touch with my two brothers.

Ralph and Maureen were renting an old, rambling house in an inner city suburb and when their landlord put it on the market they decided to buy it. As they had plenty of spare rooms my friends and I often dossed down in sleeping bags on spare mattresses so I saw quite a lot of them. As a result I shared in the wedding plans.

Because Maureen's parents were fairly conservative and strait-laced, a church wedding followed by a formal reception was planned. Maureen asked me about seating arrangements with regard to our mother and father. I suggested, rather facetiously, that they be placed at opposite ends of the room, as I knew Dad still felt a sense of hurt and anger towards Mum and positive hatred of Fred. In his chauvinistic way he felt Fred had somehow stolen Mum from him. Although I sort of joked about it I was worried that our parents' animosities could spoil the day for Ralph and Maureen.

On the day of the wedding Bruce and I left Canberra early so that we could be in Melbourne before noon. I should mention something about Bruce, as by this time he had become the most important person in my life.

I find it quite hard to write about us without it sounding like something from a Mills and Boon novelette, but this is what happened. He was my supervisor at work and when we were introduced I was instantly attracted to him. As soon as I looked into his vivid blue eyes and felt his warm handshake I knew I wanted this man. As I came to know him better I was impressed with his organisational skills and the easy way he had with his staff, but he seemed rather sad and aloof. At times I'd catch him staring out of a window with a rather lost look on his handsome face and I wanted to cheer him up, but didn't know how. According to office gossip he was recovering from a failed love affair with a woman named Betsy, who had been working there before I joined the staff. It was said she had broken his heart when she dumped him and moved to Sydney.

Every Friday afternoon we all knocked off work a little early and went to the nearby pub for a few drinks and to unwind at the end of the week. Bruce always came and generally bought the first round of drinks, but invariably left early. I began making sure that I sat near him and we talked easily. Gradually he began staying longer until one evening we were the last to leave.

It was a cold spring night, and as we walked to the car park he put his arm around my shoulders and pulled me close to him saying, 'Let me warm you up.'

My heartbeat quickened as I snuggled willingly against his side and I thought he might finally make a move, but when we reached my car he gave me a light kiss on the cheek said, 'Have a good weekend,' and went to his car.

I was so disappointed I nearly cried as I drove home. I'm not conceited but I know I am attractive. I inherited Mum's blonde hair and curvy figure but have dark brown eyes like my father and am tall like him. When I was younger I found this embarrassing, but I came to rather like my height. Generally I had no problem attracting men, but it seemed Bruce was impervious to my charms.

When I arrived at work on Monday all the staff was abuzz with the news that Betsy was in Bruce's office. We all settled down to work but I couldn't concentrate. I wondered what was going on behind that closed door. I felt quite desolate at the thought of Bruce reuniting with his past love. It made me face up to the fact that I had let him become too important to me.

At about eleven Bruce and Betsy emerged from his office and left the building. I couldn't help but notice that he had his arm around her shoulders as they entered the lift. He returned alone about half an hour later and spent the rest of the day working as usual, but he seemed more cheerful than I had ever seen him. Obviously they were back together again.

The following Friday we all went to the pub as usual, but I avoided Bruce and spent much of the evening flirting quite outrageously with a man at the next table. Bruce left early and I figured that he probably had a date with Betsy.

The next few Friday nights followed a similar pattern but I no longer enjoyed them as I had before. My jealousy at the thought of Bruce with Betsy made me awkward when he was near, and we no longer talked as easily as we had in the past. I would often see him watching me across the table, but now it made me uncomfortable.

Things came to a head when we were working together late one night. We had a particularly tedious computer problem and when we solved it I turned to him and we gave each other a congratulatory hug. I pulled away embarrassed, but then Bruce held me tight and kissed me long and hard on the mouth.

'I've wanted to do that for so long,' he whispered.

I stammered, 'But what about Betsy. Aren't you an item again?'

He laughed, 'Office gossip is not to be believed my beautiful one. No Betsy and I split up months ago. We're now just good friends, but working in the same place did complicate things when we were together.'

'Is that why you've waited so long? I'm sure you could tell that I liked you.'

"I've been wary about becoming involved with a work mate again, but I can't help myself. I think about you all the time, and it's been breaking me up since you've become so standoffish with me.'

I pulled him to me, 'Well lets remedy that.'

We have been together ever since and I love him to bits.

Well, enough of Bruce and me and back to Ralph and Maureen's wedding. We arrived at the church and the first person I saw was Mum, looking very smart in a blue silk suit, with Fred at her side. People were milling outside the church waiting to be allowed inside. Bruce and I walked up to them and I was making introductions when, at the back of the crowd, I saw Dad arrive. With him was his latest lady-friend, an attractive divorcee named Joanne.

Seeing me he headed in my direction, but as he came closer and saw Mum he veered away. Great! I thought.

Just then the doors of the church were opened and ushers, in dark suits, began directing people into their seats. Mum, Fred, Bruce and I followed the usher to the front pew and were seated. Seconds later Dad and Joanne were shown to their seats, directly behind us. Mum obviously felt his presence and turned towards him with a tentative smile, only to be met with a grimace from Dad.

I can't say I enjoyed or even heard much of the wedding service, as I was conscious all the time of the malevolent vibes emanating from Dad to Mum and Fred. It was a relief to escape the heavy atmosphere in our part of the church.

Fortunately Ralph had told Maureen's parents of possible friction between our parents so Bruce and I were seated at a table with Mum and Fred and two other couples on one side of the room, while Dad and Joanne with Dale and his new girlfriend, Gay, were seated on the other.

I don't know whether the friction still existing between our parents affected Ralph's pleasure on that day. I don't think it did. I, however, felt worried and tense all the time, fearing that something unpleasant would happen. I decided that day that if I married I would ensure neither of my parents attended.

Towards the end of the next year Dale and Gay were married, but their wedding was so huge Mum and Dad probably didn't even see each other. Gay's parents owned a palatial property overlooking Sydney Harbour, and the ceremony was held on the expansive lawns that ran down to the water's edge.

Gay wore a sleek, stylish strapless dress and carried a huge sheaf of white and green orchids, while Dale looked extremely handsome in a dinner-suit with one green orchid in his lapel. I felt so proud of him and happy that he had found a mate as ambitious and competent as he.

After the ceremony the guests mingled in the sunshine, while being served exquisite canapés, even better than

Mum's and Carolyn's, and drinking copious quantities of champagne. Later strawberries and cream and profiteroles were served on the enormous terrace that ran the width of the house. Here brief speeches were made and the four-tiered cake was cut. During the afternoon Bruce and I spoke to both Mum and Dad but, as far as I know, they didn't encounter each other. Nevertheless, I worried all afternoon that they would meet

Bruce and I spent a long time talking to Ralph and a very pregnant Maureen. They were jubilant at the prospect of becoming parents, and were busy restoring and redecorating their rambling old house.

On Valentine's Day, the following year, Bruce asked me to marry him. We were dining out at a new Hungarian restaurant, and he had even organised a gypsy violinist to serenade us while he proposed. It was very romantic and of course I said yes.

My big problem would be the wedding. Even though Dad was now engaged to Joanne, and should have let past animosities go, I still didn't want my parents at my wedding. I didn't want to risk their past problems impinging on the beginning of our married life. Bruce couldn't understand my concern as it had now been a long time since their divorce, but he said it didn't matter to him how we were married as long as we were.

He is pragmatic as well as romantic – a lovely combination. He also had no parents to consider. He and his younger brother lost their parents in a tragic accident when Bruce was twelve and his brother ten. A wealthy and genial uncle brought them up, but he had died two years before Bruce and I met.

I decided that I would like to be married on a beach in Fiji, with only our dearest friends as witnesses. We had developed close friendships with three other couples and often spent camping weekends or trips to Melbourne or Sydney with them. Together we began planning the "Honeymoon Holiday" as it had been named. We would all fly to Fiji and stay at a resort on a beautiful beach, not far from Suva. There Bruce and I would be married, and then we would fly off to one of the smaller islands for our honeymoon, leaving the others to holiday and shop before returning to Australia.

The bookings were made and the resort agreed to organise the wedding. I wrote to both of my parents telling them about the wedding plans.

Dad wrote back wishing us a happy day and a bright future and promising a nice wedding present when we were next in Tasmania.

Mum wrote back saying she was heartbroken. She added that she felt I was cutting her completely out of my life. I think she must have had a few wines before she wrote to me because she became quite maudlin about every mother wanting to see her daughter as a bride. She wrote that she knew she hadn't always been there for me when she should have been. She finished by saying she now felt that I was punishing her for this and for putting Fred first.

It was difficult to write back to her. I still loved her, but did not feel like changing what had already been planned. To be honest I did feel that she hadn't always been there for me during my later teen years and so did not deserve the consideration due to other, more consistent mothers.

In the end I wrote a letter that was probably unsatisfactory for both of us. I said I understood how she felt, that my wedding plans had nothing to do with how she had been as a mother, that I loved her very much but that it was too late to reorganise anything.

I did not receive an answer.

In June Bruce and I and our six friends boarded the big jumbo jet and headed off to Fiji. All the cabin staff wore brightly coloured shirts or dresses, we were given delicious food and the wine flowed freely. Eight weary Australians staggered off the plane into humid tropical heat, clad in warm winter slacks and sweaters. We couldn't wait to get to our resort and change into more summery clothes.

We spent the next two days swimming in the pool and the ocean, wandering along the soft sand, eating exotic fruits and spicy fish and chicken dishes and generally relaxing.

On the third day the girls and I went shopping in Suva while the guys headed out on a boat for a bit of reef fishing. We females had a mission, to find me something suitable in which to get married. I had left the choice of the dress until then because I wanted something exotic and glamorous and suited to the location.

After wandering from one shop selling sarongs to another selling sarongs and a third much the same we finally found one that was different. An immaculate, little Indian man and his beautiful, dark-eyed wife, who was dressed in a floating, crimson sari, ran it. Both spoke very precise English so I had no problems explaining that I was looking for something really special to wear for my wedding.

The wife nodded solemnly while saying, 'I am Rani, and I will find you what you need.'

She bowed me into the changing room while my girl friends looked over the collection. They were going to wear sarongs for the wedding and busied themselves making their selections while I tried on several different garments.

During the next hour I put on floaty saris, with much help from Rani, vivid kaftans and finally the one – a silken dress in white and trimmed with gold. It was low-cut in the front and back, had a full-length skirt that swirled softly around my ankles and a wide gold belt. I looked at myself in the mirror and knew this was the dress in which I should be married. My girl friends all crowded into the changing room, and by the looks on their faces I knew I was right.

After the serious shopping was out of the way we continued down the street stopping, shopping, bargaining and giggling until we found a nice cool restaurant for lunch and wine. We then caught a taxi back to the resort and went to our rooms to try on our new clothes, and to wait for the return of the fishermen.

The guys came back, all weary and slightly sunburnt, but jubilant with their catch, and informed us that dinner would be the fish they had caught. We had a hilarious evening of good food and wine, much laughter and comradeship.

The next day the guys took Bruce into Suva to find suitable clothes for a groom and his witnesses. We girls finalised the plans for the wedding with the resort manager then swam and lazed in the pool. That night, after dinner, the guys took Bruce away for his last night of freedom and my friends and I spent the remainder of the evening drinking champagne, painting finger nails and toenails and practising hairstyles.

The morning was perfect as we breakfasted on the patio off my room that overlooked the aqua pool surrounded by gently swaying palms. Beyond was an expanse of deep blue sea that glittered in the sunlight.

The wedding was planned for eleven o'clock so that Bruce and I could catch the afternoon flight to the other side of the island. From there we would catch a ferry to Manna Island where we were to spend our honeymoon.

By ten I had showered and brushed my hair out loosely around my shoulders. My three friends were in various stages of readiness. Di was still in the shower, Rebecca was putting finishing touches to her hair and Jackie was ready, looking very beautiful in a dark blue sarong decorated with lighter blue hibiscus flowers and with an orange hibiscus behind her ear.

Someone knocked on the door and Jackie answered it to have a large box thrust into her hands. She plopped it on the table saying, 'Well I guess this is for you.'

I opened the lid and inside was a freshly made circlet of frangipani nestling golden and white amongst the tissue paper. I pulled it out eagerly and placed it on my head while realising that this was the perfect foil for my dress. As I crumpled the box I felt something heavy slip sideways and fall to the floor. There was a smaller box. I opened it and inside was a gorgeous gold necklace with a note attached which read – "For my bride with all my love. Rani said you need this to complete the dress. Can't wait to see you. Love Bruce."

I removed the circlet from my head, carefully pulled on my gown and fastened the belt. Jackie did up the clasp on the gold necklace before replacing the frangipani on my head. I was so happy with the way I looked I did a little pirouette and laughed out loud.

By now my friends were all dressed in their colourful sarongs and had hibiscus blossoms behind their ears. We left the room in a giggling group, arguing about which ear indicated if you were single or unavailable

The manager greeted us at the entryway and handed me a bouquet of frangipani and vine leaves. An island band played a haunting, drumming tune as I walked to the beach followed by Di, Jackie and Rebecca. There, waiting for me on the sand, was Bruce dressed only in a sulu with a lei of frangipani around his gleaming, golden neck. How I loved my man at that moment – not only because he looked so gorgeous, but also because he was doing something so special by acting out with me my romantic dream.

The minister was a huge Fijian man, also dressed in a sulu but with it topped by a loose white shirt. While we said our vows the drums beat softly in the background and the sea swished gently beneath our feet.

After we were pronounced man and wife we turned to our friends for congratulatory hugs. Out of the corner of my eye I saw a figure move swiftly behind a palm tree at the edge where the grass met the beach. It was my mother! I called out and ran across the sand, but when I reached the palm trees there was no one in sight.

Bewildered I walked back to Bruce, took his hand, and told him what I had seen. He assured me that if my mother were at the resort we would find her, but first we had to sign the marriage certificate.

As soon as the formalities were completed we walked back to the restaurant where a gala lunch was planned. On the way Bruce and I stopped at the desk to check if my mother was registered, but her name wasn't there. When questioned the clerk said no one fitting her description was staying at the resort.

I was baffled. Unless she was staying there she could not have known the time of the ceremony, but I was sure I had seen her. Could it be that I had conjured up her image from a sense of guilt or had she really been there? Bruce hugged me close and said, 'We'll sort this out later, but now we've got to go back to our party.'

So we joined our friends and had a most delightful lunch before boarding the plane for our honeymoon.

We had a wonderful time, swimming, snorkelling and canoeing over the colourful reef. Our beautiful bure was luxurious, with cool tiled floors, cane furniture piled with big colourful cushions and fresh flowers in vases and bowls every day. Making love on the wide comfortable bed with the ceiling fan sending a gentle breeze onto our sun and sex-warmed bodies is a memory I will hold dear forever.

A week after our return to Australia and chilly Canberra we had a get together evening at our flat with our friends. Phillip, who was our designated photographer, had collected the wedding and holiday films and we poured over them laughing uproariously at some of the more candid shots.

I was looking at the photos of the actual wedding ceremony when, suddenly, one shot made me catch my breath. It was one of Bruce and me, holding hands while saying our vows, and had been taken from the water's edge. In the background was the beach then the palm trees where a small, pale figure of a woman could be seen with her hands clasped in front of her face. Although it was only a silhouette I knew it was my mother.

'She was there,' I shouted, 'Look,' and held the photograph out to Bruce.

He looked at it closely and then said, 'Well darling, it could be anyone. You can barely even make out that it's a woman.'

I didn't want to leave it at that but was beginning to feel a bit foolish and slightly unsure. I said, 'Let's not discuss it any further.'

The evening continued pleasantly with much reminiscing about the holiday.

I couldn't get the memory of that photograph out of my mind. I still hadn't heard from Mum and we had been back two weeks, so I rang her to tell her about the wedding.

She apologised for her maudlin letter and asked numerous questions about Fiji, the wedding day and our honeymoon. She said how happy she was for me and then went on to talk about Fred and their plans for the coming year. She finished our conversation, promising to write soon. When we had hung up I was almost convinced that, through feelings of guilt, I had imagined my mother at my wedding but it was only almost.

The next day I posted off the flowered skirt for Mum and the bula shirt for Fred that I had bought in Fiji plus a couple of photographs of the wedding. Mum's answering letter was full of thanks for the clothes and the photos and plans for the coming summer when Bruce and I would spend a couple of weeks in Tasmania.

We arrived at The Cove on a clear, bright summer day in early January. Mum and Fred raced down from the verandah as soon as we drove up. Obviously they had been watching out for us to arrive, and had champagne waiting for us in an ice bucket to belatedly celebrate our marriage.

We spent the afternoon wandering around the grounds, admiring the flourishing vineyard and the prolific vegetable garden. Late in the afternoon we were ordered off to our room to dress for dinner. We had been told to bring our wedding clothes, and I felt that dressing up in them was the least I could do to humour my mother.

It was a little chilly for Bruce to just wear his sulu so he topped it with a shirt.

When we joined Mum and Fred on the big deck they were dressed in the Fijian clothes we had sent them. The pine table had been moved out onto the deck and it was covered with the most amazing spread that included curried chicken in coconut shells, char-grilled fish, baked sweet potatoes and an enormous bowl of exotic fruit.

As I walked through the doorway in my white and gold dress Mum turned to Fred and said, 'I told you how beautiful she looked.'

Fred looked uncomfortable and said, 'Yes, well I saw her in the photographs too you know.'

I let the little slip pass, enthused about the wonderful food and we enjoyed a delightful evening.

The next morning, while Bruce and Fred were pulling the net in the bay, Mum and I were enjoying an early morning cup of tea on the veranda.

I just had to ask, 'Mum, did you come and watch Bruce and me getting married?'

Mum looked at me sheepishly then admitted, 'Yes. I had to. I couldn't let that day go by and not see you. Fred knew how I was feeling and came home with the airline ticket and I just went.'

'But how did you know where and when to come?' I asked.

'You told me you were getting married at a resort near Suva so I checked all possibilities until I found the right one. When I did I swore the manager to secrecy.'

I took her hands in mine and said, 'I'm so glad you were there Mum.'

When Bruce and Fred returned with a good catch of salmon they found us crying in each other's arms.

In a peculiar way I felt that my mother and I had reclaimed each other and the rest of the holiday was lovely. When we packed up our car to leave Mum and I hugged and promised to keep in closer touch.

Communication

The next year was very busy and so happy. Being married to Bruce brought me such joy. Having seen my parents' marriage disintegrate I had been wary of making any serious commitment, but falling in love with Bruce changed me so much. I think I had always been too serious and backward looking, and he made me take life more lightly and to live more in the moment.

Towards the end of the year I had a dose of the flu, the first time I'd been sick since coming to Canberra, so I was having a rare day off work. We were going down to Tasmania in a few weeks time and I had been spending this free time rereading Mum's letters to familiarize myself with what had been happening in her life. When we were together again she would be sure to mention some of their new friends, and I wanted to know whom she was talking about.

We had written to each other regularly that year. I would have preferred to keep in touch with phone calls, but Mum was never really at ease on the phone. I guess the big advantage of letters is that you can reread them whereas you can't replay a phone call.

Most of the time she sounded very happy and she and Fred were obviously enjoying life at The Cove. Food and cooking featured in many of her letters as well as the problems associated with trying to achieve a level of self-sufficiency. She often mentioned friends she and Fred had made at the Small Landholders' Association meetings and their various social get togethers. She also said she and Fred might have been becoming a little bit insular before they joined this association and how good it was to meet like-minded people.

As I read I paused at this one written in April. It was one of the few times that she mentioned the past, and I thought of how my mothers' life had changed in just a few years.

April

Dearest Helen,

I'm sitting on the verandah writing this and it is one of those superb autumn mornings. The Cove looks an absolute picture at present as the vines are just beginning to turn golden and red and the apricot orchard is a mass of orange leaves that are fluttering to the ground in a light breeze. The contrast of the warm colours against the blue of the bay is inspirational, and I'm going to get my paints out later and see if I can capture it.

Yesterday we picked our pumpkin crop and sealed the stalks with wax before storing them in the shed on racks. We also dug the remainder of our onion crop and I am going to plait them after they have had a couple of days drying in the sun.

I feel a tremendous sense of peace living here with Fred and we work so well together in every way.

I know I caused a lot of unhappiness for you and the boys and Rod by falling in love with Fred, but I really feel we were meant to be together. Fortunately everything has worked out in the end with all of you kids happily married, and I heard on the grapevine, called Carolyn, that your father is marrying soon. I wish him well.

Carolyn and Matt came down for a weekend and we had a lovely time catching up with news about friends from the old neighbourhood and talking about books we had both read and plays she has seen. I have promised to go to town for a few days to see a show, look at the galleries and do some shopping. I really need new jeans and sweaters for the winter, and it's much more fun shopping with a friend than by yourself, as you would know. Fred will join us at the weekend.

Must close now,

Love you,

Mum.

The next one was obviously in answer to one of mine soon after Bruce and I moved into our new unit.

When we first married we had continued to live in a flat Bruce had been renting, but then he bought a beautiful new townhouse with money he had inherited. It was very spacious, close to work and also had a small garden area so I could grow some herbs. There were quite a few great restaurants near-bye, which suited us as we often worked late.

May

My Darling Girl,

It was lovely to hear how happy you and Bruce are. Your new flat sounds gorgeous and it must be great to be so close to work. I know you told me about Bruce and his brother being bought up by a bachelor uncle, but I hadn't known that he left them so well provided for.

Fred and I have spent a considerable time picking and crushing the grapes. We picked the chardonnay first, then the pinots and the bottling shed is now full of various shaped containers quietly burbling away.

Beth and Tom came and helped us with the picking and of course we put on lunch, barbecued salmon steaks with tomato and red onion salad. We finished the meal with my glace apricots and coffee. They enthused about the food, but I could see that they were not very impressed with our last year's wine.

We also went over and helped them with harvesting their grapes. They send theirs off to a vigneron who makes the wine, then takes a proportion of the bottled wine in exchange for producing the completed product. I'm' going to try to convince Fred that we should get ours made by an expert as we are making wine that is drinkable, but not as good as it could be.

Bye for now,

Much love,

Mum.

At the end of May Bruce and I took a week off work and had a luxurious holiday on Hamilton Island. I must have raved about it at length in one of my letters as I received this response.

June

Darling Helen,

It was great to get your long, newsy letter. It sounds as though you and Bruce had a wonderful holiday on Hamilton Island. The apartment you had sounds divine and so does the pool and restaurants. I agree with you that Fred and I would undoubtedly love to go there, but we couldn't afford it and neither of us really has the travel bug.

We continue to have delightful lunches with our friends and for the winter solstice celebration we all went up to Hobart for a special dinner. It was put on by Brown Brothers' Winery and consisted of a five-course meal with suitable accompanying wines. We all stayed at the casino for the night. A great time was had by all of us.

I also had my little stay in town with Carolyn at the beginning of the month and we had a terrific time together. Under her guidance I now have a much-improved wardrobe for the winter including a gorgeous blue, soft wool sweater that cost the earth but really suits me.

The days are getting shorter and colder and there is not much to do outside now that the vines have been pruned – a big job.

Fred and I are spending most of our days indoors. We go to the local library once a fortnight, and have been getting out videos as well lately as there is not much on television. We both enjoy some of the really old movies, especially the musicals.

Must close now and start dinner,

Love to you and Bruce,

Mum.

Mum's letters for June and July were rather depressing and she wrote about travelling to work on the icy roads and returning home in the dark. It was also obvious that their attempts at making money from their produce were not being very successful.

She sounded as though they were still enjoying special lunches with their new friends and wrote about a Bastille Day meal at which she and Fred served Gratin des Landes and Chou Farci Limousin. She promised to make these dishes for Bruce and me when we came down in January.

At the beginning of August I'd had a rare phone call from Dad to wish me happy birthday, but also to tell me that he and Joanne were getting married. It was to be a very small affair with only a few of their friends invited. He was a bit apologetic about not inviting his children, but Joanne's weren't going either. Evidently this was how she wanted it to be. Perhaps she shared my feelings of trepidation about weddings, especially ones that involved broken up families.

After Dad's phone call I was really pleased to receive this letter from Mum.

Darling Daughter,

I hope you had a happy birthday and liked your present. You have said how cold the winters are in Canberra so I figured a pure merino wool Tassie sweater would come in handy.

As you probably know, your father has sold the house now that he and Joanne are finally getting married. Evidently she wants to start their life together in a new house, and I can understand how she feels.

Anyhow he wrote to me and said he felt I should get something from the sale of the house. He has sent me a cheque for forty thousand dollars.

I felt guilty about leaving him and so didn't make any financial claim when we divorced. I know you and I discussed this at the time, and that you thought I was being a bit altruistic, and I probably was.

I must tell you though it came as a nice surprise to get the cheque. It means I'll be able to buy myself a decent, reliable car. It also means Fred and I will be able to do something we have dreamed about during this long cold winter.

We'll tell you all about our plans when we see you both in January.

Love to you and Bruce,

Mum.

P.S. It was nice to hear from your father and to feel that perhaps I'm forgiven at last.

Mum.

In October Bruce and I and the friends who had come with us to Fiji had a wonderful holiday sailing around the Whitsunday Passage. We hired a magnificent yacht. The guys sailed it while we females did a minimum amount of food preparation to earn our places on the boat. The weather was superb and we spent the days luxuriating on deck as the boat skimmed across the water, and then weighing anchor in little bays of uninhabited island and swimming and fishing before sumptuous dinners and boozy evening. It was so delightful and we were virtually out of contact with society. I was, therefore, shocked to receive this next letter which was in the mailbox when we returned home.

October,

Darling Helen,

I have the most awful news. I tried to ring you but didn't get an answer, and then I remembered you were going on that sailing holiday and I didn't know how to contact you.

Gordon was killed last Friday.

He was on a kayaking trip with some of his pupils and one of the boys got into difficulties when they hit some rapids. Evidently Gordon saved the boy, but was hit on the head by a log just as he was pushing the boy ashore and then he was swept away and drowned. He must have been knocked unconscious by the log because he was a strong swimmer.

It has been the most horrific shock to all of us and I know it will be for you too. The funeral was on Monday and it was a very moving service. All the children from his school were there, and one of the boys who had been on the trip gave the eulogy. I've never seen a sadder sight than that funeral. Obviously he was loved greatly by his students.

I still haven't come to terms with the fact that I won't see him again and Mum is absolutely distraught, even worse than when Dad died. She keeps saying that you shouldn't outlive your children, and I know exactly how she feels.

I don't think I could bear it if you or Ralph or Dale died.

I have stayed in town with Mum for the past week, and now Ronda has taken her home to stay with her for a while.

I am sorry to have to give you this news by letter but I did try to phone.

I wish you were here so that we could have a hug. I know how fond you were of your Uncle Gordon. I hadn't seen much of him during the past few years and I so regret that now. I still can't believe I won't ever see him again.

I'm so looking forward to you coming in January. It seems a long time since you and Bruce were here. Although your letters are a source of joy for me they don't really make up for not seeing you regularly.

Love you lots,

Mum.

As I reread this letter I cried once more for my dear uncle. He had been so vital and energetic, and we kids had always looked forward to seeing him. He really listened to you and made you feel important.

When Bruce came home from work he found me red-eyed and miserable. He made me a hot toddy of whisky and honey, cooked and served a gourmet meal then brushed my hair until I felt relaxed and sleepy.

In many of the next letters Mum sounded sad and was very concerned about Nanna, but by December she seemed to be cheering up a bit. I'm sure the thought of seeing Ralph and his family for Christmas and of course us later on was helping her get over her sadness at the death of Gordon.

The following was written shortly before Christmas and she sounded much more cheerful.

December

Darling Daughter,

I gather from your letters that you are frightfully busy at work. Hope you get a little rest and relaxation over the Christmas break, even if you do only get four days off.

Fred and I have been busy in the garden, orchard and vineyard. At this time of year the vineyard is very time-consuming as the vines are growing rapidly and need attention.

Ralph and Maureen and my beautiful granddaughter Jasmine are coming over for Christmas. They spent last year with Maureen's parents so this year it is my turn. I had a lovely expensive time buying presents for all and we have earmarked a small self-sown pine for our tree.

We received presents from Dale and Gay early, but will wait until Christmas morning to open them. Such self-control! I won't see them this year as they are spending their holidays cruising around the Greek islands for a week, and then renting a villa in Tuscany with several of their friends. It all sounds marvellous and I'm sure they'll have a wonderful time.

I've just finished wrapping their presents and will post them today. I'll keep the presents for you and Bruce here so that I can give them to you in person.

Must close now so that I can post this letter and the presents on my way to work.

All my love,

Mum.

This was the last letter I received from Mum before our holiday in Tasmania. I had been a bit concerned about how she would feel about Bruce and me only staying with her and Fred for a week but her letter was reassuring.

January,

Darling Helen,

Just a short note to say how much we are looking forward to your visit, and of course we understand about you wanting to spend part of the time showing Bruce the rest of the state.

We had a lovely time with Ralph, Maureen and Jasmine. She really is adorable and enjoyed wandering around the gardens and vineyard and helping me feed the chooks. They are such a peaceful, loving little family. They would dearly love another baby, but Maureen has now had two early miscarriages so I don't think this will happen.

Fred and I could come and pick you up from the airport, but if you are happy to hire a car from the beginning of your holiday we won't insist. It's a long drive here and back and I would rather be here to give you a big welcome.

See you soon,

Lots of love,

Mum.

Barbecued Salmon Steaks

Fresh Salmon steaks
Lemon juice
Fresh herbs
Butter

Combine lemon juice and mixed fresh herbs e.g. dill, thyme, chives, parsley.

Place each salmon steak on piece of well-buttered foil.

Drizzle over lemon juice/herb mixture and wrap securely.

Place on hot barbecue and cook, turning once.

Cooking time depends on the heat of the barbecue so check after 15 minutes.

Ready when fish no longer translucent and beginning to flake.

Do not overcook.

Glace Apricots

1.0 kg apricots   250 ml water
1.5 kg sugar   juice 1 lemon
caster sugar

Prick each apricot a few times.
Put 1.0 kg. sugar in saucepan with water and lemon juice.
Bring to boil, stirring until sugar dissolves.
Slide apricots into saucepan and simmer for 3 minutes.
Remove apricot and place in glass bowl. Return syrup to
heat and boil for 5 minutes. Pour over apricots, weight
down with a plate and leave for 24 hours.

Drain apricots. Return syrup to saucepan, adding 250 g
sugar. Bring slowly to boil, stirring until sugar dissolves.
Skim well and boil for 5 minutes.
Add apricots to syrup and return to boil then reduce heat
and simmer for 5 minutes.
Remove apricots to bowl.
Boil syrup again for 5 minutes then pour over apricots and
leave for 24 hours.

Drain apricots. Return syrup to saucepan, add remaining
sugar and bring to boil stirring to dissolve sugar. Skim and
boil 3 minutes.
Add apricots, return to boil then reduce heat and simmer
3 to 4 hours until fruit looks clear and candied.
Place apricots on rack and air dry for 24 hours then
sprinkle with caster sugar and dry in oven at 120C with
door open for 12 hours.

Store in airtight container. Keeps up to 3 – 4 months.

Gratin de Landes

2 tbsp. butter	salt and freshly ground pepper
1 ½ lbs. pumpkin, finely sliced	2 cups milk, warmed
5 slices prosciutto, roughly chopped	½ cup cream
6 oz. grated Gruyere cheese	

Butter an oven proof baking dish.

Alternate layers of pumpkin, prosciutto and cheese.

Season each layer with salt and pepper

Dot with small knobs of butter

Finish with a layer of pumpkin sprinkled with grated cheese.

Mix together milk and cream and pour over layers.

Bake in slow oven [160C] for 50 minutes or until pumpkin tender.

Serve hot as an entrée or as a light luncheon dish.

Stuffed Cabbage (Chou Farci Limousin)

1 large cabbage	1 tbsp. marjoram finely chopped
150 g ham finely cut	2 eggs
½ kg. sausage meat	salt and pepper
2 onions finely chopped	2 cups meat stock
2 garlic cloves finely chopped	

Cut cabbage in half, remove central core.
Break off leaves one by one and blanche in boiling water for 10 minutes.
Refresh under cold water and drain.

Mix together ham, sausage meat, onions, garlic, marjoram and eggs, and season to taste with salt and pepper.
Grease a heavy casserole with butter.
Cover bottom and sides with largest cabbage leaves.
Spread a thin layer of stuffing on the cabbage then cover with more leaves, pressing down firmly.
Repeat the process until all stuffing has been used finishing with a layer of cabbage.
Pour on stock, put on casserole lid and cook in oven [16-C] for about 2 hours.
Remove lid for last ½ hour.

Turn out and serve with potato/parsnip/sweet potato mash.

My Island Home

When Bruce and I arrived in Hobart it was one of those clear mild January days that only Tassie can turn on. Canberra had been hot, still and enervating. To step off the plane and feel a gentle breeze blowing across the tarmac and smell the faint tinge of salt sea air made me feel quite weepy.

After we retrieved our bags from the only carousel, we were met by the Hertz agent who drove us a short distance up the road to collect our hire car.

Bruce drove so that I could look around at the familiar landmarks. In a few minutes we had travelled up the highway to a point overlooking Hobart. That first view, as you drive down the Eastern Outlet, always pleases me. It's such a pretty city. On that day the sparkling blue river was dotted with little sailing boats and the mountain, looming protectively over the hills and houses, looked indigo with deep purple shadows down the Organ Pipes and in the valleys. A wispy, white cloud floated over the pinnacle.

There was little traffic so we were soon over the bridge and passed the wharf area, where locals and tourists wandered amongst the docked fishing boats and visited harbour side restaurants or fish punts. We headed straight up Davy Street and onto the Southern Outlet and from there turned to drive towards the Huon Valley.

Although the hills around the airport had been dry and yellow the Valley looked green and lush. In the past that area had been the heart of Tasmania's apple growing industry but changes in world trade had affected its viability for many orchardists.

Now the land on either side of the highway is planted with more varied crops – cherries, apricots, blueberries and grapes as well as new varieties of apples, most of which are now grown on trellises and are destined for the Japanese market.

We stopped at Huonville and bought crusty bread and some tasty cheeses and soon were winding along the gravel road to The Cove. Mum and Fred were waiting on the verandah and the minute Bruce stopped the car they were there with hugs and kisses. Both of them looked brown and fit so obviously the outdoor life was suiting them.

After we had been settled into the little flower-filled front bedroom Fred opened a bottle of champagne and we all belatedly toasted each other to a merry Christmas and a happy new year.

Mum served delicious cheese puffs as well as tapenade on crisp French bread. We then exchanged our long awaited Christmas gifts before settling down to the promised French meal. It consisted of a delicious garlic and bread soup, a stuffed salmon served with fennel and cucumber salad and Tarte Tatin – a superb caramelised apple tart, made of course with apples from their orchard.

They had bought a new French cookbook the previous year and had been experimenting with several of the recipes. As well, they were determined to feed themselves as much as possible from the food that they grew and proudly explained that the garlic, potatoes, cabbage and apples were all home grown.

Following dinner, and feeling totally sated from the good food and wine, the four of us went outside and sat on the deck overlooking the bay where we watched the moon rising in the darkening sky and shimmering across the water.

Suddenly Mum jumped up saying, 'Now I know that you two must be absolutely exhausted and Fred thinks I should wait until tomorrow, but I just have to show you something.'

With this Mum trotted off to the lounge room and returned with a large rolled-up sheet of paper which she proceeded to spread out on the glass, coffee table.

Bruce and I leant forward and saw a schematic drawing of the property showing the house plus two other smaller dwellings, one above the vineyard and the other further over the property and behind the dam.

I looked at her questioningly and then she said, ' This is what we plan to do. With the money your father gave me, and an investment of Fred's, we figure we will have enough to build two little holiday units. Tourism in Tasmania is increasing and even if we only get a forty percent fill-rate that should bring in enough to enable Fred and me to give up our jobs.'

Almost in unison Bruce and I spoke.

I asked, 'Will you get council approval?' and Bruce's query was, 'How can you be sure you'll get enough tourists to make it worthwhile?'

Fred put his hand up and grinned, 'One question at a time. Actually I tried to get your mother to wait until tomorrow to tell you, but you know what she's like. Let's all go to bed now and we'll tell you all about our plans and research tomorrow.'

We all agreed this was a good idea and headed off to bed. I felt slightly tipsy from the wine and tired from the travelling. Nevertheless I lay awake, long after Bruce was asleep and snoring softly, and worried if these two dreamers knew what they were getting themselves into.

The next morning, after a scrumptious breakfast of poached eggs served on a bed of steamed spinach and topped with gravadlax and a cheesy, white sauce, Mum once more brought out the plans. As well as the plan she had preliminary drawings of the proposed units showing both the external designs and the internal layouts.

We pored over them for a while and I said, 'I think I'd like to see exactly where you plan to put the units and then you can tell us all about the practical details.'

We wandered over the land for quite a while, stopping to admire the growth in the vineyard on the way and later walked back for tea and cake on the deck. Over tea Mum and Fred told us about their progress so far. They had consulted with representatives of the council, including the planning engineer. He could see no problems except for the installation of two extra septic tanks.

They had also been in touch with the tourism department and obtained quite a lot of information regarding expected fill-rates, advertising and tourist requirements. I could see that they are totally involved in this project, and if it should come to fruition how wonderful it would be for them.

After that first day they promised not to bore us with their plans any more but reckoned by the time we came down next year they would be in the tourism business.

As this holiday had been planned so that Bruce could see as much of the state as possible we went on several day trips. These included a trip to the Hartz Mountains for a day walk and a visit to Hastings Caves, where we also had a swim in the thermal pool and a barbecue lunch.

The week went quickly and I knew Mum felt she hadn't seen enough of us and me in particular. On the last day we went for a long walk – just the two of us – and later prepared the evening meal together. I made my French onion soup, Mum cooked her stuffed cabbage, or as she called it Chou Farci Limousin, and we prepared the vegetables while chatting and sharing a bottle of wine.

We had a lovely evening together and the next day wandered around the land, ate a leisurely brunch, and then packed the car to leave. I hugged Mum for a long time then climbed quickly into the driver's seat. Bruce got in beside me and we drove off.

After leaving The Cove we headed for Hobart where we had arranged to spend a night in Dad's new home. I didn't want to arrive there too early so we dropped in to visit some friends in Kingston on the way. It was late afternoon when we drove into his street, which was in Lower Sandy Bay and only a block away from the water.

As we headed up the winding drive Bruce turned to me, a quizzical look on his face and said, 'Well, it's certainly very upmarket, isn't it?"

Before us stood a huge house built of soft creamy pink rendered block. It had a wide timber garage door on one side, an arched entry to the front door and Tuscan-type tiles on the roof. On the second storey there was a deck surrounded by stylish, black wrought ironwork.

We parked in front of the garage and walked into the entryway to ring the bell. After a very short wait Dad appeared, big, handsome and welcoming. I hadn't seen him since we'd made a brief visit to him at our old home a year ago, and he looked happier and fitter than he had then.

Joanne stood behind him, looking elegant as usual and dressed in slim-line black slacks and a soft pink silk shirt.

She smiled a welcome as she took my hands saying, 'I'm so glad you could give us a night. Your father so wanted to see you and for you to see our new home.'

She seemed very genuine but I often wondered with her if there wasn't a sting in the tail – but that was probably just me being bitchy.

After we had retrieved our luggage from the car they showed us to a beautiful, big bedroom. It was painted white and carpeted in a soft green that exactly matched the colour of the brocade bedspread and heavy drapes. The ensuite was as big as most normal bathrooms and featured a white triangular spa bath, a green tiled floor and double vanity basins. It was altogether very impressive.

We unpacked our clothes for the evening then joined Dad and Joanne downstairs for a drink in the lounge room. Once again this was a big room. It was painted a soft cream colour and furnished with leather couches in a dark chocolate brown. The only other colours in the room were some bright, bitter green cushions, a bowl of green Granny Smith apples on the square coffee table and a huge, semi-abstract painting on one wall. The room had a wall of long timber and glass doors that opened onto a small, very private courtyard.

As soon as we finished our drinks Joanne excused herself to go and put the finishing touches to dinner while Dad showed us around the rest of the house. It was all very beautiful and I thought either Dad had been doing very well financially during the past few years or Joanne received a substantial divorce settlement. This was a house that would have cost serious money.

After the grand tour Bruce and I changed for dinner and joined the others in the dining room. Once again this was a very large room built at a right angle to the lounge room so that it too overlooked the courtyard and also had a wall of doors opening onto it. It looked a marvellous set-up for summer parties.

Joanne served a good but unmemorable dinner and for the first time I had a chance to see her and Dad together away from a social setting with other people around. By then they had known each other for quite a few years and were comfortable and affectionate as a couple but she appeared to kowtow to him a bit. Twice she expressed a slightly divergent view from his, and when he queried her opinions she immediately backed down.

This was only a small thing, but it made me wonder if Dad had learnt anything about being too dominating with his women.

I was glad when it was late enough for us to say our goodnights and once we were in bed I asked Bruce what he thought of their relationship.

He moved closer to me in bed, fitting comfortably against my back and said, 'Darling, they're probably as happy as most couples. They've taken quite a while to get together, probably because they were hurt before, and they are certainly old enough to know what they want in a partner. I think you can relax about them. Now let's go to sleep because tomorrow we have lots to see and do.'

We slept contentedly in the huge firm bed, and after an early breakfast served in a small sunlit room that adjoined the kitchen set off on our trip around the island.

The next day we made a brief stopover at Nanna Alice's house before heading off on our tour of the state. She looked older and frailer than I remembered her being, but she gave us a lovely welcome and served her delicious scones slathered in butter.

I had talked a lot to Bruce about Tasmania and he was interested to see the places I had described.

Because I had always loved the East Coast we first drove over the bridge and towards the east coast highway, stopping at Richmond for a brief look at the galleries, the old gaol and of course the famous bridge, reputed to be the oldest one in Australia. Our next stop was Swansea and I showed him where I had worked as a waitress for three summer vacations. Here we enjoyed a lunch of fish and chips, sitting on the beach and feeding the surplus chips to a flock of noisy, quarrelsome seagulls.

From there we drove to Bicheno where we were booked into a resort that had good accommodation and beautiful outlooks to the sea. Bicheno is a charming little town with delightful scenery, numerous resorts and holiday homes and a still viable fishing industry. It is still noted for the availability of fresh crayfish and a variety of scale fish.

The resort where we were staying had a notable restaurant that specialised in the local seafood so for dinner we had a delicious, thick fish chowder served with garlic bread and the house specialty, crayfish mornay served on the half shell.

We got up early the next morning for a walk around the foreshore with its orange and mustard coloured lichen-covered rocks and a rather spectacular blowhole that spluttered and sparkled erratically out of the dark stone. After a quick breakfast we packed the car and set out for Launceston. Here we spent two nights at an old colonial hotel and a day visiting the Gorge area, the powder mill and the museum and art gallery. Like me, Bruce thought

Launceston quite attractive but not somewhere he would like to live.

The next day we travelled to Stanley, stopping on the way for lunch at Deloraine, and arrived in plenty of time to walk up The Nut, a large rocky outcrop that dominates the town. The walk up is extremely steep, almost vertical in places, but the views from the top are tremendous. After our walk we booked into our motel, then showered and changed for dinner. We had an enjoyable meal then walked around the old town before bed.

Early the next morning we backtracked to Burnie then headed down the west coast, stopping briefly at Queenstown. Bruce was impressed with the colourful, bare hills and I described how they had been even more spectacular before the regrowth of trees on the lower slopes.

We continued down to Strahan, another fishing town and now a popular tourist destination. Here we stayed at a very expensive motel, which was said to have one of the best restaurants in Australia. We both had crayfish cocktails followed by char-grilled trevalla that had first been marinated in a mixture of lemon juice, olive oil and garlic.

Early the next morning we boarded the boat for the trip up the Gordon River. I had made this trip before but it was all new for Bruce and he was completely entranced by the whole experience, but particularly by the chance to see Huon pine growing in its natural habitat. We arrived back in time to drive to another of my favourite places, Ocean Beach, where we walked hand in hand on the hard sand and watched the huge breakers rolling in all the way from Africa.

Once again we had an early start the next day because we were booked into the Cradle Mountain Chalet and I wanted us to have time to fit in a walk before dinner. Although the trees through parts of central Tasmania are stunted, because of the montane climate, Bruce enthused over the beauty of the varied, multi-coloured low growing shrubs against the distant blue mountains.

We arrived in plenty of time to do a short, circular walk that took us through a cool fern gully, along the river to a small waterfall then back to the chalet. Our meal was delicious, Tasmanian fare, scallops in a white wine sauce and King Island beef that has been marinated in a mixture of red wine, olive oil and pepper berries and served on a garlic-flavoured mash of potatoes and parsnips. We finished the meal with ice cream surrounded by a mixed berry coulis. With the meal we had a bottle of pinot and a half bottle of sauterne plus a port with coffee. Totally replete and feeling slightly drunk we headed off to our luxury accommodation.

Although the next morning we were both feeling a little bit hung over we were still determined to get in a decent walk because I had told Bruce about the wonderful scenery and wanted to share it with him. We had a long walk, danced in the Enchanted Ballroom, circled Dove Lake and climbed a steep hill so that he could get a proper view of that magnificent place. We returned footsore and weary and enjoyed a relaxing sexy time in our spa bath before another gourmet meal.

The next morning we left straight after breakfast so that we could have a leisurely drive to Devonport, allowing for a stop at Sheffield so that Bruce can see the murals, a feature of this small country town. We arrived with ample time to drop off the hire car, board the Spirit and find our cabin before the departure time.

We had a smooth trip back and caught the plane for the return trip to Canberra. After two and a half weeks away and the many changes in accommodation that we have experienced we were glad to be back in our own space and comfortable familiar bed.

During the next few weeks, while we settled back into the routines of work, my thoughts often returned to our trip and the feelings I had experienced while revisiting some of the places I had loved in earlier years.

Bruce's thoughts were also back on the island and he raved to our friends about how beautiful and varied it was. He also kept talking to me about the different places we had been to and how much he had enjoyed the whole holiday.

One Friday night, when we were spending the evening at home relaxing after a hard week at work, he turned to me on the couch and asked, 'Do you ever feel like going back to Tasmania to live?'

I think if he had asked me this before our trip I probably would have said no, but it had stirred up a funny sort of longing in me to return to my island. I also think the fact that Mum and I had moved closer together emotionally was also influencing me.

I looked at Bruce and answered, 'Well I hadn't until lately but now I think I wouldn't mind. In fact I'd like to, but there's no way we would be able to get such well paid jobs in Tassie as we have here. Anyhow how would you feel about moving there?'

With a thoughtful look on his face he answered, 'Well I don't feel tied to any place really. As you know I grew up in Melbourne, which I don't remember much, and then when Mum and Dad died I moved here to live with Uncle David. I suppose this has been my home during my growing up years, but I've always thought of Canberra as a sort of artificial place. Seeing your little island I felt quite overwhelmed; it's so beautiful and natural. I think I could happily move there if that's what you'd like.'

I move along the couch to hug him, he looked so serious, and said lightly, 'Yes darling, I'd like to go back, but as I said, what would we do about jobs – and I mean ones where we'd both earn decent money?'

He returned my hug saying, 'Well let me think about the options. Leave it to me.'

I sort of forget that conversation although I continued to have this little feeling of longing and loss during the next few months.

One Sunday morning in May we were sprawling around on our lounge room floor, reading the weekend papers while demolishing a late breakfast of coffee and croissants, when Bruce let out a yelp, 'Wow, that would suit us.'

I moved over on the floor next to him as he read aloud, 'Computer Wise. Wanted - partner in innovative young company supplying hardware and software to businesses and the home market. Purchaser needs sound knowledge of all computer equipment and skills in installation and customer training. Based in Hobart this company is the major supplier of computer equipment in Tasmania. Contact Frank Symons for further details.' There followed his telephone and fax numbers.

Not wanting to get my hopes up before I knew more about it I murmured, 'It doesn't say how much it would cost to buy into the company,' but this didn't dampen Bruce's enthusiasm.

'I know we don't know the cost darling, but it's worth contacting this Frank Symons to find out.' He paused for a while then continued. 'You know that money Uncle David left in trust for my brother and me. This would enable me to draw my share.'

Bruce's uncle had left both boys well provided for; that was why we had been able to buy our lovely townhouse. In addition to an immediate inheritance a large amount had been left in trust specifically to buy or start a business. I suppose the old dear had wanted to be sure his boys had security and didn't just fritter the money away.

I hugged Bruce and said, 'Darling, I'd love to go back to Tasmania. Like so many of my generation I couldn't wait to get away and see the big, wide world, but it does have a strong pull. I'm more than ready to go back home if this is viable.'

The next week Bruce and Frank spoke interminably on the phone and exchanged innumerable faxes. Bruce also saw his lawyer who agreed that this project fulfilled the legal requirements of his uncle's will.

Before committing ourselves we made a whirl-wind trip to Tasmania and thoroughly examined all aspects of the company, which was booming, but needed an injection of money in order to continue its expansion.

Bruce and Frank, who had come to know each other quite well over the phone, hit it off like long lost friends and before the weekend was over we had exchanged contracts to become half-owners in Computer Wise.

Jubilantly we boarded the plane for Canberra and celebrated with numerous small bottles of champagne.

The next few months passed in a blur of activity. We handed in our notices at work, I completed a project I had been working on for most of the year and we sold our lovely townhouse.

We packed up our furniture and household effects and sent everything for storage at a place on the eastern shore in Tasmania. The last week in Canberra was spent living with our dearest friends, Rebecca and Phillip, and partying non- stop.

By the time we waved goodbye to our friends and to Canberra we were exhausted and looking forward to a couple of weeks at The Cove before starting our new jobs as directors of our own computer company.

Cheese Puffs

2 ¼ cups milk	8 eggs
160 grams butter	300 grams Gruyere cheese
2 tsp. salt	pinch nutmeg
2 ¼ cups plain flour	pinch pepper

Place milk, salt, pepper and nutmeg, with butter cut into small pieces, in a saucepan.
Bring to the boil ensuring butter has melted by time milk boils.
Remove from heat and add sifted flour all at once.
Incorporate quickly and mix thoroughly with a wooden spoon and continue mixing until mixture balls around the spoon. *(This step is done over a low heat.)*

Remove from heat; allow to cool slightly before adding eggs, one at a time. Beat each one thoroughly before adding the next.
Grate 250 grams of the cheese and dice remainder.
Stir grated cheese into mixture.
Spoon small balls of mixture onto a buttered baking tray.
Prick a piece of diced cheese into each puff, brush with a little beaten egg and bake in a hot oven for 20 minutes or until risen and golden.

Serve hot.
Great with pre-dinner drinks or champagne.
These can be frozen on trays then stored for later use.
Good way to use up surplus eggs.

Tapenade

1 garlic clove

1 cup pitted, black olives

1 tbsp. chopped capers

1 ½ tbsp. lemon juice

20 slices French bread sliced diagonally

2 tbsp. olive oil

freshly ground black pepper

2 anchovy fillets

Place garlic in food processor and blend until finely chopped.

Add ¾ of the olives and process to a rough paste.

Add capers and anchovies and pulse a few times.

Remove mixture from the processor and place in a bowl.

Add lemon juice, olive oil and pepper to taste.

Toast the bread and spread with paste.

This as a delicious mixture and can also be served on plain biscuits and goes very well with hard boiled eggs.

Garlic Soup

5 garlic bulbs [about 50 cloves]
6 slices good, white bread
6 cups water
salt and freshly ground pepper
2 tbsp. chopped parsley
cream for garnish

Peel garlic

Place in large saucepan the separated garlic cloves, bread slices and water and boil for 20 minutes.

Remove from heat and puree soup, season to taste and reheat.

To serve drizzle on cream and sprinkle with parsley.

This is a great way to use garlic if you have grown too much.

Tarte Tatin

5 firm apples [Cox, Golden   85 g butter
Delicious]
140 g sugar   1 tbsp. water
sheet short crust pastry

Cut butter into small pieces

Place sugar, butter and water in solid 20cm. tin.

Peel, core and halve apples, then pack tightly on top of sugar/butter with round side down.

Place on top of stove, low heat and cook until sugar/butter begins to caramelise, approximately 5 minutes.

Place in oven and cook for 15 minutes.

Remove from oven, cover with pastry trimmed to fit circle.

Return to oven and cook further 20 – 25 minutes until pastry is golden.

Allow to cool then turn [invert] onto a flat serving plate.

Serve warm with cream or ice cream.

There are many variations of this dish. Can be made with puff pastry and raw or brown sugar produces richer caramelisation.

Gravadlax

2 kg. Atlantic salmon – 2 large fillets
1 heaped tbsp. salt
1 tbsp. sugar
1 tsp. black peppercorn, crushed
1 tbsp. brandy
1 tbsp. fresh, chopped dill

Mix together all pickling ingredients.

Place ¼ mixture in flat dish.

Place one fillet, skin side down, on mixture.

Spread over half remaining mixture

 Place other fillet, skin side up, on top and cover with remaining mixture, rubbing it into the skin.

Cover with foil. Lay a board on top and weigh it down with something heavy.

Chill for at least 12 hours before serving but it is best left for 2 days. Can be left longer [up to 5 days].

Drain well and slice.

Gravadlax can be served on toast with crème fraiche, with avocado and seafood sauce on shredded lettuce, cut up into creamy pasta or as a spectacular breakfast with spinach, cheese sauce and poached eggs.

World Of Our Own

We arrived at The Cove during the second week in September. Mum and I had continued to write to each other regularly so I thought I knew what to expect as far as changes were concerned.

As we drove up Mum and Fred were, as usual, waiting on the verandah to greet us and give us a big welcome. While Mum hugged me she said, 'You can't imagine how happy I am to have you back in Tassie again.'

When I moved out of her arms I saw tears in her eyes so I hugged her again and said, 'And I'm glad to be back too Mum.'

We really didn't see how much things had changed until we had unpacked our gear from the car, dumped it in the bedroom and then were positively dragged outside again and around the house. From there we could see the two little units, one sitting above the vineyard and the other further over the land, with the dam in front and a big old pine tree behind.

The units were like miniature replicas of the old farmhouse before the extension had been built on the side. Both buildings were weatherboard with sloping iron roofs and little verandahs in front. Each had a tiny garden of geraniums and boronia.

Mum and Fred had done an enormous amount of work to the land and had laid paths that wound from the house up to the first chalet then along to the second one. Lavender bushes were planted on either side of the path, and although they were still small they were already beginning to flower and perfume the air with their amazing scent.

I was tremendously curious to see what they were like inside but Mum said that we could only look inside the Chardonnay Chalet because the Pinot Pension currently had, 'A lovely young couple staying there who are on their honeymoon.'

Bruce and I looked askance at each other on hearing the names. To me they sounded rather twee and slightly absurd but I wouldn't have said this for the world. Really only Mum could have thought them up. Fred just smiled benignly and led us across the top of the vineyard to the first chalet.

When Fred opened the door we stepped inside and were in a long lounge/dining room that had a small kitchen at the back. To the right side of this room a door opened into a beautiful bedroom that shared the lounge room's view of the vineyard. Behind this room, concealed by a partial wall was the bathroom, containing a large spa bath, an elegant vanity unit and a toilet.

Although the whole area was probably only about five squares it felt spacious because both the lounge room and the bedroom had large windows that encompassed the magnificent views over the vineyard and out to the river and the hills beyond.

The colour scheme also increased the feeling of spaciousness because the entire chalet was painted in a soft grape-green with blending carpets. The kitchen and bathroom areas had tiles that exactly matched the carpet and the drapes were a deeper shade of green. Brilliant paintings on the walls, vivid orange and golden cushions on the couches and a colourful duvet on the bed provided the only contrast.

I looked around with admiration and said, 'Mum it's lovely and it all blends so well with the views.'

She appeared pleased with my approval, 'Well I had a lot of fun planning this and it works, I think.'

Fred joined in with, 'She's being modest. Your mother certainly has an eye for colour. Most of our guests rave about how lovely the units are. But wait until you see inside the other one. It's really spectacular.'

We left the unit, after briefly admiring the view from the small verandah, and then walked back to the house. When we were all seated around the pine table with cups of tea and homemade cake I broached the subject of how successful their project was proving to be. From Mum's letters I knew all about the problems they had experienced with the building and, more particularly, in getting permission to install two extra septic tanks. She had, however, told me very little about the past few months since they had been open for business. From this I had the impression that there had not been the demand they had expected.

In answer to my query, Fred pulled out a big, impressive-looking book from one of the drawers in the dresser and put it on the table in front of Bruce and me saying, 'This is our accommodation book and, as you can see, it's been a slow start but it's picking up.'

He opened the book to July then flipped over the pages to August and then September. From a quick look it seemed that they were not reaching the expected forty percent fill-rate.

Fred then turned to October, then November and December saying, 'The first few months were slow, but we are picking up and we reckon we'll have about eighty percent occupancy from November through to February.'

Bruce and I turned the pages and it was indeed impressive. All the weekends were booked for the next five months and in many cases the bookings were for the whole week.

'We didn't have our advertisement in the phone book until this month, so up until now we've relied on ads in the paper and publicity through Tourism Tasmania and the RACT. I reckon we'll get a lot of returns and word of mouth publicity so we think things are looking good.'

Fred stood there with a big smile on his face.

Mum came round the table and gave him a hug and smiled, 'And we reckon that by the end of the year we'll both be able to give up our jobs and finally stay here all the time.'

The following day the guests in the Pinot Pension left and we had a chance to see inside. It was more colourful and exotic than the other unit, and frankly more to my taste. The walls were all soft mulberry red and blended with the deep purple-red carpet, which was the colour of pinot grapes just before they darken to purple. Once again the tiles in bathroom and kitchen matched the carpet and the duvet was a riot of colours, reds, mauves and purples.

During the next week Bruce and I slept in both the units at Mum and Fred's instigation. They wanted us to give them a test run, so to speak, and both passed with flying colours. Actually I loved the pension best and Bruce preferred the chalet's colour scheme, but we were in total agreement that they were lovely spaces in which to spend time.

Before returning to Tasmania we had checked out some real estate agents in Hobart and had lined up several properties to look at in the second week of our return to the island.

Mum and Fred came with us and we had a couple of days looking at so many houses it became confusing. Was it the house with the swimming pool that had the horrible wallpaper, and which one had the laundry cleverly concealed in the kitchen? We decided that we had to begin making detailed notes about each property that we saw to avoid this confusion.

As it happened this proved to be unnecessary because on the third day we found it, the one that was just right for us. It was on the eastern shore, and from the front deck there was a magnificent view of the Derwent River and Mount Wellington. While living in Canberra the two things I had missed were mountains and real water, as opposed to artificial lakes. The view sold it to me, but it also had a wonderful kitchen, big, generous rooms and a master bedroom with a huge spa bath in the ensuite.

Bruce and I looked through this house then looked at each other and nodded with silly grins on our faces. This house said hello to both of us. We signed to buy it that day, and as it was vacant and we had our finances already arranged we settled promptly and moved in the following week.

For the next few months Bruce and I were flat out, moving into our new home and buying furniture but also learning as much as we could about the new business in which we were now half-owners.

The staff was only small and everyone worked hard including Frank. Bruce and Frank worked together with regard to purchasing, contracts and the organization of installations. I took over the team involved in training company and business groups, as well as private clients in the usage of their computers initially and also when new programmes were installed.

Because of our busy lives we rarely made it down to The Cove, but a couple of times Mum and Fred came up to town and we went to dinner and a show and they stayed the night. I think Mum was a bit disappointed that she didn't see me more, now that I was back in Tassie, but she said she understood.

During that first year back I managed to see my little Nanna Alice quite often. Because she lived in New Town I could drop in and see her between visiting clients. She had aged considerably during the past couple of years. I had seen her at Christmas time, a few months after Uncle Gordon had drowned, and she had naturally still been very upset. However I don't think I had really understood the terrible impact his death had had on her. She seemed to have sort of shrunk in on herself; she was smaller and frailer than she had been. I found it hard to recognise her as the warm and welcoming Nanna from my childhood who hugged and loved us. Neither was she any longer the vibrant, active Nanna from my teen years.

Now she gave me a paper-thin cheek to kiss and I feared if I hugged her too tightly she might break. She often talked to me about how she couldn't believe Gordon had really gone forever and said that she still expected him to come back. I told her about the Buddhist belief in reincarnation. I said that as he had been such a lovely man and had died doing something heroic he would come back with good karma, and have an extra good life. She seemed to take comfort from this idea.

While she made tea for us I reminisced about the happy times that I'd shared in this dear, old house with my cousins. I talked about the fun we'd had playing hide-and-seek around the gardens or helping Granddad in his vegetable patch and enthused about the feasts she prepared for us, the hot scones and kiss biscuits and wonderful corned beef sandwiches. She brightened up when I talked of those past days and the next time I dropped in she gave me her recipe for kiss biscuits written in her beautiful, flowing copperplate handwriting.

Sometimes Nanna Alice talked about the Depression years and the problems of feeding her growing family She amazed me when she quoted the prices for groceries such as butter and tea and I praised her good memory.

She laughed at this and said, 'I can remember things that happened fifty years ago as clear as day, but can't remember where I put my glasses or what I had for dinner yesterday.'

When she talked about her years as a young wife and mother I thought of how different life had been then compared with now. In a way it had been uncomplicated because there was so little choice and I guess that led to the acceptance of circumstances as they were. Women of my generation can choose to have children or not. We have equal rights to an education and almost equality in the workplace. Despite these differences Nanna Alice seemed to have had a contented and fulfilling life, and I sometimes wonder if we have lost as much as we have gained.

I am so glad that I had those times with her because in June Nanna Alice died suddenly and unexpectedly from a heart attack. I am also glad that I was around to comfort Mum as I felt my being close during those first few weeks helped her cope with her loss.

By September Mum and Fred were becoming busier with their venture and, as the holiday period approached, they always had both units let, not just for the weekends but also for the whole week. We went down to spend the week between Christmas and New Year with them and on two occasions were joined by guests from the units for barbecue lunches. Both Mum and Fred were enjoying this new phase in their lives They had left their other jobs so were feeling very free.

The previous year Mum had convinced Fred they should have their wine made by a vigneron because they would be so busy with their building project. As a result their wine was now very good, and Mum had decided that by increasing the accommodation tariff they could offer a complimentary bottle of wine to their guests. This had proved to be quite a money-spinner as often their visitors wanted to buy another bottle before leaving. Many of them also bought fruit or Mum's garlic plaits and this saved the time of getting produce to the market or setting up the roadside stall.

In February of 1990 Gay and Dale had their first child, a boy whom they named Nicholas. Dale paid the airfare for Mum to go over to see them two weeks after the birth. Fred stayed at The Cove, as there were guests in both units. Mum drove up to town and I took her to the airport. She was as excited as a kid at the prospect of seeing her little grandson and of course catching up with the parents. Despite this she was worried about Fred being on his own so I promised her Bruce and I would go down for the first weekend that she was away.

We arrived early on the Saturday morning and Fred greeted us with his laconic grin and cups of tea. After we had done our usual tour of the vineyard and gardens we retired to the barbecue area and Fred soon had foil-wrapped fish cooking away while he brought out salads and bread.

It was funny being there with him and without Mum and at times the conversation became stilted. This seemed ridiculous because, by now, I had known him for nearly a decade and he and Bruce had always got on. The thing was we had always seen him with Mum and it was as if, without her there as a sort of conduit, the relationship was altered. It was almost as if part of Fred was missing.

Gradually we relaxed together and the old familiarity returned. We talked about our company and of what we were doing and Fred brought out the accommodation book to show us how things were progressing. Later Bruce and Fred went fishing together and I prepared a piece of beef that I have brought with us. I served it with a salad of rocket, beetroot and horseradish cream. Fred said he enjoyed it but I think the beef may have been too rare for him.

We drank a couple of bottle of their 1989 pinot noir, which was really good, followed by coffee and liquors. We then retired for the night, but not before Fred had said how much he missed Mum and that he'd be glad when she came back the following weekend.

'I'm just sort of marking time until she returns,' he sighed before going to his room.

We left early the next morning because we had household chores to catch up with before the start of another busy week. As we drove away and I waved a fond farewell to Fred I thought how alone he looked without Mum next to him.

Later that evening I rang Mum and told her about going down to see Fred. She said she had spoken to him and he told her how much he had enjoyed our visit. She also raved about the baby and about how happy Gay and Dale were, but she finished by saying that she was missing Fred. This had been the only time they had been apart for more than a couple of days since their marriage, with the exception of when she went to Fiji.

It made me wonder how dependent you should let yourself become, and if I would miss Bruce as much if we were apart for two weeks. I didn't think I would although I love him very much.

I asked Bruce how he would feel and he hugged me and said, 'Of course I'd miss you, but life goes on, and think of the home-coming.'

This was reassuring because it was much the same as I felt. I suppose all the talk today about co-dependency, unhealthy relationships and dominant and passive roles has led my generation to analyse too much what Mum's lot accepted naturally. Perhaps the pendulum has swung too far, and we now protect and value our innate independence too much, particularly we females.

Mum was due to return the following Saturday. Although we said we'd pick her up from the airport Fred insisted on driving up, even though it meant that they would have both cars in town. We let him have his way and when they arrived at our house to collect Mum's car they were like teenagers, hugging each other and sitting close together while we had a cup of tea, before they drove off in their separate cars.

That was the last time they spent apart during their marriage. When Gay gave birth to another boy in November the following year Fred went with Mum to Sydney. A neighbour welcomed visitors and serviced the units for them while they were away and made sure that the hoppers in the fowl house were replenished.

Despite the closeness they shared their relationship was certainly not exclusive. They loved having Bruce and me to visit, enjoyed frequent lunches with their friends and also appeared to adopt many of their paying guests. Frequently when Bruce and I went down for a weekend we would be joined for dinner or a barbecue by tourists who were staying in the units. The easy-going friendliness that they showed towards guests certainly paid off because their occupancy rate kept increasing, and many of the bookings were repeats or from word of mouth by satisfied customers.

During the following year Mum decided that she would like to have all her family together in 1993. She had only been seeing her siblings on very rare occasions when they happened to visit Nanna Alice at the same time. Nanna had been the lynch pin holding the family together and with her gone the sisters had even less contact. I think Mum wanted her children and grandchildren with her, if only for a short while, as a sort of reassurance of continuity.

After numerous phone calls between Mum, the boys and their wives the second and third weeks in January were selected. I looked forward to this time with some trepidation, as it would be the first time that my brothers and I would live together since Mum and I had moved into the flat.

I had spent weekends with Ralph and Maureen and the odd day with Dale and Gay, while living in Canberra, but the boys had only seen each other briefly at their respective weddings and at funerals, the last one being Nanna's.

Would we be like three casual acquaintances with Mum expecting more rapport between us than we felt? And how would I cope with two small children and a toddler around the place for really I didn't like children very much?

Kiss Biscuits

4 oz. butter	1 ½ cups plain flour
½ cup caster sugar	½ cup cornflour
1 egg	1 tsp. baking powder

Biscuits

Cream butter and sugar, add egg and beat well.

Add flour, corn flour and baking powder and mix to a fine dough.

Roll out thin and cut into circles.

Bake 10 minutes in a moderate oven.

Butter Icing

2 oz. butter	2 cups icing sugar
1 tsp water	

(lemon juice can be used instead of water for lemon icing)

Soften butter.

Add icing sugar and mix well.

Add water carefully to achieve desired consistency.

When biscuits are cold join together with raspberry jam and ice with butter icing.

Family Affair

Bruce and I went down to The Cove the day before my brothers and their families were due to arrive. I knew Mum and Fred had been planning this for months but we thought that we might be able to lend a hand with any last minute preparations.

Because we didn't have children we had been consigned to the front bedroom where we usually slept, and the families had each been allocated a unit. I asked Mum if there was anything that I could do to help.

She just waved a hand airily saying, 'No darling, everything is under control. This is your holiday too you know, so take that lovely man of yours out onto the deck and I'll call you as soon as lunch is ready.'

Fred had been working in the vineyard, retying the vines, and when he joined us he looked hot and dusty.

'Anyone want a beer?' he queried, raising one of his bushy eyebrows, and we both agreed that this was a good idea as the day was warm, and even with the air conditioning on it had been stuffy in the car on the way down.

We lounged idly on the deck, sipping our beer, until Mum called us for lunch, a duck terrine with salad and crusty bread. I enthused over the terrine and Mum explained how they had swapped some chickens for two ducks. She had made them into two terrines, one to share with us and the other for a meal sometime later in the week. She had found the recipe in her French cookery book and evidently this dish kept very well in the refrigerator.

After lunch I once more offered to help with any last minute chores saying, 'I know I'd be in a flap with six adults and three children to house and feed for two weeks.'

Mum laughed, looking so light-hearted and happy, 'I am in the tourist business you know darling. No, everything's ready. I'm putting Dale and Gay and their little boys in Pinot Pension and Ralph, Maureen and Jasmine in Chardonnay Chalet. I think the colour schemes will suit the girls' tastes best and I've put the cot in the pension and duvets on the lounges for Jasmine and Nicholas. I've also bought a port-a-cot for when little Bradley needs a daytime sleep. It could come in handy in the future if we have two little ones staying in the units at the same time.'

Still not completely reassured I persisted, 'Is there anything in the food line that you've forgotten? Bruce and I could go and get it if there is.'

Fred chuckled, 'I think you'll find that we are well provisioned. Your mother and I spent a small fortune at the supermarket the other day, not to mention the dishes she's been cooking and freezing during the past fortnight. You don't have to worry Helen.'

After we had finished lunch and tidied up the kitchen Fred and Bruce left for a spot of fishing, and to give Mum and me time alone.

We settled on the deck with a bottle of wine and Mum talked excitedly about the boys, their wives and the children and the coming holiday. She was so looking forward to it, but I was concerned that she would be disappointed if my brothers and I didn't relate well to each other, and frankly I could see this happening.

Although Dale and Ralph look somewhat alike, having both inherited Dad's dark good looks, they had always been very different as boys. From the little I knew of them now they had grown to be even less alike as men. I had always been the little sister and, although I cared for them both, I hadn't seen them much in the past years and no longer felt closely bonded to either of them.

To still my growing qualms I refilled our glasses and said, 'Come and show me your preparations. I'd like to see how the pension looks with a cot in it and a bed made up in the lounge.'

To my mind the units were ideally suited for romantic couples and I hadn't seen them prepared for family groups, although I knew that they have accommodated numerous families.

We stopped first at Chardonnay Chalet and Mum unlocked the door. The lounge was furnished with two wide couches set at right angles to each other and there was a circular dining table near the kitchen. One of the couches was now covered with a pretty duvet in various shades of green. It blended with the existing décor perfectly.

Mum led the way to the kitchen and, opening the refrigerator said, 'I've stocked both units with milk, juice, butter, eggs and bacon, plus there's bread and cereals in the cupboards. This way the little families can have their breakfasts whenever it suits them and will have some family time alone.'

She had also put in supplies of coffee, tea, biscuits and several varieties of homemade jams as well as the essential vegemite.

There was a large floral arrangement of green leaves and cream roses on the dining table and in the bedroom small vases of jasmine on the bedside tables scented the room.

I gave Mum a hug, 'Oh darling, you've thought of everything; even the flowers match their daughter's name.'

She laughed, 'Well that is actually accidental. I wanted something that would match the décor and would smell nice, but now you mention it that is good. Now come and see the pension.'

We walked along the path that skirted the top of the vineyard and came to the next little dwelling. Mum once more unlocked the door and led the way in. Here she had again matched the duvet on Nicholas's couch with the décor and it was a vivid combination of deep reds, lilacs and purples in a swirling pattern. She opened the bedroom door to reveal the cot that was covered with a matching, miniature duvet. On the bedside tables were slim specimen vases, each holding one deep red rose and on the dining table was a large, bowl-shaped vase of multi-coloured roses.

I lifted my now nearly empty glass to Mum and toasted her, 'Well I'd say you've thought of everything. Let's go back and finish off the bottle and see if the men have caught our dinner.'

The next morning Bruce and I were up early and after breakfast we went for a long walk. I think we both felt that for the next couple of weeks we wouldn't have much time alone so we made the most of the peaceful morning

By the time we arrived back it was mid-morning and Mum and Fred were already seated on the verandah, eagerly awaiting the arrival of the two families. The boys had arranged to meet up at Tullamarine Airport to catch the same Melbourne to Hobart flight. They had also booked a big people mover that was roomy enough to seat four adults plus three children in their rather bulky child restraint seats.

Mum was on edge and kept getting up from her chair, walking around the front garden and then coming back to perch on her seat again. Seeing her growing agitation Fred went inside and came back out with yet another cup of tea for her.

The people mover came up the drive at exactly twelve o'clock, and it had scarcely stopped before Mum was off the verandah and waiting expectantly for the doors to open. Dale, who had been driving, was the first out of the car and gave Mum a big bear hug. Ralph had been in the front passenger seat and was the next one to receive a kiss and a cuddle.

The men then turned to the task of freeing their children from their car seats and my two sisters-in-law stepped down from the back seats. Mum gave them both a hug, but her eyes were on the middle seat where Jasmine was being unbuckled. As soon as she was freed she headed straight for Mum saying, 'Nanna, Nanna,' and Mum swept her up into her arms.

The next little person to emerge from the van was obviously Nicholas. I hadn't seen him before but I knew that he was about three. He was dressed in jeans and a navy top and looked like a miniature Dale. At first he seemed very shy and clung to his daddy's hand but when Mum put Jasmine down and dropped down on her knees in front of him he cried, 'Nanna' and put his little, plump arms around her neck.

Meanwhile Gay had picked little Bradley out of his seat and walked towards Mum with the toddler in her arms. Still cuddling Nicholas Mum gazed at Bradley, a rapt look on her face, and said to Gay, 'Oh, hasn't he grown. Let me hold him.'

As I watched this scene and saw the joy on Mum's face I felt a bit guilty that I had chosen not to have children, but then you don't have children to please your mother.

Dale and Ralph came up the steps together; both give me a hug and shook hands with Bruce and Fred. Mum and her daughters-in-law were oohing over the children and I think Fred noticed that Bruce and I were looking a bit awkward because he said, 'Let's go through to the deck and crack a bottle. You won't get Liz away from those kids for a while.'

On the deck was a magnum of champagne, cooling in an ice bucket, and the round glass table was covered with glasses, juice, plastic beakers and plates of biscuits and cheeses and a bowl of fruit. Mum, Gay and Maureen eventually joined us and the mothers busied themselves pouring juice for the children and helping them to biscuits and cheese before accepting glasses of champagne.

I had settled myself in a chair with my drink when I felt a small hand touch my arm. Beside me stood Jasmine. She was a pretty, little girl with strawberry blonde hair like her mother's. I had met her briefly the previous Christmas, but didn't expect her to remember me.

She smiled at me and said, 'Hello Auntie Helen,' and kissed my cheek

Feeling quite pleased I pulled her towards me saying, 'Hello little girl. I didn't think you'd remember me.'

She smiled up at me, 'Yes I do. I met you and Uncle Bruce last Christmas. You gave me a doll.'

I felt absurdly happy to be remembered by this little person, and even more so later when we are being seated around the big pine table for lunch and she asked if she could sit next to me. I thought that perhaps the holiday would be all right after all.

When we had finished lunch the men unpacked the van and carried everything across to the units. Mum had gone ahead with Gay and Maureen and I tagged along to see what they thought of their accommodation. Both women enthused about the colour schemes and I could see how right Mum's choice of units for her daughters-in-law had been. Maureen was dressed in a soft green linen pants suit and Gay wore cream slacks, a deep rose silk shirt and had a multi-coloured scarf knotted elegantly at her throat.

When the men arrived with the luggage Gay greeted them with the laughing remark, 'Isn't your mother clever? We even match the décor.'

I began to see why Mum had such a soft spot for her. They obviously shared a concern for detail and a love of colour.

Mum bustled from one family to the other, showing them where everything was and stopping to give first Jasmine, then Nicholas a cuddle. Little Bradley was tired from the trip so Gay heated him a bottle in the microwave and put him to bed in the cot.

Bruce and I, and I think Fred also, felt a bit in the way so we went back to the deck and opened another bottle of champagne.

During that first week we settled into a routine wherein the families had their breakfasts in their units and joined us at mid-morning on the deck for tea and biscuits. I slowly become reacquainted with my brothers and Maureen. I also began to get to know Gay and the children better.

We spent the days lazing about; going for walks and on warm days some of us swam in the bay. I had one lovely afternoon fishing with my brothers while the others minded the children and Fred and Bruce repaired a fence.

Another day Maureen, Jasmine and I went for a bush walk and collected wild flowers while Mum and Gay set up easels on the foreshore and painted the view across bay. The men had been left to mind the little boys and when we returned we found Fred, Ralph and Bruce playing hide-and-seek in the orchard with Nicholas while Dale watched from the verandah, nursing his sleeping toddler.

One of the best days was when we all went oyster and mussel gathering at a bay near Dover. We needed the people mover and Mum's car to take us all, plus the collecting gear of buckets, hammers and knives as well as snacks and juices for the kids and a blanket, pillow, sunshade and nappy changes for Bradley. Being with children made me realise once again how much simpler life was without them.

It was one of those clear, golden days that make you feel good to be alive. We arrived at the pretty bay early in the afternoon. Gay opted to stay on the sand with her little boys, Mum, Maureen, Jasmine and I walked around the rocks where mussels were to be found and the men waded into the water where dozens of oysters were attached to under water rocks.

We females soon had two buckets full of good-sized mussels and returned to the beach. The men were still at work, as they had to prise the oysters off the rocks with knives and sometimes use a chisel and hammer.

Eventually they also had their buckets full so we all piled back into the vehicles with our bounty from the sea and drove home.

Once again the men had the hardest task because they had to open the oysters while Mum simply put all the mussels into two big pots of water to boil and we pulled them out as they opened.

After the mussels had all opened Mum took half of them plus a little of the cooking water and began preparing a soup by frying off leeks and garlic in butter, adding diced potatoes and skinned tomatoes, a little white wine and her own fish stock.

She set me to work making a sauce with lemon juice, soy sauce, olive oil and a little chilli to go with the remaining mussels.

Gay had settled Bradley to sleep in the port-a-cot and Nicholas, tired out from the sun and sea air, had dropped off to sleep curled up peacefully in an armchair. Relieved of motherly duties, Gay volunteered to make a cocktail sauce to accompany the oysters and Maureen and Jasmine decided that they would collect vegetables from the garden for a salad.

The evening was still and mild and we sat around the pine table with the doors leading to the deck open. We feasted on the raw oysters, dipping them first into the cocktail sauce. These were followed by mussels in the cheese sauce I had made served with a tossed green salad. The finale was Mum's mussel soup that she had thickened with cream at the last minute. This was served with a warm crusty loaf of bread.

We all felt a little sunburnt and weary but it had been a memorable feast. The little boys slept through it, and for once Gay didn't seem too concerned about the change in their routines.

When Jasmine's eyes began to close Ralph and Maureen said their goodnights and Dale and Gay also left, carrying their sleeping sons.

Mum sighed, as she watched them all walk away along the path in the moonlight, 'Oh what a lovely day it's been.'

Although for most of the fortnight the weather was fine and mild we did have a couple of wet dreary days. On one such day it was too cold for the children to be outside so Mum and Maureen assembled paper, glue, pencils, stickers and blunt scissors. They planned to keep Jasmine and Nicolas entertained at the big table. Bradley had had an unsettled night and Gay had taken him back to the unit so that he could have an uninterrupted daytime nap. I think she also planned to catch up on some sleep herself.

Bruce and Dale were locked in combat over a very intense game of chess and Fred was having a read in his armchair by the fire.

I was sitting on the verandah, watching the waves pound against the rocks on the point and the heavy grey clouds building up across the river when Ralph came out and joined me saying, 'Do you want to go for a walk little Sis?'

As children we had enjoyed wandering in the bush and walking along the fire trails on rainy days, and it is something I still enjoy doing so of course I said yes.

We borrowed Fred and Mum's wet weather gear and set off at quite a rapid pace, up the gravel road, down into a dip then up again until we were overlooking a rather desolate little bay.

'Will we go to the next bay?' Ralph asked, looking at the gathering storm clouds. 'We might get a soaking on the way back.'

'Well it won't be the first time will it?' I answered, remembering days from our childhood, 'Let's go. I'd like to see the deer farm that's been started since Bruce and I were last here.'

We didn't talk much on the way, partly because we were getting slightly out of breath, but also I think that we were enjoying the quiet after being around people for the past few days. I was also remembering walks on the fire trails of our childhood. The trails were narrower than this road, but there were the same eucalypts and wattles and similar native shrubs along the verges and the same pungent smell of dark, damp earth in the air.

The rain still held off. After inspecting the extremely high fence surrounding the farm, pondering how high a deer could jump and trying to spot the distant animals, we sat on a jetty that went from an old, derelict shed out over the water.

Ralph turned to me and said, 'You and Mum seem to be getting on well these days.'

Somewhat taken aback by his remark I asked rather shortly, 'What do you mean? We get on wonderfully well.'

He looked at me with his kind dark eyes and answered slowly, 'Well I suppose that this is the first time I've seen you two together for any length of time since those lunches we shared with Mum when we were both at university. My memories of that time were of Mum being a little bit diffident with you, and you being fairly off-hand and sort of brittle with her. I'm so glad for you both that things seem to have changed.'

I thought back to how we had been at that time and how we'd come back to an easy, loving relationship. Of course Ralph would notice the difference.

I put my hand on his arm, 'Sorry if I was a bit abrupt then and you are right. Mum and I have sorted out a lot of angst in the past couple of years.'

Then I told him about Mum coming to my wedding, and how this had been a sort of turning point in our relationship.

He murmured, 'Yes, I can see how that would have cleared the air between you. I guess it made you both realise how much you meant to each other,'

Turning to him I then asked, 'But what about you? I think you went through the worst of it when Mum and Dad separated, and seemed to be the most affected at the time, but now you seem so bloody normal and calm as if nothing could or has ever upset you.'

He grinned at me, 'Well, I wouldn't say that, although it does take a lot to stir me up. Some of the kids I have to deal with worry me, but I think my misspent year helps me understand many of their problems better.'

'So you think you need to go through parental divorce, drug taking, drinking to excess and whoring around to make you a good student counsellor?' I asked rather sarcastically.

'No,' he answered, 'I wouldn't put it as baldly as that, but I do know I have more empathy with my problem students because of the unhappiness and loss of purpose that I experienced back then than I would have if I'd just gone along living in my safe little bubble.'

'I can see your point there but I think we've gone away from what I asked you or at least what I wanted to know. You were as angry with Mum as I was, but you get on together now as if nothing ever happened. What caused the change for you?'

'You're right Sis,' he replied, 'I was still carrying a chip on my shoulder towards her until we came down for Christmas a few years ago. As I watched Mum with Jasmine and saw the joy they had from being together it reminded me of how she was with us. She had given us so much love and care when we were children, and it seemed time for me to forgive her for splitting up the family that way.'

He gave a big stretch and opened his arms to the sky then turned to me, 'At this stage in my life I am very happy. I adore my big girl and my little girl. Although Maureen and I would have loved more children it's not to be, so that makes us cherish Jasmine even more.'

I nodded, 'Well she's certainly a delightful child. She's so enthusiastic about everything and she's also so good. I haven't heard one grizzle or complaint out of her.'

'Praise indeed, little sister, coming from you,' he laughed,

'Am I that bad?' I retorted, 'You know I don't like children much, but I'm becoming quite fond of Jasmine. She's so affectionate and self-assured and not at all spoilt.'

'Well thank you again. We're pretty proud of her and love her utterly. You know I wasn't sure what sort of father I'd be. I don't think Dad was much of a role model but when I held Jasmine in my arms, as soon as she was born, I felt such love for her I can't even begin to describe it.'

We had been so engrossed in our conversation we hadn't noticed the storm front moving across the river until raindrops began dimpling the water and landing heavily on our hands and faces.

Ralph stood up and put his hand down to me saying, 'Come on. We'd better head for home or we'll be totally drenched.'

The wind increased and the rain changed to an icy sleet that froze our faces and filtered down our necks until we were quite soaked. By the time we reached the house we were freezing. The only warm part of me was the hand Ralph had held all the way back, as he had sometimes done when we were children.

Mum hustled Ralph off to his spa bath and ran water into the claw-foot for me. Once we were warm and dry again Fred made us hot toddies of whisky and lemon juice, and because we had missed lunch Mum heated up soup and made us toast.

We ate sitting side by side at the table, and I felt so happy to have had this special time with Ralph and the chance for us to really reconnect.

After more than a week of Mum and Fred preparing all the meals we began to feel thoroughly spoilt, but also that we should give them a break. We decided that each couple would take it in turns to prepare the evening meal and, to make a game of it, the meals had to be a total surprise. We three couples went off and planned our menus and wrote out our shopping lists.

While Mum and Fred minded the children we all piled into the people mover, having first removed the kiddie seats, and went shopping. We had a surprisingly good time as we joked around the supermarket, pretending to spy on each other and we made sure each couple went to the nearby butcher at different times.

Mum had told us to stay away as long as we wanted to, so after everything was packed in the van we drove to a restaurant near the river. We chose to sit outside and had beautiful platters of seafood followed by sticky date puddings served with cream and ice cream. We spent the luncheon joking about what we were going to cook, and trying to outdo one another with ghastly, inedible combinations. I think the best was Dale's suggestion of chocolate stuffed crayfish on a bed of garlic-flavoured prunes.

When we arrived back at The Cove the others secreted their purchases in their units and Bruce and I put ours in the house fridge with strict instructions that there was to be no peeking. We also opted to go first as it would be harder for us to keep our meal plan a surprise with our ingredients in the communal refrigerator.

That evening Mum and Fred cooked a barbecue and we sat around outside, talking and drinking, until Nicholas and Jasmine were half asleep snuggled up in their fathers' arms. Little Bradley had been sleeping in the port-a-cot and hardly stirred when Gay picked him up before we all said our goodnights and went to bed. It had been a fun day and I really felt that my brothers and I had regained some of the affection and familiarity we had lost.

The next day, after a casual lunch of sandwiches, Bruce and I banished everyone from the kitchen so that we could begin preparing our meal for the evening.

Gay said that she had to start two of her dishes in advance and left, taking Bradley back to their unit for an afternoon nap.

Fred, Ralph and Dale decided that they would take Nicholas fishing and Mum, Maureen and Jasmine went for a walk.

While Bruce and I chopped and diced we wondered what Gay might be planning that needed such early preparation. We both really liked her and this holiday had been a chance to get to know her better. Unlike Maureen, who was a very peaceful, relaxed person, Gay was full of verve and energy and obviously an ambitious and competitive woman. She had been running her own interior decorating firm from the time she turned twenty-one. As I understood it her parents had given her financial help to start the business and their wealthy friends had been the initial clients. Nevertheless it was her talent and hard work that made the business the success it was. I had always thought how suited she and Dale were, but previously I had only seen them as a couple. It was interesting to watch them in their parental roles.

Anyhow we were curious about what she would come up with the next night because she was a bit of a perfectionist, but basically we concentrated on our own preparations. We had decided on a Chinese Banquet and together prepared the vegetables, meat and poultry for chicken with cashews and sweet and sour pork then mixed the marinade for Asian-style fish. We planned to accompany these dishes with plain boiled rice. For dessert we were serving a simple but refreshing dish – melon balls and lychees in a brandy and orange flavoured syrup served with ice cream.

By four o'clock we had the desserts completed, looking very attractive in long stemmed glasses. The fish was marinating and everything else was ready to cook. We decided to reward ourselves with a glass of wine and sat on the deck enjoying a quiet time until the men and Nicholas returned with a bucket full of cleaned flathead that Fred said would make a great breakfast. Maureen,

Jasmine and Mum also came home, their arms full of wildflowers, which they proceeded to spread around the house in vases and bottles.

When Gay came back from her unit with a bright-eyed Bradley in her arms, Bruce and I returned to the kitchen to complete our food preparations.

We put on the rice cooker, placed the fish in the oven and, while I cooked the sweet and sour pork Bruce made the chicken dish.

Bruce and I work well together in a kitchen because we often prepare meals together, and always when we are having a dinner party. By the time everything was cooked Mum had set the table and we brought out our dishes to noisy applause.

The adults appreciated our meal, and Jasmine tried everything. Nicholas decided that he only wanted rice, although he did eat some of the melon balls. All the food was deemed unsuitable for Bradley so Gay made him vegemite and cheese sandwiches.

I was pleased with our meal and it's reception, but wondered what Gay was going to produce that would please the adults but also suit her two sons.

The next day Gay seemed very relaxed about her meal. Dale did not appear to be involved. Although he had offered to lend a hand she said she didn't need any help when she went inside at about three o'clock to start cooking. She returned an hour later, looking cool and collected and announced, 'Dinner will be served at six-thirty.'

We had all spent a relaxed afternoon, sitting in the sunshine, playing with the children and enjoying a couple of bottles of the "house" wine.

At six Gay and Dale went to their unit and returned carrying two containers, then Dale set the table. Exactly at six-thirty we were called in from the deck and served a veritable gourmets' delight – venison terrine with crisp toast and dill pickles, followed by rich Beef Bourguignon with minted, new potatoes. For the finale there was strawberry sorbet decorated with fresh berries.

It was a delightful, sophisticated meal and the little boys both had some terrine on toast and small serves of the beef with potatoes. The three children enthused over the sorbet and little Bradley giggled, 'Icy pole.'

I decided there must be an art to cooking food that was suitable for adults and children; an art that Bruce and I lacked.

I was also impressed with the efficiency of my sister-in-law, but couldn't help thinking, rather sarcastically, that she had needed time the previous day to prepare the terrine and start the sorbet.

Maureen and Ralph were by far the most relaxed about getting their meal ready when it was their turn. They left the deck, where we had all been sitting, at about four to commence their food preparations, and of course Jasmine was included in their work.

By six thirty they called us to the table for a delightful meal of roast lamb served with masses of vegetables, baked potatoes, pumpkin and parsnips, cauliflower cheese and a medley of julienne carrots and snow peas.

Once we were seated Maureen served us the vegetables of our choice, Ralph brought around the lamb, beautifully carved and presented on a large platter, and Jasmine followed him with a jug of rich, brown gravy. It was all very good, and once more the little boys ate the meat and their choice of vegetables.

For dessert we had baked apples, flavoured with nutmeg and cinnamon, stuffed with dates and served with pouring custard.

Fred proposed a toast to all of us for our culinary efforts and we joined in with self-congratulations. When the hilarity had subsided Mum said she wanted to make an announcement and we all quietened down.

'Well my darlings,' she began 'Because you have all prepared such spectacular meals Fred and I have decided to reward you. We've booked you into The Grill for dinner tomorrow night, and we will mind all the children in the Pinot Pension so that they can get an early night.'"

We all thanked them for the offer and decided to dress up and make it a gala event.

I thought it an excellent idea of Mum's because Gay had been getting a bit uptight about the children's routines being upset by the late nights. Little Bradley usually just slept in the port-a-cot, but often Nicholas had been fractious before going to sleep in the arms of one or the other of his parents.

On the night that Bruce and I had cooked the meal his grizzling had become too much for her, and she had turned to Dale and said, 'Doesn't it bother you seeing your son upset?'

Dale had actually been talking to Bruce and me about a new computer that he wanted installed for his company. With a quizzical grin he had risen, walked around the table and picked up Gay and Nicholas together and answered, 'It will worry me more if my woman gets upset so let's take this child to bed and leave the grown-ups in peace.'

Turning he'd said to Ralph, 'Will you bring Bradley across?' and left the room, a giggling wife and a silent son in his strong arms.

In the morning Gay and Dale had been very affectionate towards each other so obviously his he-man tactics paid off.

Evidently Mum had worried about this minor upset and I think that was why she had organised for us "young people" to go out to dinner together.

The next evening we all dressed up in our best casual gear and once more removed the kiddie seats before getting in. Ralph drove but Bruce volunteered to be the designated driver for the return journey.

We didn't take long to get there as it was only about a twenty-kilometre trip. Although Gay and Dale looked dubious about the external appearance of the place they brightened up when we got inside. It was attractively decorated, the lighting was soft and a large, freestanding wood heater warmed the room.

The owner/chef was a big, welcoming bear of a man who lived nearby and enjoyed cooking the local produce. He had a good memory for faces because he remembered Bruce and me although we had only been there once before with Mum and Fred. He gave us a cheery welcome and asked how the units were going. He also enthused about the locally produced venison he was featuring that night so we all decided to try it.

The entrée specialties of the day were honey brown mushrooms served with a dipping sauce and salmon patties with wilted rocket and cream and tarragon sauce. We ordered three of each and shared them around.

For the main course we all had venison steaks served with a plum and cranberry sauce and accompanied by potato wedges and a mixed green salad.

Ralph and Maureen chose the blueberry tart for dessert while the rest of us settled for the locally made ice cream served with fresh strawberries.

We drank quantities of Tasmanian Pinot, except for Bruce who was very good and only drank one glass. On the way home was sang, rather drunkenly, nonsense songs from our youth.

We had one more day together, and the next morning the two families packed up, settled children in their seats – after Mum had kissed each child several times – and then we adults said our goodbyes before we waved them off.

Bruce and I were staying for another two days, theoretically to help them tidy up, but I'd thought Mum might need my company to help her adjust after the departure of her sons, daughters-in-law and grandchildren.

All things considered it was a good holiday and I'm so glad to have the memory of those days because I didn't see Dale during the next year and only caught up with Ralph and Maureen and Jasmine briefly at Christmas time.

I rang them occasionally, but I usually finished up talking to their wives, as they were either absent or busy elsewhere in their respective houses.

The next time we three siblings were together was at Fred's funeral the following June and it was a very distressing time. We were all so concerned about Mum, but somehow lacked the closeness to share our worries about her.

My brothers could both only stay for two days as it was term time for Ralph, and Dale had a business trip planned. I understood why they couldn't be with us longer but it meant that I was left, with help from Bruce of course, to cope with Mum in her desolation and it wasn't easy.

Duck Terrine

1 duck, about 2 ½kg. boned with liver

½ cup Calvados [apple brandy] mixture of lean and fat pork that equals weight of boned duck

1 tbsp. coriander, finely chopped

salt and freshly ground pepper

400 g. pork fatback or bacon

1 fresh thyme sprig

1 bay leaf

1 tbsp. parsley, finely chopped

Slice duck breasts thinly and marinate with strips of pork fat, half the Calvados, the thyme and bay leaf for two hours.

Finely chop the remaining duck meat, liver and pork then add remaining Calvados, coriander, parsley, salt and pepper.

Line an 8-cup terrine with slices of pork fatback. If bacon is used leave excess hanging to fold over terrine.

Add half chopped duck and pork mixture and pack down firmly.

Cover with half slices of duck breast and some fatback then add remaining duck/pork mixture.

Top with rest of duck breast and slices of fatback or bacon. Cover with aluminium foil.

Cook in a bain-marie. Bring to boil on top of stove, then place in oven [200C] and cook for 1-½ hours.

Remove from bain-marie and cool.

Refrigerate for at least 4 days before serving

Mussel Soup

Boil a quantity of mussels in large saucepan of water until open.

Remove from shells and set aside.

1 litre fish stock *(see below)*	1 tbsp. butter
2 leeks finely sliced	3 tomatoes skinned
3 cloves garlic minced	½ cup white wine
2 diced potatoes	cream

Melt butter in saucepan, add leeks, garlic and potatoes and cook for a few minutes, stirring to prevent sticking.
Add cut tomatoes, white wine and fish stock.
Cook until potatoes and leeks softened then mash roughly.
Return to heat, bring to boil and add mussels.
Cook to heat through, 2 – 3 minutes.
Add a little cream and serve.

Fish Stock

1 onion	1 carrot
1 stick celery	1 kg. fish bones or ½ kg. white fish fillets

Put all ingredients in saucepan with 2 litres water and cook for 30 minutes.
Remove from heat and strain.
Return to heat and cook until reduced to 1 litre.
When cool pour into container and freeze.

Chicken with Cashews

4 chicken breasts cut into bite-sized chunks
bunch spring onions, chopped
small piece fresh ginger finely cut
1 green and 1 red capsicum, deseeded and cut into small
squares
2 tbsp. olive oil
110 g. cashew nuts
2 tbsp. soy sauce
2 tbsp. sherry
1 tsp. corn flour
salt and pepper to taste

Heat oil in wok. Add onions and ginger and cook for 1
minute.

Add chicken pieces and cashews and stir-fry for 3 minutes
or until chicken is tender.

Add capsicums and cook further 3 minutes.

Blend together soy sauce, corn flour, and sherry then add
to mixture in the wok.

Stir-fry for 1 minute or until mixture thickens.

Season to taste then serve with rice or noodles.

Sweet and Sour Pork

1 tbsp, soy sauce	1 red pepper cut in strips
1 ½ tsp. sugar	4 oz. mushrooms sliced
1 tbsp. sherry	1 medium cucumber diced
1 egg yolk	1 can pineapple
2-½ lbs. pork fillet	¼ cup vinegar
2 onions sliced	salt and pepper
4 spring onions sliced diagonally	oil
corn flour	1 dsp. tomato paste

Mix together soy sauce, sugar, sherry and egg yolk – stir well.

Cut pork into cubes, place in this marinade and leave for 1 hour, stirring occasionally.

Heat oil in wok and fry onions until transparent.

Add pepper, mushroom, spring onion and cucumber in that order and cook approximately 5 minutes.

Drain can of pineapple, keeping the juice aside.

Add drained pineapple pieces to wok.

Cook for a further minute then remove from heat, empty into bowl and keep warm.

Drain meat from marinade, toss in corn flour.

Add oil to wok and cook meat until cooked through.

Add vegetables.

Mix together marinade, vinegar and tomato paste and heat.

Blend 2 tsp. corn flour into pineapple juice, add to marinade mixture and cook until thickens.

Pour over meat and vegetables and serve with boiled rice.

Asian Style Fish

12 fish fillets [any good, firm, white fish]
2 tbsp. oil
2 tbsp. soy sauce
1 tbsp. hot chilli sauce
1 tbsp. lemon juice
1 tsp. fresh ginger, grated
2 tbsp. fresh coriander, finely chopped

Mix together all ingredients except coriander.

Place fillets in flat baking tray and pour over the ingredients.

Place in preheated moderate oven and cook until fish beginning to flake – approximately 20 minutes.

Sprinkle with chopped coriander and serve with boiled rice.

Melon and Lychee Delight

1 tin lychees	1 cup water
honeydew melon	1 cup caster sugar
watermelon	juice of 1 orange
1 tbsp brandy	

Boil water and sugar over gentle heat until sugar dissolves.

Add orange juice and tbsp. brandy [optional] and set aside to cool.

Make melons into balls using a small scoop.

Arrange melon balls and lychees in individual, glass bowls.

Pour over syrup and top with a scoop of ice cream.

This is a very simple but attractive dessert to serve on a hot day or after a heavy main course.

Venison Terrine

Make at least one day ahead.

1 kg lean minced venison
2 onions finely chopped
250 g pkt. frozen spinach defrosted and squeezed dry or
fresh equivalent
1 cup fresh breadcrumbs
1 tbsp. juniper berries crushed
3 eggs beaten
salt and black pepper to taste
2 tbsp. fresh thyme leaves finely chopped
¼ cup cream
200 g prosciutto

Mix together venison mince, onions, spinach, breadcrumbs
and juniper berries in a large bowl.
Add eggs, seasonings, thyme and cream and mix well.
Line a buttered terrine or oblong tin with prosciutto,
overlapping the slices and leaving enough to fold over.
Fill with venison mixture, smooth over then fold
prosciutto over top.
Bake in moderate oven [180C] for 1 ¼ hours or until
cooked.
Remove from terrine, wrap in foil and place weight on top
while cooling.
Refrigerate covered overnight.

Serve with toast and pickles.

Beef Bourguignon

2 white onions, finely chopped
2 carrots, finely chopped
2 sticks celery heart, finely chopped
3 tbsp. oil
1.3kg beef [round or topside] cut into 2-inch cubes.
Salt and freshly ground black pepper
Bouquet garni – bay leaf, 1thyme sprig, 5 parsley sprigs
1 bottle Burgundy style red wine
2 tbsp. plain flour
3 tbsp. softened butter
2 tsp. chopped parsley

Heat oil in large, heavy saucepan and fry meat with chopped vegetables for 6 minutes stirring frequently.

Season with salt and pepper, add bouquet garni and pour in red wine.

Bring to the boil, cover with lid and simmer gently for 3 hours.

Mix together softened butter and flour and add to saucepan, mixing until well blended.

Cook uncovered for a further 10 minutes.

Sprinkle with parsley and serve with boiled, new potatoes.

Strawberry Sorbet

1 kg fresh strawberries	300 ml water
250 g caster sugar	juice 1 lemon

Hull and halve strawberries and put in blender. Process until smooth.

Put sugar and water in saucepan.

Bring slowly to the boil, stirring occasionally until the sugar is dissolved.

Reduce heat and simmer slowly for 2 minutes.

Remove from heat, add lemon juice and allow to cool completely.

Mix together cooled sugar syrup and blended strawberries.

Pour into container, cover and freeze for 1 ½ hours or until semi-frozen.

Remove from freezer and whisk with an electric mixer until smooth.

Return to container, level surface, cover and freeze a further 4 hours.

Transfer to lower shelf of refrigerator 15 minutes before serving to soften slightly.

Little Boxes

Mum was completely heartbroken. She walked around the land as if she was trying to find him and I worried for her sanity. It was as though she didn't believe he had really gone.

She knew he was lying in the funeral parlour being somehow treated so that, on the day of the funeral, people would be able to view him and see a rough facsimile of how he had looked in life, but she couldn't cope with the thought of that. She hadn't wanted to know anything about the funeral arrangements, so it had been good to have Dale and Ralph here. They had been wonderful and organised everything. They also notified Fred's son about the arrangements but he didn't attend.

Two days after the funeral Mum and I sat in the kitchen drinking too much red wine, and finally she talked about her loss.

She looks at me, her face streaked with tears, and said, 'I have loved and been loved completely but now I feel so alone. I don't know how I can go on living without him.'

I hugged her close, murmured soothing words and finally suggested that we go to bed, which we did, but I lay awake for hours worrying about how she would be during the ensuing months.

A week after the funeral the phone rang at Mum's and I answered it. I had been fending off calls from friends and family, as Mum was still too upset to talk much.

An unfamiliar male voice said, 'May I speak with Mrs. Elizabeth Davidson please?'

I identified myself as her daughter and asked the caller why he wanted to speak to her.

I heard throat clearing at the other end of the line before he answered, 'I am Reginald Pickering, the late Mr. Davidson's lawyer and I need to discuss with your mother the matter of his will. Can she come to town in the next few days?'

'She isn't able to cope with either travel or business matters at present,' I said rather brusquely. 'Perhaps I could come instead of her?'

Once again the throat clearing, followed by a pause, and then he said, 'If you can get your mother to sign a paper saying that you are currently attending to her affairs I will be happy to talk with you.'

I agreed to follow this procedure and made an appointment with him for the following Thursday as I knew Carolyn was coming down then to stay for a few days.

She arrived early on the day and breezed into the house looking elegant, as usual, in slim fitting jeans and a russet coloured sweater with a golden scarf draped casually around her neck.

Because of her visit Mum had made an effort, and for the first time since Fred's funeral had put on makeup and dressed in good jeans and the blue sweater that Carolyn had helped her choose a few years before

They greeted each other with a long hug and then Carolyn started chatting about all the goodies she had brought with her. I left them, talking happily, and drove away to keep my appointment with Mr. Pickering, feeling better about Mum than I had for days.

When I was shown into the lawyer's office he was seated behind a large untidy desk but stood up immediately to greet me. He was a tall, gaunt man dressed immaculately in a dark suit, white shirt and plain dark tie.

After we were both seated and I had handed over the paper signed by Mum he looked at me rather solemnly and said, 'This may come as a shock to your mother but I have recently received a copy of your stepfather's will, and in it he leaves all he owns to his son, Julian Davidson. This, of course, includes the property known as The Cove.'

There is a horrible American term that had infiltrated the English language, "gob smacked." I had always detested this expression but it described exactly how I felt.

Baffled I stammered, 'But surely Mum has a share in it? It has been their home and business and, in fact, Mum put quite a lot of money into it.'

The lawyer rubbed his chin reflectively, 'Unfortunately for your mother the property is only in Fred's name. I did discuss with him the need to make a new will when they commenced the business, but he just didn't get around to doing it. He made this one many years ago with another law firm but had never altered it. I think he felt there was no urgency about the matter.'

I must have looked shaken because he rang his secretary and asked her to bring in tea and then turned to me saying, 'Of course your mother can contest the will in court, but from my experience it is unlikely that it would be overturned. The law generally favours progeny over second spouses.'

I lost my cool and shouted, 'And what does the bloody son plan to do? Kick Mum out of her home?'

The lawyer came around his desk put a hand on my shoulder and said with a sigh, 'I'm afraid that's exactly what he does plan. He has informed me, through his lawyer, that he would like the property vacated in two months. He will then put it on the market, and from the sale will recompense your mother for the money she invested in the business.'

Just then the secretary entered the room with a tray, and I thankfully drank a cup of tea while trying to get my head around this information.

The lawyer commiserated, 'I'm sorry to be the bearer of such bad news and I do feel for your mother, but legally there is nothing I can do unless she decides to appeal. Let me know her decision and I will set the wheels in motion if she wishes to but, as I have said, in my opinion the chances of her getting a favourable decision are slim.'

I left the office, my legs still shaking from both the shock and anger at Fred for being so thoughtless. On the way back to The Cove I practised ways in which I could break the news to Mum.

In the end I just burst into the kitchen, where she and Carolyn were sharing a bottle of wine, and blurted out, 'Fred didn't make a new will so everything goes to his son Julian.'

Mum just looked at me calmly. 'I'm not surprised. We talked about making new wills, but somehow we didn't get around to doing it.'

I shouted, 'Mum, this means you'll lose your home and business, just because that useless, bloody cretin couldn't get around to changing his will. Where was his sense of responsibility to you?'

Mum's head reared up, 'Don't talk about Fred like that. He was a good man and both of us felt we had years ahead together. Changing wills didn't seem a priority. At any rate I don't think I'd want to live here without him, so it's probably for the best.'

During this conversation Carolyn had been sitting stiffly on her chair, her big eyes going from one to the other of us.

She rose elegantly, came towards me, put her arms around my waist and said, 'Calm down Helen. I don't think Liz is up to this at present. Let me pour you a wine. I've brought down some very special bottles.'

I accepted her offer of a glass, and then went for a wander through the vineyard to get my anger under control. When I returned the two old friends were reminiscing about a time they had shared in the past and the will wasn't mentioned again that day.

Obviously Carolyn was the catalyst Mum needed to jerk her out of her deep depression because during the next few days she improved, and by the end of the week had discarded her sleeping pills. We even had some fun, cooking absurdly elaborate dishes, eating whenever we felt like it and drinking far too much.

I couldn't get over my anger with Fred for leaving my mother unprovided for but she appeared to bear no rancour. As she had said she probably wouldn't be happy staying there without him.

Nevertheless it was hard to watch when Fred's son Julian arrived, a man with a twisted mouth and the cold, empty eyes of the unloved. He strode around the property, appraising it like a real estate agent and was barely civil to my mother when making arrangements about when she could move out.

Nearly all the furniture belonged with the house but Bruce and I went down to help move my mother's few possessions; a favourite armchair, the second bed that she had bought for visitors, a coffee table that had travelled from the big house to our flat and then to Fred's house and a small freezer.

Most of her treasured things were in the kitchen – her heavy, copper pans, pottery casserole dishes, her prized set of chef's knives, and of course all the fruits of her and Fred's labours from the past autumn. I wondered what she would do with all those lovingly made sauces, jams and pickles and the frozen vegetables and fish, but Bruce and I dutifully pack them all in cartons and the frozen food in large Eskies.

Mum had applied for a Housing Department unit and one had been allocated to her in Kingston. I had gone with her to inspect it the previous week, and although it was small it was in fact quite appealing. It was an end unit in a block of five with five others across a bitumen courtyard. Being at the end meant one less neighbour and also provided a lovely view of the mountain from the lounge room and the upstairs bedroom.

Upstairs there were two bedrooms, one very small but the other was generously proportioned and there was a bathroom/ toilet combined across the narrow passage.

Downstairs was one long room comprising a tiny corner kitchen, a dining area and a lounge room with high, glass, double doors that opened onto a small courtyard. This was currently overgrown with weeds and a few struggling climbers.

My mother appeared reasonably cheerful about it so I agreed with her about the positives, but I secretly worried about how she would get on, alone amongst strangers and with such a tiny, cramped kitchen.

Bruce and I had invited her to live with us but she had refused, saying that we needed our privacy and she her independence. We were secretly relieved by her decision but I felt a slight sense of guilt when we left her, surrounded by boxes and such meagre furnishings.

To salve my conscience I took her shopping during the following week and bought her lovely lounge suite and a circular Blackwood table with four matching chairs.

Over the next few weeks I dropped in frequently to see how she was getting on and was amazed at how quickly she transformed the place.

She had befriended a rather haggard-looking youth who lived in the next-door unit. Although he was unemployed and looked incapable of any physical work she had managed to get him to put up extra shelving in the kitchen. These shelves were now bright with her pickles and jams and beneath them she had hung her copper pans on sturdy hook. Pots of herbs lined the ledge below the window and a vivid, potted cyclamen glowed pinkly on the coffee table.

The freezer had proved impossible to fit into the kitchen so had been relegated to the second bedroom. I thought this would be a great inconvenience but Mum seemed to think that it wouldn't. As she pointed out she was still agile and quite capable of dashing up and down stairs.

Bruce and I went on a long-planned holiday to America and Japan a few weeks after Mum's move. Actually it was a combined working holiday, as we wanted to check out other IT companies as well as see something of both countries. We were away for nearly two months and had a marvellous time as well as getting a lot of ideas for our business.

As soon as we had unpacked I rang Mum to tell her we were back and to see how she was. After thanking me for the postcards I had sent her during our trip away she invited me to afternoon tea the next day. She sounded bright and cheerful.

The following day, feeling slightly jet-lagged and weary and not a little guilty about leaving her alone at a fairly critical time in her life, I made the trip down to Kingston.

I knocked on the door and walked into the unit to be greeted by a cacophony of sounds, a child giggling, a man coughing, adult laughter and soft music. The room smelled of gingerbread and the sweet, distinctive aroma of marijuana.

On the lounge was the skinny youth from next door, a cup of coffee in one hand and a smoke in the other. In front of him on the coffee table was plate of gingerbread. At the dining table sat a rather bedraggled young woman nursing a cheery, rosy little girl who was laughing at something that the elderly, unshaven man sitting opposite had said to her.

Mum rushed over and hugged me tightly. She then introduced me to her neighbours, Ben, Marianne and her daughter Cherri and Bob, before bustling off to the kitchen for a cup and plate for me.

I'm not sure whether I had appeared unfriendly or the visitors were being tactful, but within a matter of minutes of my arrival Ben unfurled from the couch and wandered off, Marianne remembered that she'd left a load of washing in the communal laundry and Bob also left with a nod of his shaggy head.

As the door closed behind Bob's shambling back I turned to Mum and asked bewilderedly, 'What are you doing Mum, entertaining those dropkicks?'

She turned to me, her blue eyes as cold as ice, 'They're my friends and if you're going to insult them you can leave.'

'But Mum,' I mumbled. 'Surely you can't like them?'

'As a matter of fact I do,' she retorted, 'They've made me welcome and helped me to adjust to this new life I'm leading.'

I ate humble pie along with my slice of gingerbread and talked about the trip to America and the places that Bruce and I had seen until I could leave without seeming too abrupt.

I fumed all the way home, angry at Fred whose thoughtlessness had left Mum in such a dire financial state, and also at my father who had happily taken advantage of my mother's lack of interest in material matters at the time of their divorce. Most of all, though, I was angry with the freeloaders who were apparently taking over my mother's life and space.

Bruce made soothing noises and rubbed my tautened shoulder muscles when I told him about my visit, but I don't think he realised just how my mother was living and how much it had upset me to see her surrounded by life's losers.

We were very busy at work during the next couple of weeks. Stimulated by what we had seen in the United States and Japan we were implementing changes to our business, and I barely had time to ring Mum let alone visit her.

Two weeks after I had last seen her I was working on some new schedules when my personal assistant, Dianne, came into my office looking rather flustered.

Di said, 'There's a young woman in reception. She insists that she must see you and refuses to make an appointment or leave.'

Baffled and annoyed I followed Di out to the reception area, and there was Marianne, standing at the counter looking nervous but very determined.

I dismissed Di with an offhand, 'I'll see to this,' and after greeting Marianne led her into my office.

Her agitation was obvious, so to help her relax I took her to the little conference area that was sited away from my desk and furnished with comfortable lounge chairs. After she was seated I hardly had time to say, 'Now what can I do for you?' before she stumblingly began, 'It's your Mum. I'm real worried about her. She don't answer the door to anyone and we haven't seen her outside for days, not even in her courtyard.'

My heart fluttered and then steadied. How long was it since I'd last spoken to her on the phone? Thinking back I realised it had been nearly a week.

Trying to sound calm I said to Marianne, 'It's probably nothing to worry about. She may have the flu. Anyhow, I'll just let my husband know what's happening, and then I'll take you home and we'll see what's the matter.'

I drove quickly down the highway to Kingston, wondering why my normally out-going mother would suddenly become reclusive. She had seemed fit and happy the last time I'd seen he, and subsequently had sounded all right on the phone, but who ever really knows another person's innermost feelings? I had been surprised by how quickly she'd seemed to bounce back after the first terrible weeks of grieving for Fred. Perhaps I had let myself be convinced of her adaptability because it was the easiest route.

By the time I reached the units I was as flustered as Marianne and nervous about what I would find.

Using the key that Mum had given me when she first moved in I let myself into the unit, not knowing quite what to expect.

The big room was tidy but cold, warmed only by a weak stream of sunlight that filtered through the glass doors. On the coffee table were piles of photo albums and Mum was lying on the couch, wrapped in an old, mohair shawl. I rushed to her. She opened her bleary, swollen eyes, and then closed them again.

I put my arms around her and cried. 'Mum, what's the matter? Are you sick?'

Slowly she straightened in my arms, looked at me sadly and answered, 'No darling, not sick, just sick of trying, of being alive without Fred, of being alone.' Then she burst into tears

I held her for a long time in that still, cold room making shushing, comforting noises until her wild, hysterical crying turned to sobs and finally stopped. When I felt that I could disentangle myself I gently settled the mohair around her shoulders, turned on the heater and made us both a cup of strong, hot tea. They say tea is the universal panacea, and it proved to be for I watched as she sipped and slowly regained control of herself. Gradually I saw my usually strong, capable mother re-emerge from her broken shell.

I was anxious to know what had caused this apparent breakdown when she had seemed to be coping so well, but was wary of shattering her fragile calm. I turned to the photo albums, and soon she was reminiscing and even laughing about some of the photographs.

Later, while she went upstairs to wash her face and comb her hair, I rang Bruce, described how Mum was and told him that I would stay the night with her.

There seemed to be surprisingly few supplies in her kitchen cupboards, so I insisted on taking her out to dinner at a nearby vegetarian restaurant where the food was reputed to be very good.

After we returned to the unit, slightly tipsy from the wine we had consumed with dinner, we settled on the couch with Glayva and coffee. I felt I could at last ask what had happened during the past couple of weeks to cause her breakdown.

Mum sighed, the longest sigh, and said, 'I don't know if I can explain properly. I suppose I've really been pretending that Fred wasn't gone forever and would come back.'

I felt a shiver in my body as I remembered what Nanna Alice had said to me about Gordon dying – I felt a sort of déjà vu – then listened closely as Mum continued.

'Last week I accepted this wasn't going to happen and that I'd never see him again. Then I became quite strange. I could feel myself changing, but couldn't do anything to stop it. I became obsessed with watching couples; young ones on the street kissing openly, old couples helping each other shop in the supermarket. Even the ads on television were all about couples, sitting on new couches, eating pizzas, driving in new cars. I became eaten up with a kind of jealousy of all those couples and began thinking how I'd never again be part of a couple. I'll never again have a man look at me with love, or shop with me, or do all the dozens of things that couples do together. I just didn't want to be part of the world of couples so I shut my door and let myself sink into a morass of self-pity.'

It was now my turn to cry and we hugged for a while, but then she pushed me away gently.

'I'm going to be all right though you know. I've hit the bottom and now I'm on my way up.'

With a grin she stood up and moved to the little side table saying, 'Now let's have another Glayva to celebrate.'

I slept on the couch and in the morning woke to the sounds of Mum rattling around in her little kitchen preparing breakfast for us.

I know my mother continued to mourn the loss of Fred but she never again reached that level of despair. However, I felt she would benefit from some form of grief counselling, so with a lot of pressuring from me she finally agreed to join a self-help group.

The results of this were hilariously sad if that is not a contradiction of terms. As she described it to me the group members met in a bare, white room and were greeted by a lovely smiling lady who looked like a refugee from the hippie seventies. She wore tights, a huge hand knitted sweater and had long, dark greying hair partially held in place with bone clips.

This woman was the group leader and the evening commenced with the participants holding hands in a circle. Then, horror of horrors, they were all asked to introduce themselves and say why they were there.

Mum told me later about some of the people and their problems.

There was Alice, a slim tense woman with an arm in a sling, who had been forcibly and violently ejected from her home by her husband of twenty-five years, Gloria, a plump young woman concerned about her self-image, Anne and

Tony, a plain couple who said that they were deeply in love but concerned about a ten year age gap and Garth, a teenager whose dog had died.

Mum said she found it totally impossible to describe her feelings to this group, as was expected, so simply said that she was recently widowed.

As the evening progressed she joined in with the calming and self-affirmation exercises, but was seriously wondering what she was doing there.

At the end of the session each person was given a contact buddy and told to get in touch with that person during the week.

Mum's first "buddy" was a nice middle-aged woman who was going through the trauma of a divorce. During the following week they met for coffee and talked about everything but their problems.

At my instigation Mum returned the second week for more of the same; handholding, self-affirmation exercises and baring of souls. The woman with the broken arm had not returned, so Mum volunteered to be her phone buddy to save her from the dog-less teenager or someone equally unsuitable.

With some reluctance she rang this woman who said that she was definitely not coming back to the group. She said she felt out of place because her problems were so much more serious that those of the other participants. Mum said she quite understood and commiserated with her. They evidently finished up having a good chat about what really are life-changing events or problems.

Mum returned for the third session with great feelings of trepidation. This was not helping her at all. The evening began with a reporting back on the buddy-bonding phone calls or meetings.

The group then formed a handholding circle and were instructed by the leader to turn to the person on their left and say, 'I love you inordinately.'

At this Mum lost her cool, stepped out of the circle and said, 'This is ridiculous. I'm not going to say that. I love my children and grandchildren inordinately. I love my best friend inordinately and I suppose I love my siblings inordinately, but apart from those people I love no-one inordinately and especially not anyone in this room.'

With this she picked up her handbag and left.

During the following week she received a call from the leader who said she was sorry Mum had found her methods unhelpful, a call from Tony who wanted her to know how much he admired her stance and one from Garth to tell her that he had bought a new dog.

So much for my suggestion of counselling.

Shortly after Mum had curtailed her disastrous counselling sessions she rang and invited Bruce and me to lunch and we accepted happily. The day was warm and sunny as we left home for the trip to Kingston, taking with us a good bottle of red wine and a bunch of freesias that scented the car and added to our sense of well being.

Mum must have been watching at the window because she opened the door as soon as we arrived, and after hugging both of us led us straight through the lounge room to the courtyard.

In my agitation on my last visit, three weeks earlier, I hadn't looked out to this area and now saw that a transformation had taken place. The weeds were gone and had been replaced by neat, raised beds that contained delicate plants, Asian greens and herbs. The straggling climbers had been pruned and were already showing pale green tendrils of new stems and young leaves.

In one corner a small paved area had been installed and was surrounded by a lattice wall on which new climbers – jasmine and happy wanderers - were already beginning to twine. On the pavers stood a long wooden table with benches on either side.

I looked in amazement, then hugged my mother while exclaiming, 'Why, this is wonderful Mum. How have you done this in a few weeks?'

She smiled, not a little smugly, and replied, 'Well I've had help, and I wanted you and Bruce to share this "thank you" lunch that I'm giving for my family and friends.'

As we returned to the lounge room I handed Mum the freesias, which she smelled lovingly before arranging in a pretty pottery vase on the coffee table. The delicious aroma of garlic bread wafted from the oven and a large pot bubbled on the stove.

A tentative knock sounded on the door and then Ben strolled in, looking clean and neat but unbelievably thin. He shyly shook hands with Bruce then headed out to the courtyard.

Mum whispered, 'He's very shy and probably needs a smoke to relax himself.'

I looked across at Bruce, my eyebrows raised, silently querying his opinion of Mum's friend, but he just shrugged and grinned.

Another knock was followed by a rush of air as the door flew open and Cheri raced in on chubby legs; a ragged bunch of flowers clutched in her little hands. She ran to Mum for a cuddle, thrusts the flowers at her, and then danced through to the courtyard. Marianne followed close behind looking less haggard than when I had last seen her and dressed in an array of floating layers of colours.

Behind her stood Bob, clean-shaven and dressed in a crisp white shirt and grey slacks. He clutched a bottle of wine to his chest. He waited diffidently until Mum called, 'Come in, come in Bob and meet my lovely son-in-law.'

When introductions had finished Mum led us out to the courtyard and seated us at the long table before bustling back inside. We sat in silence, a strange disparate group, until Mum reappeared, a large platter of garlic bread in one hand and her best blue bowls in the other.

Bruce opened the wine, brought it back to the table and filled glasses all round while Mum returned from the kitchen with the large pot and a glass of juice for Cheri. Soon we were all served with large helpings of her magnificent minestrone and, with shared appreciation of her food, conversation began to flow as we all relaxed.

I was still amazed at the transformation of the courtyard and asked Mum once again how she had done it.

Smiling around the table at everyone she answered, 'Well Marianne and Cheri and I soon cleared the garden and pruned the climbers. Ben can do anything,' she continued, beaming fondly in his direction. 'He paved this area with bricks we found in the Tip Shop and he also put up the lattice. Bob and I found the outdoor setting in a second-hand shop and he sanded it down and stained it for me.'

After this lengthy explanation she stood up and raised her glass, 'So this is my "thank you" lunch to my dear family and friends for helping me make a new life for myself. Thank you all.'

We responded in unison, 'To your new life.'

Now our little gathering was completely at ease and everyone helped clear the empty bowls and reset the table with plates. Mum appeared with a cheesy, bubbling lasagne in one hand and a colourful Greek salad in the other.

We all served ourselves, Bob opened the bottle of wine he had brought and we relaxed in the sun enjoying the good food and wine and surprisingly pleasant company.

Bruce and I went home from that luncheon feeling much happier about Mum. Her new friends seemed a bit strange to us, but they were supportive and caring and appeared to be helping her adapt to her life without Fred.

Mum settled contentedly in her unit and through the years she fed and nurtured a passing parade of fellow unit-dwellers. Bruce and I met some of them; others only stayed for a few months and then moved on before we got to know them.

Of her first four friends I know that Ben moved back home and began working with his father in his handy-man business.

Marianne met a man, who she felt she could trust, and she and Cheri moved in with him. I don't think all went well with her life. She continued to visit Mum, but sometimes looked tense and bruised although she insisted she was happy.

Bob continued to battle his need for alcohol, sometimes going for days without a drink and then spending a week in an alcoholic haze. He was eventually deemed unable to look after himself properly and placed in a supervised home. Mum visited him, but she worried about how he was fading away and he died within a year of going there.

Others replaced her first neighbours and Mum ran a virtual open house for all those in need of a friend, a willing ear to listen to problems or a good feed. She cosseted and fed them and taught many of the young women and some of the young men how to prepare cheap but nutritious meals. Her little kitchen became the heart of that soulless block of flats and her courtyard a place where people met and shared good food and cask wine.

Bruce and I often joined her for Sunday lunch and during that time her cuisine changed once again. Everything she cooked seemed to be made in bulk, to be eaten by a crowd or frozen into smaller portions. She made huge pots of minestrone or farmhouse soups, lasagnes that filled her biggest platter and fish cakes by the dozen.

Mum also experimented in making several meals from one chicken and was pleased with how cheaply she could feed herself and the people who dropped in for a visit.

There was a very good market a short walk from the units and her fridge was packed with varied vegetables and meat and fish that have been on special. Her freezer was filled with instant meals of her making.

In time it had proved to be inconvenient to have the freezer upstairs so it was brought downstairs by a couple of young artists who lived in one of the units. They decorated it beautifully with stylised flowers and it stood near the dining table with a large climbing plant trailing over the top and down the sides.

In no time her garden was prolific with herbs and vegetables and she had strings of home grown garlic and chillies hanging from pegs on the walls. She had always been expert at producing nourishing stir-fries at short notice and rarely ate alone.

Bruce and I relaxed about how and where she lived, and told each other how great it was that she had adapted so well to such a change in her life. I suppose we were pleased we didn't have to worry about her, and I rationalised that I did much more for her than either of my brothers.

I haven't mentioned them much with regard to this time in our mother's life, but then they were not around much. They were both still living happily on the mainland, and I kept in touch with them through phone calls and so did Mum. Whenever Bruce and I joined her for Sunday lunches she'd tell me about their calls, but I felt that they could have kept in contact more frequently than they did.

During the second year that Mum was in the unit Dale and Gay moved into a magnificent house overlooking Sydney Harbour, and from then she visited them once a year to catch up with them and the precious grandsons.

They rarely came to Tasmania and when they did they stayed at a hotel. They usually took Mum out each day of their holiday so we didn't see much of them. I know Mum found their visits tiring, but she adored their little boys and was grateful for the attention.

Because Ralph and Maureen were both with the Education Department they could come down a couple of times a year during school holidays. They always stayed in the unit, and Jasmine shared Mum's bed while her parents dossed down happily on the new futon in the small bedroom.

I still enjoyed Ralph's company, was very fond of Maureen and really liked Jasmine so Bruce and I made a point of getting in touch when they were at Mum's.

Despite the great family holiday we had shared the year before Fred died I felt my brothers and I had drifted apart once more, and these occasional meetings didn't bridge the gap that was there.

During the years that Mum was in the unit we all managed to get together only once as a family.

It is at the end of 1999 and 2000 was to be the year that we decided to recognise as the beginning of the new millennium. I'm still not sure whether it officially began in 2000 or 2001, but we decided to spend that Christmas and New Year together.

Mum, Bruce and I met the families at the airport and ferried them to Kingston, Dale, Gale, Nicholas and Bradley to the best hotel in the area and Ralph, Maureen and Jasmine to Mum's unit.

The boys were then about ten and eight and seemed to be spoilt and demanding. In contrast Jasmine was a beautiful willowy thirteen year-old with the serenity of her mother and the warmth of her father. I think if I had ever chosen to have a child I would have wanted a daughter, so I had a special feeling for Jasmine.

I took the day before Christmas off work and spent it with Mum, in her tiny kitchen, preparing for Christmas lunch. Together we made the trifle, a family favourite and different from any others I have tasted because of the way the jelly partially permeates the sponge cake. We scored, decorated and baked the ham and prepared the stuffing for the turkey that was defrosting in the refrigerator. We had a wonderful time cooking together, but for me the next day did not live up to expectations.

On Christmas day Bruce and I arrived at Mum's with presents for all and a suitably good bottle of wine in hand. Mum and Jasmine were dressed and excitedly putting finishing touches to the meal. Ralph and Maureen were still bumbling around, not quite with it after a heavy drinking night with friends, but eventually they showered and dressed.

At exactly twelve o'clock Dale, Gay and their boys arrived loaded down with enormous gifts.

I don't know how to describe the rest of the day without sounding a bit bitchy. It was the first time we had all been together for some time, so things were a little strained. Nevertheless the food was marvellous, and we ate it in sunshine beneath the beautiful flowering jasmine and happy wanderer. No one argued, the children behaved impeccably and the presents ranged from highly suitable to totally over the top.

I think Mum was much happier with the pottery vase Bruce and I gave her than the computer from Dale and Gay or the microwave from Ralph and Maureen, but I might have still been haunted by sibling rivalry.

Anyhow the rest of the week went off all right and we had some family bonding time. We visited Port Arthur, went to Richmond and wandered around the maze with the kids and spent a happy but slightly frazzled New Year's Eve at Mum's unit, where we welcomed in what we had chosen to call the New Millennium.

The next day Bruce and I took Mum, Ralph, Maureen and Jasmine to the airport and Dale and his family arrived shortly before takeoff in a stretch limousine.

I waved my siblings, their wives and progeny off and took Mum back to her unit. I really didn't know how she felt, but as we three shared a coffee in her lounge room she breathed a huge sigh and looked a little sad. I wondered if she was thinking of the previous holiday when she'd had Fred by her side and all her family in her own home.

As the years passed Bruce and I continued to be very happy and our business was highly successful. Every year we had a holiday overseas and we loved trying the different foods in the countries that we visited. Because we both enjoyed cooking we had a large collection of recipes garnered from places we had been to around the world, and we really liked giving dinner parties with an ethnic flavour. Sometimes I thought back on Mum's first attempts at French and Italian cooking and had a little giggle.

Mum was still happily feeding her waifs and strays as I sometimes referred to her fellow unit dwellers, but only to Bruce. She continued to be quietly content and remained active. She walked most days, attended art classes one day a week and continued to read voraciously. She was enmeshed in the lives of many of her neighbours and leading a fulfilling life. Her biggest heartache during that time was when Carolyn died of cancer after a relatively short illness.

She had spent nearly a decade in the unit and was pleased with her home and loved her little courtyard and garden.

Suddenly all this changed when she fell.

Golden Gingerbread

½ cup golden syrup
⅓ cup sugar
3 oz. butter
3 cups self-raising flour
1 tsp. ginger

1 tsp. cinnamon
1 egg
1 cup milk
1 tsp. bi-carb soda

Place in saucepan golden syrup, sugar and butter.

Stir over low heat until sugar has dissolved and butter melted.

Cool a little

Sift together flour, ginger and cinnamon.

Make a well in the centre of dry ingredients and gradually add the golden syrup mixture with well-beaten egg.

Heat the milk to lukewarm, add the bi-carb soda and stir until dissolved.

Add to cake mixture, beating well.

Turn into greased lamington tin and bake in a moderate oven 30 to 35 minutes.

Minestrone

1 tbsp. oil
I onion chopped

2 potatoes cubed
2 carrots sliced
3 sticks celery sliced

2 cloves garlic finely cut up
1 tin tomatoes
1 tin haricot beans

1 tin red kidney beans
6 cups beef or chicken stock
1 tbsp. tomato paste
100 g. French beans sliced
¼ cabbage roughly shredded
salt and pepper to taste
grated Parmesan cheese

Heat oil in large saucepan, add onion, then potato, carrot, celery and garlic in that order stirring, and cook slowly for 5 minutes.
Add tomatoes, haricot beans and kidney beans.
Add stock and tomato paste and simmer until potato is softening.
Add French beans and cabbage and cook for a further 10 minutes.
Season to taste and serve sprinkled with Parmesan cheese.

Accompany with crispy, garlic bread.

Suitable for vegetarians if beef or chicken stock replaced with vegetable stock and tastes just as good.

Farmhouse Soup

few bacon bones or pork hock
8 oz. split peas
6 cups water
1 onion finely chopped
1 carrot finely chopped
Add any of the following in season – swede, pumpkin,
parsnip, kohl rabi, broccoli, skinned tomatoes.

Chop all vegetables finely and place in a large saucepan
with other ingredients.

Cook slowly for two hours. Skim during cooking.

When peas are soft remove soup from heat and push
through a coarse sieve.

Return to stove to reheat.

Season if necessary.

Serve with oven baked croutons or toast.

Lasagne

6 oz. lasagne sheets

Cook lasagne sheets in boiling, salted water until softened.
Keep separate in pan or they can stick together.

Meat Sauce

1 lb. mince	2 cloves garlic
1 tbsp. oil	Crushed fresh oregano and basil leaves
1 ½ lbs. tomatoes	2 tbsp. tomato paste
1 onion finely chopped	1 tsp. salt
4 oz. mushrooms	½ tsp. sugar

Fresh herbs can be replaced by dried herbs

Heat oil in pan, add mince and brown then add peeled,
chopped tomatoes, onion, chopped mushroom, garlic,
paste and seasonings. Cook until meat is tender.

Cheese Sauce

2 oz. butter	2 cups milk
3 tbsp plain flour	4 oz. grated cheddar cheese

Melt butter, stir in flour and cook 2 minutes. Gradually add
milk then grated cheese.

Topping

½ cup grated Parmesan cheese

½ cup cream

Place layer of lasagne in ovenproof dish, then half meat
sauce and half cheese sauce. Repeat layers.

Top with cream and Parmesan cheese and cook 15
minutes in moderate oven.

Fish Cakes

500 g. firm white fish
500 g potatoes cooked and mashed
3 spring onions finely sliced
½ cup mixed fresh herbs – parsley, coriander and dill
1 dsp. lemon juice
1 dsp. chilli sauce [*optional*]
salt and freshly ground black pepper
1 egg
breadcrumbs

Select fresh, firm fish, boil until soften

Allow to cool and remove fish from bones.

[*The water can be seasoned and used as fish stock*].

Mix together fish, mashed potatoes, spring onion, herbs
lemon juice and chilli sauce.

Season to taste with salt and pepper and roll into balls.

Dip balls into beaten egg, coat with breadcrumbs and fry
in moderately hot oil until cooked and golden.

Serve with avocado salsa, green salad and crispy, fresh
bread.

Chicken, Chicken and More Chicken

The following three meals can all be made from one medium to large chicken.

Choose a free-range chicken for value and flavour.

Initial Preparation

Cut chicken breasts from bird and set aside. These will be used in the Chicken Breasts recipe that follows.

Joint remainder of chicken.

Place jointed chicken, minus breasts, in a large saucepan, cover with water and cook for 30 minutes.

Remove chicken pieces from water and allow to cool then remove cooked flesh from bones.

This should produce approximately 4 cups stock and 3 cups cooked chicken.

Chicken Breasts

2 chicken breasts	1 tbsp olive oil
juice of 1 lime	2 tsp chilli sauce
1 clove garlic, minced	½ cup finely chopped coriander

Flatten breast and place in marinade of olive oil, lime juice, chilli sauce, garlic and coriander.

Marinate for 2 hours covered.

Prepare suitable filling.

Filling Suggestions
Spinach and fetta cheese.
Spring onion, sun dried tomatoes and fresh herbs.
Lightly cooked mushroom slices and chopped ham

Flatten breast, top with choice of filling.

Roll up, tie with string.

Melt a small amount of butter in a hot pan.

Seal outside of chicken breasts in the hot pan. Transfer to a baking dish.

Bake in moderate oven for 20 minutes or until fully cooked.

Chicken Casserole

30g. butter
8 mushrooms sliced
2 spring onions sliced
1 tbsp. plain flour
1 cup milk

2 cups cooked chicken
1 tsp. paprika
salt and pepper to taste
mashed potatoes
grated cheddar cheese

Melt butter in saucepan, add mushroom and onion and cook 1 minute.

Add plain flour and cook 1 minute stirring all the time.

Remove from heat, add milk then return to heat and stir until thickened.

Add chicken and seasonings and stir in.

Pour into a casserole, top with potato and grated cheese.

Place in moderate oven and heat until topping is golden.

Chicken Soup

1 small onion finely sliced	1 dsp. butter
1 large leek sliced	1 cup cooked chicken
1 carrot cut into circles	4 cups chicken stock
2 potatoes cubed	chicken stock cube
	[optional]

Melt butter in saucepan, add vegetables and cook 1 minute.

Add stock and simmer until vegetables are soft.

Add cooked chicken and stock cube if needed.

Can be served immediately or frozen for later meals.

Trifle

½ round sponge cake
raspberry jam
1 tbsp sherry

1 pkt. raspberry jelly

½ litre custard
2 bananas
cream, sweetened and
whipped

Make jelly and place in refrigerator to set.

Spread cake with jam, cut into small squares and place in glass bowl.

Sprinkle with sherry.

Make up custard and allow to cool until just warm.

Remove set jelly from refrigerator, break up and place ¾ over sponge.

Pour on ½ custard and mix through jelly and cake. This is the most vital step as the custard must be just warm enough to partially dissolve the jelly so that it permeates the sponge.

Slice 1 banana evenly over the mixture.

Smooth on remaining custard.

Top with whipped cream and decorate with remaining jelly and banana.

Don't Get around Much Any More

So far Helen has been telling this part of our family's story and I think she is doing a good job. She is a dear sensitive, caring girl, even if she is not at all maternal and can be a bit of a snob at times.

This next part of our story can really only be told by me because I was the only one there when this accident happened, and my resultant incapacity had such a profound affect on me not even the most sensitive daughter could describe it adequately.

To go back to that fateful day, I was standing on a chair to reach a case that was stored on the top shelf of the wardrobe in my spare bedroom. Dale and Gay had sent me an airline ticket so that I could visit them. Although my little holiday was still a few days away I had decided to start working out which clothes I should take. I always found it difficult to travel light when I visited them, as I needed to take dress-up clothes as well as more casual ones because they always took me out to fancy restaurants and to shows.

Anyhow I had to stretch to get the case, and suddenly the chair tipped sideways and I come crashing down with the suitcase on top of me. As I fell I must have hit my head on the edge of the bed because I was knocked out.

I came to and at first I couldn't work out where I was. My sight was blurry; I had a thumping headache and the most excruciating pain in my leg. When I tried to get up the room span and I felt faint, so I slumped back down on the floor. I lay there feeling a bit like a beetle that had been tipped onto it's back and couldn't turn over. The case had fallen sideways and was now wedging me between the bed and the wardrobe. I didn't feel I had the strength to move it as even the smallest movement sent a stabbing pain down my leg. I must admit that I started to cry from the pain and the frustration of not being able to get up.

While I lay there, wallowing in self-pity and wondering how I could make it down the stairs to the phone, I heard my outside door open and a young voice calling, 'Mrs. Davidson, are you about?'

It was Janice from next door. Oh the relief I felt to hear her!

In a pretty feeble voice I called, 'Up here.'

And really that's the last thing I remember for a while.

I must have blanked out for quite a long time because the next thing I knew I was on a stretcher and two ambulance officers were manoeuvring it down the stairs. They reached the bottom and lowered the stretcher gently to the floor, and then one of the men came and shone a torch in my eyes and said, 'Ah good, so you're back with us again. How are you feeling?'

Well I ask you, how did he think I'd be feeling?

I tried to focus on his face and answer the question, but somehow my tongue felt too big for my mouth and the words I tried to say came out as a sort of garbled sound.

Meanwhile the other officer was pulling up the sleeve of my sweater and attaching a blood-pressure band around the top of my arm. He watched my face as he took the reading then said, 'Not bad considering; 145 over 90.'

He leaned close and asked, 'Where do you hurt?'

This time I managed to mumble, 'Leg,' before I drifted off again.

The next time I came to I was strapped firmly onto the stretcher, and was obviously in an ambulance because I could feel the movement and hear the siren very close and very loud. It vibrated through my head, but then it stopped. I was so relieved.

I heard a voice saying, 'Elderly lady, definite concussion and probably a broken leg, but nothing more serious. We'll be there in about ten minutes.'

'Well,' I thought, 'How serious is serious? This feels bad enough to me.'

My head was throbbing, I couldn't seem to think clearly and my leg was agonisingly painful. I tried to turn around to see where the voice was coming from, but was so firmly strapped I couldn't move. I lay there silently hoping the jolting trip would soon end.

After we arrived at the hospital two men came out and I was moved, very gently, from the stretcher to a trolley thing on wheels. One of the ambulance officers came around to my head and said cheerfully, 'You're in good hands now dear. They'll soon make you comfortable.'

A young man wheeled me off through a wide door and along what seemed like endless corridors. I heard him say to an unseen person, 'I'm to take her to X-Ray first for the leg. According to the chart she hasn't had a stroke, but she's a bit concussed from a bang on the head. Her blood-pressure and pulse rate are slightly elevated but no more than you'd expect.'

The next few hours were a blur. At one stage I saw Helen and Bruce with worried looks on their faces, but I can't quite place when this was. I recall lying for quite a while on the trolley and feeling very cold. After a while someone put a blanket over me and I felt better, but then it was removed again and I was taken into a dark room. Here I was rolled onto a high, narrow bed and told to lie very still. Later I was put back on the trolley and once more wheeled along endless corridors and into a very bright room.

I asked someone if I could have something for the pain in my leg and heard voices saying, 'She may be concussed,' and, 'Check with the admitting doctor.' Later a bright light was shone in my eyes and a young nurse asked me my name and age.

I told her my name but said that my age was no concern of hers. She laughed and said I must be feeling okay, and then gave me a couple of tablets and a sip of water. After that I drifted off again.

I woke with a start as I was being rolled onto a bed and heard a young voice saying, 'Ease her over gently. That's right,' then the speaker was standing above me holding a couple of tablets and a glass of water. She smiled down at me and said, 'Here dear, take these and I'm sure you'll be feeling much better in the morning.'

I tried to tell her that I'd already had two tablets, but the words still wouldn't come out clearly so I swallowed them as well with a little drink of water and soon felt myself dozing off again. At least my leg wasn't hurting so much anymore although it felt very heavy.

When I woke the next morning a fine ray of sunlight was just lightening the room and my head felt clear although it still ached, and I could feel a big bump at the side of my temple. I looked around and saw that I was in a room with four other people, all of whom were sleeping soundly. Next to me was a wizened old lady with white hair so thin I could see her scalp beneath it.

I tried to pull myself up into a sitting position so that I could look out the window and see the sunrise but my right leg, which was now plastered, felt too heavy for me to move. I lay there hoping someone would soon come in and help me sit up.

I've always woken early and love to see the start of the day and watch the colours changing in the sky, so I felt very frustrated lying there like a helpless bundle.

I was so relieved when a nurse finally came in, looked at the chart at the bottom of my bed and then moved around to take my pulse saying, 'And how are we feeling this morning?'

I can't stand the way some nurses talk in the plural so answered rather sharply, 'I'm feeling much better thank you, but I would like some help to sit up.'

She adjusted the blood-pressure cuff around the top of my arm and answered, 'Doctor says we have to lie still for a couple of days. We've had a nasty blow on our head and we're better off lying down until everything settles.'

As she removed the cuff she added, 'Our blood-pressure is coming down and our pulse is back to normal, so if we are good for a day or so we should be able to sit up.'

I seethed quietly at this slip of a girl patronisingly telling me to be good and using the annoying "we" all the time as if she were sharing my body.

I lay there, longing for a cup of tea, and thinking of the logistics of drinking it while lying down. I found out the answer to that when a jolly plump aid arrived with the tea trolley and handed me a cup and a sort of double bended straw. This was bad enough and took away much of the enjoyment of that first cup of tea for the day, but worse was to follow.

When breakfast arrived I had to go through the humiliating experience of having a young lass spoon porridge into my mouth. At least I could feed myself toast and decided, there and then, that I wouldn't eat anything but sandwiches or toast until I was allowed to sit up.

Shortly after breakfast Helen and Bruce arrived bearing a large bouquet of roses.

Helen kissed me and said, 'Oh Mum, we've been so worried all night. You looked so little and frail on that trolley, and didn't even seem to quite know who we were.'

To reassure her I said 'Well, except for the leg I'm feeling good,' but then I spoil it by moaning about not being allowed to sit up and being spoken to as if I were a child. I gradually worked myself up into quite a disgruntled state, and I know they both left feeling unhappy and concerned about me. That was not what I had intended.

For lunch I ate ham and cheese sandwiches and drank another unsatisfactory cup of tea through a straw. At the nurses insistence I also had a juice and a couple of glasses of water that way. When she told me I should have the casserole or fish for dinner I said I wanted sandwiches again so that I could feed myself.

The painkillers the nurse had given me made me feel drowsy again and I slept for much of the afternoon. When I woke Helen was sitting beside the bed reading a book, which she put down as soon as she saw that I was awake.

She kissed my cheek and asked, 'How are you feeling Mum?'

Determined not to be as grouchy as I had been in the morning I answered, 'Much better darling. I'm sorry I was such a grouch this morning. The pain-killers are a big help, and I had a long sleep this afternoon, but it is a drag having to lie down all the time, and the main nurse who I have seen insists on saying we should do this or feel that as if we're Siamese twins. And I would prefer to be in a room by myself.'

Helen giggled, 'I'm so pleased that we're not going to be a grouch,' and I joined in her laughter.

We were giggling away when the nurse came into the room and said, 'You must be Helen. Perhaps you can talk your mother into eating a sensible dinner. We won't get our strength back if we only eat sandwiches.'

This set us off laughing again and my Siamese twin left in disgust after taking "our" temperature and "our" blood-pressure in silence.

'See what I have to put up with,' I moaned.

Still grinning Helen answered, 'Well I really do think that we should have a nourishing dinner. It will do us good and I'm sure we can manage it together.'

When dinner arrived I had been given the casserole and Helen joked about feeding "us". She is a great girl and cheered me up no end. She promised to see what she could do about getting me moved to a private room. She also told me she'd talked to both Dale and Ralph about my accident and that they both sent their love

That night I slept intermittently. Despite being given more tablets my whole body felt uncomfortable from lying on my back. All night I drifted in and out of sleep, listening to the clatter and chatter of the night staff and the snoring and little moans of my roommates. I was glad when the first rays of sunlight filtered into the room.

Helen arrived shortly after breakfast and said she had asked about me moving into a single room, but had been told that there were none available. Her good news was that Dale had said he'd catch an early morning plane down and should get here soon.

Just as she was saying this in he walked, my big handsome son, with a huge bunch of liliums in his arms. He hugged Helen then bent to kiss me, a worried look in his dark eyes, and asked, 'How are you feeling Mum?'

'Not bad, considering.' I answered, 'The leg is hurting a bit, but not too much. The worst thing is having to lie on my back and the lack of privacy."

Helen broke in, 'Mum would really like to be in a room by herself but they say there are none available at present. Anyhow I'll leave you two to catch up and I'll be back this afternoon. How long can you stay Dale?'

'Just today I'm afraid. I'm booked on the seven o'clock plane out because I have to be at a board meeting tomorrow.'

She left with a cheery wave and Dale filled me in on what the boys and Gay were doing. He kept looking around the room with a critical eye, and when the nurse came in to give me a wash he left, promising to return in half an hour.

When he came back he had a big grin on his face, 'All fixed Mum. They have found that there is a single room available, and will be in soon to move you.'

I don't know how he did it, but before long two aids came in, made some adjustments to my bed, then wheeled me out along a corridor and into a dear, little room. Dale followed looking very pleased with himself.

When Helen returned that afternoon she looked around my room and gave Dale a light punch on the arm saying, 'What did you use, threats or bribery? This is great, and it will be one less thing for Mum to grouch about.'

He grinned, "I'm sure our mother wouldn't grouch and I used neither threats or bribery, just charm.'

They chiacked a bit about that and it was a lovely visit.

Hospitals are ghastly places and I know I was a terrible patient but things got better once I could be propped up in bed. By the third day visitors, other than family, were allowed to come.

Little Janice arrived early on that day and I finally had a chance to thank her for coming to my rescue. During the week others from the units dropped in with fruit, chocolates and bunches of flowers. My room was beginning to look lovely and smelled like a florist's shop.

Vincent and Meg visited me one afternoon and Ronda sent a big bunch of roses and a get-well card but I didn't hear from Joan.

I received a card and flowers from Matt and I had a weep that afternoon, something I don't often do. Hearing from him after so long reminded me of Carolyn and those terrible months Matt and I had shared, four years ago, while she was dying of cancer. She had always been there for me, and I had loved her like a sister, maybe even more. Watching her beautiful face and body fading away had been heartbreaking. Now, in my weakened state, I cried once again for her and a little bit for myself.

Matt and I had not seen each other since the funeral. I think it would have been too hard for both of us without Carolyn there. Now I was touched by his get-well card and the flowers, and wondered how he had known about my accident.

I learnt later that Bruce had met him by chance in the street and told him. It was so sweet of him to send the card and flowers and I was touched.

By the second week I was allowed to sit in a chair near the window, and being able to look outside made me feel more cheerful.

Towards the end of the second week I was presented with crutches and encouraged to try them around my room. They felt ghastly. I was sure I would fall at every step and the tops hurt me under the arms. The physiotherapist who was helping me with them was very patient, but often our sessions finished with me back in the chair declaring that I would never get the hang of them and weeping.

I began dreading the time of day when she would arrive for a session, and was sitting in my chair, feeling edgy, when the door was suddenly flung open and my beautiful Jasmine ran across the room, followed by Ralph.

I had received flowers and cards from them and Maureen, but there had been no mention of them coming down. As it was term time I hadn't expected them.

Jasmine was now a young woman, and so pretty with her strawberry blonde hair and big green eyes. Ralph stood back while she gave me a cuddle and then came over for his turn.

He said laughing, 'We had to come, even though it's only for the weekend. She wouldn't give me any peace until she'd seen for herself that her Nanna was going to be all right.'

They asked me when I would be allowed out and I told them of my troubles with the crutches and how useless I was with them. Jasmine tried them out and we all finished up laughing at her efforts but then Ralph said, 'Perhaps you would be better off with the elbow ones. At least they wouldn't hurt you under the arms.'

I hadn't heard of these but when the physiotherapist came in Ralph asked her if I could try them. She agreed that some people found them easier to use but warned that they didn't give quite as much support.

Once she returned with these different crutches I tried them, and instantly felt more comfortable and could move around more confidently. I spent the afternoon trying them out, and by the time Ralph and Jasmine were leaving I walked with them to the lift.

That evening they came in again with Helen and Bruce, and were all in such happy moods it was contagious. Jasmine said they were going to a very special place for dinner, and that they would come back the next morning and she would tell me all about it.

I was awake early the next day and took myself to the toilet for the first time on my new crutches. They felt so much better than the others I was sure that soon I would be mobile enough to leave hospital.

I had scarcely finished breakfast when my family arrived. Jasmine enthused about their evening out, described what she had eaten and proudly showed me the new belt that Auntie Helen had given her. We had a lovely visit but they had to leave at twelve to catch the one o'clock plane back to Melbourne.

Helen told me she and Bruce would be in again that evening and I said hopefully, 'Now that I can get around on these new crutches they should let me out. We'll talk about it this evening.'

When they returned we discussed my convalescence. I really hadn't thought much about it. Just getting out of hospital had been uppermost in my thinking. Helen and Bruce vetoed my returning to the unit because I wouldn't be able to get up the stairs. I realised they were right, but pointed out that their house was not much better with its upstairs bedrooms.

Helen suggested that the downstairs guest room would be ideal as it was close to the kitchen and I would be able to make myself tea early in the morning before they were up.

I was missing my own space, but knew I would not be able to look after myself and felt grateful for their love and concern. For the first time in my life I felt old and dependent and I didn't like it. It's frightening how one moment in time can change one's life so suddenly and completely.

In a few days I could walk to the end of the corridor and back on my crutches and was told, much to my relief, that I could be released.

As I have made very clear, I don't like hospitals or doctors or nurses very much, but I quite liked Dr. Ramsey. He had been encouraging without being falsely cheerful when he'd visited me each day, and was very understanding about my difficulties with the crutches.

On the last day I was sitting in my chair, my plastered leg stuck out in front of me and the crutches to hand, when Dr. Ramsey came in for a final check. He sat on the bed across from me and said laughingly, 'Well I can see you're in a hurry to leave us so I won't delay you. You've made good progress and, if you take care, you should be able to have the plaster off in four weeks time. You do realise, though, that you are going to need quite a lot of physio to get that leg moving again, and it's possible you will always walk with a bit of a limp.'

I must have looked pretty shocked at the idea of a permanent limp because he came over and patted my shoulder saying, 'Look, I don't want to upset you, but as we get older our bones become more brittle and don't knit as well as when we are young. We can't expect to mend as well or get around as we did when we were younger.'

With that he said a last goodbye and left the room on his two strong, young legs. I glowered after him for using the detested plural knowing full well that it did not apply to him. Perhaps I didn't like him after all.

Helen and Bruce arrived soon after the doctor had left and they collected my gear, saw to the booking out procedure and soon had me settled in the back seat of their car. My efficient daughter had thought to bring a cushion for my head, a throw in case I was cold and even gathered up the freshest flowers from the room for me to have at home.

I was so glad to be out of that wretched place but was feeling vulnerable and dependent and not at all sure how I would cope with having to be looked after.

All My Life's A Circle

After seeing Mum on the elbow crutches during Ralph and Jasmine's visit I thought that she would soon be allowed out of hospital.

The following Monday I went down to the unit and collected most of her clothes as well as her duvet and pillow. Almost as soon as I arrived her friends from the other units were at the door, asking how she was and when would she be coming back. Even though it was a Monday most of her neighbours were home because few of them worked.

I had met some of them at Sunday lunches so I invited them in for a cup of tea. Janice, the young couple who had painted the fridge and an old guy called Don sat around the table with me drinking tea. I told them about her progress and said it could be a long time before she would be walking properly again.

They helped me load her clothes and bedding into the car, and assured me they would keep an eye on her place and car and look after the little garden. As I drove away I felt touched by their concern for my mother, but I rather doubted that she would ever be able to return to her unit and reclaim her independent life.

Now the big day had arrived and Mum was finally released from hospital. She had hated being there and hadn't been a very good patient, so she was relatively cheerful when Bruce and I collected her and took her home. We soon had her settled into the spare bedroom on the ground floor. It's a nice room with an ensuite, and we had installed a plastic seat and altered the shower rose so that it was hand-held.

Gradually we developed routines that enabled us to care for Mum and not miss too much work. We are lucky our hours are flexible and that we work together because one of us needed to go home each lunchtime to make Mum a cup of tea and get her something to eat. Although she was now getting around quite well on the crutches she couldn't really pour boiling water into a cup or bend to get things out of the refrigerator. Of course we didn't mind doing this, but I knew Mum hated being so helpless.

Another problem was the shower and for that she definitely required assistance. In the evenings she undressed, and then I covered the plastered leg with plastic and helped her into the shower.

Mum had never been particularly concerned about my seeing her nude when she was younger but she now seemed more self-conscious. She said that she felt ridiculous with one leg plastic wrapped while the rest of her was bare. I tried to joke her out of this, but knew she didn't like it and would be very glad when the hated plaster was removed and she could, once again, shower in private.

As well as this problem Mum was not eating with her usual gusto and seemed to be losing weight. Although she hadn't said so I don't think she enjoyed some of the meals we served, and I suppose some of it was different from what she was used to.

Bruce and I had travelled a lot, both for business and pleasure. As we both love food and are interested in trying new tastes we have incorporated many dishes that we have enjoyed in other countries into our daily meals.

When we first married I discovered that, among his many talents, Bruce was a first-class cook. Apparently his uncle had been quite a food and wine connoisseur. He also loved to cook, and had taught his two orphaned nephews all that he knew.

I, of course, have always enjoyed preparing good food and sharing it with friends. Obviously I inherited the cooking gene, but also picked up Mum's attitude to this important pastime.

Throughout our marriage Bruce and I had cooked together and we happily peeled, chopped and sautéed while enjoying a relaxing glass of wine. Because of our travels we cook many Asian–inspired stir-fries, we both love Indonesian curries and often make sushi or tempura, two dishes that we tried and loved during a memorable trip to Japan.

Although Mum had embraced foods from European countries, and had moved away from the meat and three vegetables of her youth, she had never branched out into the Asian cuisine that Bruce and I favoured. She seemed to quite enjoy our tempura fish and vegetables but struggled with sushi, a dish we love. She also found some of our Thai and Indian curries too hot and spicy and was missing the familiar tastes of her own cooking.

It is also possible that, seeing us cooking together, may have reminded her of the way she and Fred had been.

I told Bruce about my concern that Mum didn't seem to be eating well and was losing weight, and we decided to revert to more Australian cuisine while she was convalescing.

Mum had been living with us for a few weeks when it would soon be her seventieth birthday. After what she had been through, I decided to give her a big family party and invite her sisters and brothers as well as any of their children who were still living in Tasmania. Her brother, Bob, who had moved back to Sydney sent a formal unable to attend card but Ronda, Joan and Vincent happily accepted along with several of my cousins, and of course Ralph, Maureen and Jasmine. Dale and his family would not be able to make it because of prior commitments, but send cards and presents and an enormous bouquet of flowers on the day of the party.

I had decided to make it a buffet lunch, and with a lot of help from Bruce prepared a veritable feast. We roasted several chickens, glazed and baked a ham, prepared lamb and beef curries, and make innumerable salads as well as fried rice. We also bought a beautiful big smoked trout and arranged it on a platter with asparagus spears and avocado salad, and made platters of sushi because we knew how popular this would be with the younger set.

I cheated a bit and bought cheesecakes and Pavlovas and had a large, square, chocolate mud-cake made and decorated for the birthday cake.

Mum had just had the plaster removed and was having problems walking unaided but she seemed to be looking forward to the party and to seeing some of her family again.

The first to arrive was Ronda, looking hale and hearty, compared with her younger sister. Obviously the country life suited her, for although her skin is a bit leathery she moved like a woman half her age. The two sisters hugged and kissed and seemed pleased to see each other.

The party was good. After returning to Tasmania I had renewed my friendships with three of my cousins, Allie and Sal, who are Uncle Vincent's daughters and Auntie Ronda's daughter, Jennie. Because we all worked in town we often met for lunch. Many of the other cousins had not seen each other for years but the friendship between the four of us made it easier for them to reconnect.

Some of the cousins had brought their children, but fortunately for Bruce and me Ralph and Uncle Vincent take over responsibility for the younger set. They organized a snooker competition in the rumpus room for the older ones and other games outside for the younger children. This left Bruce and me free to concentrate on feeding everyone and seeing that the party was going smoothly.

Despite the obvious enjoyment of the cousins I had been aware of certain frostiness between my mother and her sister Joan. They hadn't seen much of each other since Nanna died, and I knew Mum was hurt that she had not visited her in hospital or bothered to come and see her since her accident.

I was, therefore, so pleased when I saw the three sisters seated on a couch in the lounge room, champagne glasses to hand, and seemingly enjoying a lively conversation. It made me think, as I have often done, about what it means to grow up in a home together, and to share the genes from the same parents. Does it bind you for life, even though time and circumstances seem to break those bonds completely?

I know that through many of my adult years I have felt completely divorced from my brothers. Nevertheless when I see them, there is always this strange pull of familiarity that I don't think you ever feel for anyone else, not even your dearest friends.

Following the party Mum became more positive in her outlook and generally more cheerful. During the weekends Bruce busied himself outside in the gardens or retired to his office so that Mum and I could have some "girl time" as he called it.

We'd sit in the kitchen, drinking tea and chatting. She had begun helping with the preparation of meals and in this way was gradually familiarising herself with my modern kitchen and the numerous labour-saving devices I have and love. She continued, however, to be dubious about the gas cook-tops, but approved of the fact that I had an electric oven.

As I mentioned the week prior to the party she had had the plaster removed from her leg, and although she still walked with a limp I could see an almost daily improvement. Bruce or I had taken her back to the hospital twice a week for physiotherapy. We didn't mind doing this at all, but she hated being what she called, "a drag" and bemoaned the fact that she couldn't drive herself. Being Mum she had thrown herself whole-heartedly into the exercise programme that she had been given and was following it enthusiastically.

One lazy Sunday morning Mum was peeling potatoes to bake with an old-fashioned roast leg of lamb that I was preparing. It was nearly three months since the dreadful day of the accident, and during those months Bruce and I had discussed almost daily what would be best for Mum's future living arrangements. We were concerned that something similar or worse could happen if she lived alone again, and she might not be found so quickly another time.

Although before the accident she had been active and spry it had taken its toll on her, and she seemed less confident and somehow frailer.

We had still not concluded whether it would be better for her to stay with us or move to some nearby units on the flat. We live on a steep hill, a long way from public transport, and there were no easy walks for her in the vicinity. We also didn't know if she would drive again.

However, while we had talked and worried and planned, in her own inimitable way my mother had come up with her ideal solution and she presented it to me that Sunday.

Mum had invited an old guy, called Joe, to lunch. She had met him at the hospital where he was having physiotherapy following a knee implant operation, and lately he had been driving her home. This had saved Bruce or me having to pick her up after a physio session, and so we were grateful and looking forward to meeting him.

Mum was wearing a pretty pink dress instead of her usual slacks, and I had been teasing her about dressing up for her "boyfriend".

It was while we were sitting comfortably, having a pre-lunch sherry, that she suddenly broached the subject of moving out.

Her opening sally was, 'Well darling, now that I can move around reasonably freely again I think I should move on and leave you young ones in peace.'

I hugged her and said, 'Mum, you know we love having you and that you're welcome to stay here with us. Why are you talking about moving out? This house is plenty big enough for you to have your own space. Our only concern has been that you're a bit isolated here.'

She patted my hand, 'Look, you and Bruce have been wonderful, and I can never thank you enough for the way you've looked after me. I know it hasn't been easy running me to the doctor and then to the hospital twice a week for physio, but neither of you has ever made me feel that I was a burden. I do appreciate all you've done and I love you both very much.'

'So why are you talking about leaving?' I asked

349

Looking slightly sheepish she answered, 'Well Joe has invited me to share his house. It's a dear, little cottage in Glenorchy, on the flat and close to the shopping centre, the library and the picture theatre.'

Taken aback I spluttered, 'But Mum, you've only known each other for a few weeks. Are you mad?'

Looking at me with those eyes that can change from soft sea blue to steely grey in a flash she answered, 'I know what I'm doing. I haven't lived this long to not be able to sum people up, and Joe's a good man. From the first time we met we clicked and I'm sure that we can give each other the companionship and friendship we both need for however many years we still have left.'

During the previous months, while I had been caring for my mother, I had felt our roles were reversed and that she would continue to need my care. Boy, had I been fooling myself. She'd been dependent temporarily and in need of mothering, but now she was reasserting her independence and I must admit I was quite shaken by this sudden reversal.

To give myself time to recover I pulled the lamb out of the oven and placed the potatoes and parsnips around the browning meat.

As I turned, flush-faced from the stove, Mum came towards me and hugged me close saying, 'Darling, please be happy for me. I know this is the right thing to do. Wait until you get to know Joe and see where I'll be living. I'm sure you'll see that this is for the best.'

Just then Bruce came into the kitchen, hot and sweaty from mowing the lawns. Sensing the rather strained atmosphere in the room he said, 'I'm off to the shower. Will you bring me a cold beer Honey?'

Relieved that he had given me a reason to follow him out I grabbed a beer from the fridge and almost beat him to the bathroom. Breathlessly I told him about my mother's plans. I was almost in tears, feeling that she wouldn't be making such a rash decision if I had been a better daughter and made her feel more welcome.

Bruce shushed away my concerns, 'Darling you've done everything you possibly could and I know your Mum appreciates all the help you've given her. But she's a strong-minded woman in complete control of her faculties. If she's decided to do this there's nothing we can do except get to know Joe better, and check out exactly how and where your Mum's going to be living.'

With these words of wisdom he took a large gulp of beer and headed for the shower, leaving me only slightly reassured.

While I was walking slowly down the staircase I heard the doorbell ring and entered the passage to find Mum already there and welcoming Joe inside. He carried two bouquets of roses and presented one to each of us with a courtly bow. Mum's were a deep, velvety red and mine had golden centres shading to an apricot colour at the tips. We both thanked him profusely as we shepherded him into the kitchen. Before searching for suitable vases in the large, pantry cupboard, Mum offered Joe a sherry or a beer, and while we arranged our roses he sat comfortably at the kitchen table enjoying a sherry.

I had seen Joe when I took Mum to physiotherapy but had only really talked to him twice before, once when he brought Mum home from physio and another time when he came to take Mum to see a movie. I had thought he seemed quite nice, but now I began looking at him in a different light. If my mother was going to live with this man I really needed to get to know him better.

He had grey, very curly hair above thick black eyebrows and dark brown eyes and looked very Italian or Greek to me. Although he was only about medium height he gave the impression of being bigger because he had broad shoulders and a wide chest and he carried himself very erectly. He'd had a knee transplant, but evidently it had been very successful because he walked without the trace of a limp. He now sat looking relaxed in my kitchen, evidently a man at ease with himself and the world. I knew this was a good way for one to feel as Bruce is like that and I have always loved this about him. Nevertheless, I still had my doubts. Perhaps Joe had a temper and would resort to violence if aroused, or maybe he was a hopeless alcoholic. We really knew nothing about him.

During lunch I watched him closely, and despite my critical eye he seemed nothing but charming. He complimented my mother's pretty dress and my cooking. He had brought an excellent bottle of red wine, which we drank and enjoyed very much with the meal. He was easy company and talked intelligently about a book that he and Mum had both read and seemed to share our concerns about the lack of choice in the upcoming elections. He obviously felt real concerns for the environment and expressed a wish for stronger Greens candidates, an attitude that echoed the sentiments of our household.

The afternoon passed happily and as he was leaving he said in his rather old-fashioned way, 'I hope that you will let me return your wonderful hospitality by joining me next Sunday for lunch.'

We eagerly accepted as we had enjoyed his company, but we also wanted to see where Mum was planning to live.

Mum escorted Joe out to his car and, being a sticky-beak, I watched their farewell from an upstairs window. He put his hand on her shoulder and gave her a chaste kiss on the cheek. 'Well,' I thought, 'that doesn't tell me much.'

Bruce and I waited eagerly for the next Sunday to come. I knew Mum and Joe had seen each other twice during that week because one day they went to the library and another on a drive down to Richmond for lunch. They were both enjoying being freed from the hassle of the twice a week physio sessions and also being able to walk without assistance.

When Sunday finally arrived Mum was as excited as a teenager and kept saying that Joe had a surprise for her and she wondered what it could be.

We easily found the house, with Mum giving directions, and my heart sank when Bruce pulled up outside a tiny cottage set close to the road. The small front garden was ablaze with geraniums, lavender and colourful annuals. Mum led the way happily down the narrow paved walkway and knocked on the door, which opened almost instantly. Joe must have been listening for our arrival.

He didn't seem to have quite the confidence and ease that had impressed me the previous week as he ushered us along a rather narrow passage that opened out into a colourful kitchen.

I could tell instantly that this was a cook's kitchen from the solid copper pans along one bench, the braids of garlic and chillies hanging from screws fixed to the walls and the pots of fresh herbs that filled a small bay window that had evidently been built for just that purpose. The walls were painted a soft, golden yellow and this colour was picked up in the crockery, decorated with purple grapes and red apples, and displayed on the shelves of a pine dresser. The muted wood of the dresser matched the floor tiles and the blending colours made the room seem larger than it was.

Joe had a bottle and four small glasses arranged on a little, circular timber table and as we stood around, rather self-consciously, he began filling the glasses with an amber liquid.

He handed them round saying, 'You must try my apricot liquor. I find it an excellent pre-dinner drink.' Then he said, 'Now let me show you the rest of the house and Elizabeth's surprise.'

Off the kitchen was a small but neat bathroom containing a big bath with a shower over it and a long, timber vanity with a square basin fitted in the top. On the other side of the kitchen was a lounge room, once again small but it looked comfortable with a chintz-covered lounge suite, a small television and a large, high bookcase.

We then all trooped into the passage to be shown Joe's bedroom, which contained a single bed, a built-in wardrobe and another high bookcase. It was rather Spartan and painted a deep olive green with a mottled floral carpet on the floor.

Crossing the passage Joe pulled Mum towards the door and said, 'You look first.'

Mum entered the room, and then gave a shriek of pure delight. 'Oh you darling man,' she said enthusiastically and planted a kiss on his cheek.

When Bruce and I finally got to see inside the door we understood her enthusiasm – it was a beautiful room.

In the centre of the wall facing the door was an exquisite bed with a beautifully carved headboard. The bed was covered with a prettily flowered spread. The walls were painted white and running around the centre, where dado boards joined plaster walls, was a frieze of roses that exactly matched the bedspread. There were also vases of pink roses on both the bedside tables that perfectly matched the lamps. A generous wardrobe took up one wall and on the remaining wall was the window that faced the front garden. This window was curtained with a white, filmy material that gave privacy without blocking too much light.

Mum started explaining her surprise. 'When I first saw this room it was full of boxes and dust and I couldn't imagine how it could be changed. Oh, it's lovely Joe. Thank you so much.'

Joe beamed down at her happily and said, 'I've really enjoyed doing it, and now perhaps your daughter will be happier about you living here with me.'

I felt slightly put on the spot and said, 'Well it certainly is a beautiful room,' before taking a face-saving sip of my aperitif.

Joe then led the way back through the passage and out the back door.

'This is where I spend much of my time. It keeps me busy and I love being out of doors.'

Bruce and I stared in amazement. The block stretched forever it seemed and every part of it was in use. To the right was an arbour covered with grape vines, and underneath stood an enormous timber table with benches on either side. On the other side, but set back so that it didn't shade the kitchen, was a long white building divided into three compartments. Nearest to the house was the toilet, then the laundry and the final compartment contained winemaking equipment and looked like a mini-cellar.

Past the building on that side of the block were fruit trees, apricots, apples and plums, and further up the path a miniature vineyard. On the right hand side of the path was a prolific vegetable garden that ended in a fowl house containing five fat, brown hens.

'These old blocks are very big. Many have been subdivided,' Joe commented, 'but I love the space even if it does mean I have many neighbours.'

He looked contentedly around his domain and I suddenly lost all qualms about my mother's hasty decision. She would be happy here with this gentle, uncomplicated man who obviously shared much that had been important in her life - love of books, gardening and preparing good, healthy food.

There were bits that were reminiscent of parts of her earlier homes – the colourful crockery from her young married years, the vegetable garden of her Cove years and the grape arbour, which was similar but better than the arbour she'd made at her unit.

After this tour we sat outside under the arbour and Joe magically produced magnificent bubbling cannelloni from the oven, hot garlic bread and a beautiful, crisp salad made of produce from his garden. We drank the bottle of red wine that we had brought and finished the meal with good strong coffee and a sweet plum wine Joe had made.

Totally replete and feeling happier than I had for a week we said our goodbyes, thanked Joe and drove home. Fortunately there were no booze buses on duty because Bruce said later that he had felt quite light-headed after the glass of plum wine. He took himself off to bed early, which gave me a chance to talk to Mum alone about something that was bothering me just a bit.

We were settled in the kitchen drinking our usual last cup of tea for the evening when I blurted out rather bluntly, 'Will you and Joe sleep together, Mum?'

She looked at me quite seriously and answered, 'I don't think so, and certainly he hasn't ever suggested that. We are great friends and I like him tremendously, but I think we may both be past that sort of thing. Actually that's something that should concern only Joe and me and no-one else, not even you my darling daughter,'

Thoroughly put in my place I finished my tea and bid my mother goodnight after first telling her how much I had enjoyed the day, and that I could see now why she would want to move in with Joe.

A few weeks before that all happened I had been contacted by the Housing Department who asked if my mother would be returning to her unit. They had been quite good about it and had even waived the rent for two months, but said they could not leave a unit left empty indefinitely. I hadn't known what to do about this, but now I sat down with Mum. I told her about the situation and asked her what she was going to do with all her stuff.

She had obviously been thinking about this because she answered, 'Well, as you've seen, not much will fit into Joe's place. He and I have talked about this and he's said we can replace anything that he has with my things, but I don't really care. I thought I'd share it around amongst my friends at the units, that is as long as you and Bruce won't be upset with my giving away some of the things you bought me.'

I assured her that it was entirely up to her and offered to help her with what she planned to do.

The following weekend we went down to the units. Mum had written to all the unit dwellers and invited them to a party. We brought cold meats, cheeses, olives, loaves of crunchy bread, crisps, biscuits and quantities of wine and arrived mid-morning. By noon her unit was crowded and

Janice and her little girl handed round the nibbles while Bruce and Don kept everyone's glasses topped up.

When everyone was relaxed and the party in full swing Mum called for quiet.

With her arm around Janice's little girl she said, 'You've all been so wonderful to me. We've shared our worries and problems as well as our joys. Because of changes in my life I won't be coming back, but I want to give you all something that will be useful for you.'

The young artist couple that had been sleeping on a mattress on the floor received her bed, Janice became the proud owner of the lounge suite and another young couple gratefully accepted the dining setting. When all her possessions had been distributed, except for a very few treasures that she valued, Mum and Bruce and I drove away amid cheers, farewells and a few tears.

Many years have passed and Mum and Joe continue to be wonderful companions, They cook and garden together, go to the library and share many of their books and have always seen the latest films as the picture theatre is virtually only a block away.

I have grown very fond of both of Joe's sons, young Joe, who is about my age and Mario who is a couple of years older. They feel almost like brothers to me. Both men are solid dark Italianate men like their father and share his easy humour and gentleness. I also like both their wives so we have spent many happy boozy Sundays beneath the arbour. Mum and Joe prepare great feasts for us, which can be Italian, or Australian or even French, but more often are a combination of tastes. Sometimes Joe cooks the whole meal and it can be very Italian and other times Mum might make what she calls Old Australian, a roast with lots of baked vegetables followed by one of her past favourites like golden syrup dumplings.

After one of these lunches Joe called us all to halt our chattering, as he wanted to make an announcement.

I thought, 'Oh no, they're not going to say they're getting married now at the ripe old ages of seventy-seven and eighty?'

Joe looked solemnly at us all around the table before saying, 'I have first talked to my two sons about this and they agree completely. Last week I made the deeds of my house over to Elizabeth. I may die before she does, and in fact I hope I do, and if I do I want her to feel secure that she will always own this home. I think she has not had that security before in her other relationships and I have thought it was not fair, but I have gone on for seven years doing the same thing to her. Today we celebrate seven wonderful years in this house together and this is my gift to her. I just hope she lets me stay here with her.'

Mum's eyes filled with tears and she put her hands over her face, totally overcome with emotion. Seeing her seeming distress Joe hurried around the table and put his hands on her shoulders saying, 'Elizabeth, I thought this would make you happy and feel secure. Why are you crying?'

Mum turned her face to him and said, 'I cry from happiness and gratitude Joe. Thank you so much,' and with that she kissed him resoundingly on the lips.

I know it's none of my business but, after seeing that kiss, I will always wonder if their friendship remained platonic, or if on cold windy nights or after a particularly happy day in the garden together they snuggle up in Mum's beautiful bed and make love. I hope they do.

Biography – Barbara Knight

After many years as a teacher, housewife and mother I completed a Bachelor of Arts at UTAS, majoring in English Literature and History in the 1970s. I followed this with a graduate Diploma in Librarianship and worked in public libraries for sixteen years before my retirement.

During retirement I spent several years attempting to become partially self-sufficient by fishing and growing a huge variety of vegetables and fruits before turning to the more cerebral pursuits of writing and painting.

I am an avid reader, a long term member of book discussion groups and have been writing seriously for many years. I have had six short stories published in anthologies or magazines. I have also written a number of novels and a memoir.

www.ingramcontent.com/pod-product-compliance
Lightning Source LLC
Chambersburg PA
CBHW061938130726
47909CB00013B/2030